David Bishop and
the Mystic of Creation

BOOKS BY T.C. CRAWFORD

THE DAVID BISHOP SERIES

David Bishop and the Legend of the Orb
David Bishop and the Mystic of Creation

David Bishop and the Mystic of Creation

by

T.C. Crawford

David Bishop and the Mystic of Creation

This book is dedicated to everyone out there with a dream - don't give up on it, you never know what kind of adventure it could take you on!

Acknowledgements

A special shout out goes to my parents and wife – your input was extremely valuable, and I really appreciate the time you spent working with me to make this dream become a reality.

A special thanks to my wonderful wife and children, who were very patient with me while I dedicated nearly all of my free time working on finishing David's story. Your patience and support mean the world to me, I love you so very much.

Table of Contents

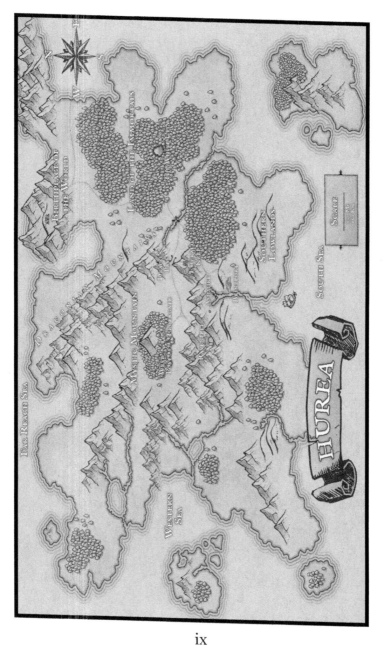

Chapter I

David Bishop stood in awe, watching helplessly as the Defiant One rose from the Dark Abyss, stopping just over the Royal Palace. He could barely hear Orin yelling for him to run, but his feet wouldn't move - he was paralyzed with fear.

The thunderous cheers and stomping of the demon army was deafening and filled David with a dread unlike anything he had ever experienced. What's worse – he knew he was responsible for their awakening. Without his powers, none of this would have happened.

He had gone into the battle with the intention of stopping General Krauss from harnessing enough energy to perform the ritual and breaking open the rift between the world of the living and the Dark Abyss. Instead, he only brought the General the power he needed to bring his plans into fruition.

His gaze fixated on the green star-like light shining brightly above the Royal Palace. It was mesmerizing. He briefly wondered why he even tried resisting – what could he, an orphan from nowhere, possibly hope to achieve against such a powerful foe.

To his side, David could see that Erin was screaming something – her face distorted with her mouth open wide in an endless array of screams. He couldn't hear what she was saying over the deafening roar of the demons, but he could see on her face that she was terrified and that her message was urgent. She kept pointing behind him and pulling on his sleeve, trying to get him to go with her, but he just couldn't muster the strength to comply.

Suddenly, the green star seemed to zoom into focus – David could see him for the first time, as clear as if he were only feet away. The first thing he noticed was his eyes – they were empty and lifeless, devoid of everything that David was accustomed to seeing in a person. But he knew that the Defiant One was no person – he was a Mystic. The Mystic of Destruction...and he was hell bent on revenge.

Just as quickly, David realized those empty eyes were focused directly on him. His heart stopped and his breath failed him as the Defiant One rushed toward him with such insane speed that he had no time to react. He was inches from crashing into him and there was nothing he could do to stop it – it was over, he had failed.

"David! David, wake up!" came a distant, familiar voice.

David opened his eyes and was nearly blinded by the intensity of the light.

He was in his bed back in Ravenfell, and the morning sun was shining brightly through his window and onto his face. Erin was standing by his bed, franticly shaking him, trying to get him to wake.

"David!" she cried, shaking him fiercely again, "You're having another nightmare, wake up!"

David slowly blinked away the dream, relieved to see he was safe in his bed until he remembered the harsh reality that his sense of security, too, was a farce – he wasn't safe, no one was. The Defiant One had been released from the Dark Abyss, and it was all his fault. There was no one else to blame.

"I'm up, I'm up!" he said, waving his arm at Erin as she tried to shake him once more for good measure.

"It was the same dream again, wasn't it?" she asked, a hint of concern in her voice.

"Yeah..." David said, nodding, a distant look in his eyes as he recalled the events of the dream.

It was always the same dream. Every night since the Awakening, David had been plagued with nightmares – always the same, always taunting him for his failures, always reinforcing them with the realization that he was solely responsible for unleashing the greatest evil the world had ever known.

"It will be okay, David. We will find a way to defeat him, I just know it!" said Erin reassuringly.

She had been so supportive since they returned from the battle of Eldergate. She knew he blamed himself, but she also believed in the prophecies that said he would be the one to seal away the Defiant One and defeat the coming darkness. David suspected that the prophecies were wrong, given the circumstances they now found themselves in, but he appreciated Erin's support, nonetheless.

3

"You keep saying that, but I can't help but feel like it won't be okay. Ever since the battle, I've lost my connection to the Orb. It just sits there, lifeless – much like how I feel." said David, looking down at the image of the orb in his hand.

The orb softly glowed in the back of his hand, as if it were mocking him and his impotence.

"Don't worry about it." said Erin reassuringly, seeing the look on his face. "You are the warrior from prophecy, that much I am sure of! It never said you would be successful right away, only that you *would* be successful. Prophecy is not always as it seems, this much I have come to expect!" she said, smiling at her friend.

It had been nearly a week since the battle of Eldergate where David had faced General Octavian Krauss and inadvertently given him the surge of power necessary to unleash the Defiant One and his army of demons from the Dark Abyss. David couldn't help but blame himself for the outcome of the battle, knowing that without his powers, the General may have never unleashed the Mystic of Destruction from his prison, and therefore, the world would not currently be facing the threat of extinction.

Since his release, the Defiant One had completely destroyed everything within the Northern Kingdom. The small, isolated settlements throughout the Outer Woods from Eldergate to West Post had all been abandoned at the end of the battle, with only a few stubborn-willed citizens staying behind while the rest fled to the safety of the city-kingdom of Ravenfell.

Those who chose to stay behind were slaughtered mercilessly by the Wolf Guard and the demon army, not a single life was spared.

King Eldergate and his loyal followers had fortunately made it out safely before the raids began and were now within the castle walls of Ravenfell, but they knew it was only a matter of time before the Defiant One and his demon army set his sights on Ravenfell, eager to squash the remaining resistance within its borders.

"Rex and the others are gathering in the meeting room. They told me to make sure you were up and ready." Erin said gently to David as he struggled to get out of bed, "I know you've had a rough night. We've all struggled sleeping lately...but we need you, the world needs you."

She gently lifted David's chin and looked deep into his eyes. She could see the pain he kept hidden locked away as he feigned a smile. She kissed him gently on his lips, longing to take away his pain, but knowing only one thing ever would – defeating the Defiant One and fixing the mess that he felt solely responsible for.

Sensing that her work had been done, Erin started towards the door. "The meeting is starting soon, don't be late!" she called back to David as she exited the room.

David flung himself back on his bed and sighed deeply before mustering the will to get up and face the day.

He made his way to his dresser where he found a small serving dish with a plate of warm eggs and biscuits that Erin had left for him when she arrived.

He quickly inhaled them before getting dressed and heading for the meeting room.

When David arrived, Erin was already seated towards the middle of the long table listening to Rex and the others discuss the defenses of the valley.

Rex was the king of Ravenfell and had been a loyal friend to David and Erin since their flight from Eldergate during the General's coup. He had defended them from the Royal Guards who had been sent to capture them in West Post and had played a vital role in helping the loyalists face the undead army and gain access to the capital city during the battle of Eldergate.

He now stood at the end of the long table bent over a map of the valley, deep in discussion with King Eldergate, Tyrius Vanderbolt, and General Ryan.

David made his way across the room towards Erin, sharing a brief intimate smile with her before taking the seat to her left. He felt her fingers intertwine with his own beneath the table and reveled in the comfort that it gave him.

"David, glad you could join us!" said King Eldergate in his deep booming voice.

He was an elderly king, tall and wide, but strong despite his old age. He had a thick, bushy white beard and equally white wavy hair that rested just below his wide shoulders. Despite having just lost his kingdom, he seemed in relatively good spirits.

Like Erin, he was a firm believer in the prophecies of old – prophecies that predicted the dark times that they now found themselves in – and whole heartedly believed that David would find a way to defeat the Defiant One and his armies and help restore peace back to the lands as the prophecy foretold.

David wished everyone would stop putting so much faith in the prophecy – he felt he had already let everyone down and didn't know how he would ever live up to their expectations.

David nodded respectfully to the King and focused his attention on the discussion at hand.

"We must focus our efforts on the mountain pass to ensure the demons never make their way into the valley," continued Rex. "That is our best chance of survival. If we allow them to break through the pass and into the valley, they will have more room to spread out and their numbers will quickly overwhelm our forces."

"He's right," said General Ryan, looking over the maps spread out across the table. "Our best chance is to bottleneck their forces at the top of the mountain here. If we can do that, we may just have a chance at holding them back." he said, pointing towards the entrance into the valley.

"But for how long?" asked King Eldergate, "We can't hold them off forever!" he said, to which everyone nodded in agreement.

"No...we can't" confirmed Tyrius, "That is why it is important for David to do whatever he can to prepare for the moment when he must face the Defiant One and defeat him, sending him back into the depths of the Dark Abyss once again. He is our only hope if we are ever to survive this conflict." he said, causing everyone to turn and look at David.

David felt like a child under the gaze of so many powerful men. He knew what they expected from him, but he felt he could never live up to them. He had tried to, once, and had failed – now he couldn't even access the powers of the orb. They were locked away, completely unresponsive to his call.

"I know what you expect of me," said David, looking around the room, "but I don't know how I can do it. I'm sorry..." he said, ashamed and averting his eyes from their gaze.

"Do not worry, my boy." said Orin. He had just walked into the room and had quietly come up behind David, placing his hands on his shoulders in an encouraging way.

"We will find a way to get your powers back. In the meantime, stay positive. Your attitude has more to do with your powers than you might think! Come now, let the kings and generals worry about the defenses. We have our own matters to attend to!" he said, pulling David away from the table.

David got up and said his goodbyes to Erin and the others before following Orin out of the meeting room and down the hall. They made their way down the central stairway and to the second floor Library where Orin sat down at a desk that was piled high with several ancient tomes.

"We're wasting our time here, Orin. We've looked through almost every book in the Library already." said David, tired of spending day after day pouring over old textbooks that were getting them nowhere.

"Patience, David. You will find that it will only take but one book with one answer to change the course of this war. It is not our responsibility to

8

question when the answer will come, but only to look for it, so that when it does come, our eyes and our minds are open and ready for what it has to tell us!" said Orin in his usual mentoring way.

David respected the old mage, after all, he had proved to be invaluable when it came to helping David unlock his powers the first time, but his incessant desire to look for answers in texts that were nearly as old as he was left David's head spinning and his eyes heavy.

"Can't we try looking for answers somewhere else for a day or two and give my eyes a break?" asked David, already feeling his eyelids start to close as he opened the first book Orin handed him titled *Hurea: A Brief History.*

"No! There is nowhere else that holds the knowledge of the ages, well...nowhere except my mind..." said Orin, chuckling. "But, alas, my mind fails me at the moment – so we must look to the books for our answers of what has passed, so we will know what is to come!"

David let out a sigh and admitted defeat, knowing he would never win this argument – Orin was as stubborn as an ox. Once he had his mind set on something, nothing was going to change it.

David walked over to the corner of the library and plopped down against the wall, resting the open book on his knees, and allowing the light from the outer windows to illuminate the pages.

He began to read a section about the start of the Mystic Wars:

The time had come when the Mystics of Creation could see that they could not sway their brother but would have to take up arms against him in order to stop him from carrying out his plan of destruction and to save the race of Man from extinction.

In the days leading up to the first battles, the Mystics began their campaign of recruiting the various races of the world in their effort to amass an army large enough to defeat the growing darkness of their brother's creation.

Two Mystics traveled East to the Land of the Immortals where they aimed to convince the Elves of old to come to the aid of Man, while another two traveled to the mines of the Draconian Mountains, just South of Draco's Pass, to meet with the Dwarves in their emerald halls to enlist their aid in the coming battles.

The final two Mystics of Creation, the eldest brother and sister, stayed with the children of Men, assisting them with their preparations, forging them magical weapons and armor that would protect them in the coming days against the evil of their brother – knowing he would be pouring his heart and soul into his army of demons, giving them weapons of unimaginable horror.

David paused for a moment while he rubbed his eyes, trying to fight away his drowsiness. As interesting as the history of Hurea was, he had been pouring over similar texts for days on end in a futile effort to find the key to defeating the Defiant One and his armies.

He looked over to see Orin pouring over a book of his own, seemingly lost in the pages within. He swore that old man could read from dusk to dawn without a break! He shook his head and renewed his focus back on his book before picking up where he had left off:

With the might of the six Mystics of Creation, along with the combined forces of Men, Elves, and Dwarves, the Mystics felt they were at last prepared to face off against their brother and his army.

When the attack finally came, they discovered they had been woefully unprepared.

Their brother had amassed such a force, that he outnumbered them a hundred to one. He had convinced some of the race of Man to betray their own and pledge themselves to him for the promise of power beyond their imagination – creating an order of dark mages. They possessed terrible black magic and fought alongside his ferocious demons, providing them magical protection and artillery that were cutting down the forces of men by the hundreds.

His army was led by terrible wolf-like beasts with the intelligence of men but the savage strength and ferocity of an animal, striking fear into the hearts of everyone they encountered.

Their armies were outnumbered and out matched, but together they fought bravely on while the Mystics waged war above the battlefield, clashing time and time again in an endless array of power.

Finally, when all seemed lost and their forces were waning thin, the eldest Mystic did the unthinkable – severely wounded, he gathered what was left of his lifeforce and released it in a powerful spell that enveloped the Mystic of Destruction in an all-encompassing shroud of light.

The spell entangled him and imploded, causing a massive explosion and a blinding light that could be seen for miles and miles.

When the light subsided, the Mystic of Destruction was gone, and in his wake was left a giant vortex in the middle of the battlefield. It was swirling around viscously, pulling the army of demons toward its center and swallowing them whole, one by one, as they fell into its depths. In a matter of moments, the entire army had been consumed, and all fell silent.

When the remaining Mystics rushed to their fallen brother's aid, he was unconscious and fading fast – so they quickly brought him to the Holy Altar in an effort to utilize the healing properties of the Crystal Caverns, hoping to enhance their powers and allow what little strength they had left to heal his wounds and bring him back from the brink of death.

Alas, their efforts were futile, and their brother began to fade from existence. In a last-ditch effort to preserve his life and power, the remaining Mystics were able to consolidate his fleeting life force into a magical artifact made from the Mystic Crystals within the cavern walls, sealing away his power.

As they assessed their wounds, they knew their time was fading. Their injuries were great, and their combined powers had been depleted from the battle they had waged with their sinister brother. Knowing their time was short, they put into motion a plan that would seal their powers and lifeforce away along with their brother's, until a time when another would come that was worthy of taking their place as the final Mystic of Creation.

They chose a select few Men who had proven to be courageous and pure of heart to inherit some of their powers and hold onto their secret, passing it down from generation to generation, until that day arrived when the warrior they prophesied would come to claim their powers and once again defend the world from their evil brother, fearing he would one day find a way to escape his prison and wreak havoc once again on the world of the living.

And so the Elder Council was formed and the Orb of Power was sealed away within the Temple at the foot of the Mystic Mountain, deep within the Outer Woods, until the day when its call would be heard and the one worthy of its power would arrive.

David sat up, blinking the tears from his eyes. He didn't realize he had been holding them open for so long, leaving them dry and irritated from the strain.

He had never heard the story told so eloquently, and the part of the story about the Crystal Caverns really stuck out to him. Tyrius had told him that the Master Elder had taken him and the King to a cavern filled with Crystals in the Birthplace of the World. He also said it was where the Mystics had placed their brother to rest in a temple deep within the mountains, within a Crystal Cavern. Could it be the same cavern that the book had mentioned? If so, did it really possess properties that enhanced the Mystics Powers? He decided to get up and tell Orin what he had found.

He walked over to the old mage, who was still too entranced in his own pages to notice David's approach, and tapped him gently on his shoulder.

"Woah! Hey oh!" said Orin, jumping up in surprise. "Oh, David! It's just you! You know better than to sneak up on me like that while I'm reading!" He picked up his walking stick to whack David on the head, something David had grown accustomed to – and David quickly ducked just in time to avoid being struck.

"Hey! Watch it, old man!" teased David, "I found something I think you may want to hear." he said, cautiously stepping closer and handing Orin the open book he had been reading. He pointed to the part where the book had mentioned the Crystal Cavern and their magical properties.

His eyes began to widen as he read the text over and over, until finally he looked up at David with eyes as big as an owl. "My boy... I think you've found it!" he said.

"Found what?" asked David.

"Our answer!" replied Orin, with a grin.

Chapter II

Hmm...yes, this does sound a lot like the crystal caverns I saw in the Birthplace of the World" said Tyrius, rubbing his beard thoughtfully.

Tyrius and Orin were pouring over the text from the book *Hurea: A Brief History* shortly after David had discovered the reference while searching through the books in the Library.

"What do you think it means? Could it be that these same crystals are in fact the source of the Mystic Crystals?" asked Orin.

"I'm not sure, but it does seem a logical conclusion. I knew I felt a powerful energy within those caverns, but at the time I didn't think much of it and attributed it to the holiness of the site – after all, it is the burial tomb of the Eldest Mystic of Creation. Sites as holy as those tend to radiate with energy, which I presume is why they were chosen in the first place." replied Tyrius, deep in thought.

"Sorry, but how do you think these crystals would help us against the Defiant One?" asked Erin, trying to follow along.

She was sitting by David in the dining hall as they snacked on various dishes prepared for them by the kitchen staff while discussing the news.

"It's just a thought, but I believe these crystals, if they are in fact the ones that were used to forge the Mystic Crystals, could help David reestablish his link with the Orb. Those crystals were the only known materials that could store the incredible powers of the Mystics of Creation long ago. They not only harnessed their dwindling lifeforce and magic, but they restored their power to its former glory so that when David arrived and bonded with it, he effectively became the bearer of the consolidated power of all six Mystics of Creation.

"If David can reestablish his link to that well of power, and those crystals can enhance his connection to it, he may be able to access those powers in ways he never dreamed possible before." he said, turning to David.

"David, if this is true, the answers you seek can only be found in those caverns. If you want to redeem yourself like you say and play your part in stopping the Defiant One and his armies, this is your chance."

David sat silently for a moment thinking over the task at hand.

"If by going to this place there's a chance it will help me regain my powers and stop the Defiant One, then I must go as soon as possible." said David, making up his mind. "The only thing is, I don't know the way."

"In this, I will help you" said Tyrius, "I am the only one who has been there before, so I will help you find the way back. I only wish that the Mystic Crystal the Elder Master had entrusted me with still had the power to send us there like it had before. Ever since the Defiant One has returned I can feel its power being drained. It is nearly spent, I'm afraid. Perhaps by going to the Crystal Caverns, it too will be restored? This alone is worthy of exploring." he said.

"Well, if you think you're going anywhere without me, then you're crazy!" said Erin, grabbing David's hand firmly. "I'm going too!"

"I wouldn't have it any other way!" said David, squeezing her hand gently, a smile breaking across his face.

David was relieved that Erin was volunteering to come along so easily, as he wasn't ready to part ways from her once again. The last time they parted, it had been in the middle of the night and they didn't even get to say goodbye. Erin had snuck away while he was distracted by a sound in the middle of his watch in her attempt to get back to Eldergate and rescue her friend and mentor, Tyrius.

After they were together once again, having both been through many battles and tribulations on their own separate journeys, David had promised Erin he wouldn't let her out of his sight again, and he didn't intend on going off without her by his side.

Not to mention, David didn't like the thought of being away from her again – he cared about Erin deeply, and the thought of parting from her left a dull throbbing in his chest. She was the closest friend he'd ever had, and their growing romance had lit a fire in his heart that he had never known before. Something he had been missing his entire life – love.

While they were discussing their plans, Reginald, the head steward to Castle Ravenfell and dear friend of the Royal Family, opened the door to the dining hall and in entered King Reximus Kane, his two closest friends Reingard and Holzer, Orin, his General, Cornelius Owen, and King Eldergate with his General Nathaniel Ryan of the Eldergate Royal Guard.

They each proceeded into the room and took a seat at the long table next to David and the others, all except General Ryan, who chose instead to stand behind his King, always at the ready in the event of an emergency.

Tyrius had sent for Reginald to find Rex and the other leaders when Orin and David had told him of their findings so that they could discuss their path going forward.

"Well, what news do you have for us?" asked Rex, his deep bellowing voice nearly shaking the glasses on the table.

He quickly pulled up a chair across from David and Erin and started piling his plate high with various meats and bread, Reingard and Holzer following suit. One would think they had all been starved the past week with how they were digging into their food, but that was far from the case – they always ate like this, as if it were an unspoken contest between the three barbarians, seeing which one could eat the most and the fastest.

"Well..." said Tyrius, clearly a little displeased by the manners of the barbarians, while David, Erin, and Orin were chuckling silently to his side. "We think we have found a clue that may help David restore his connection to the orb."

With this, Rex stopped chewing and looked up, "You mean, he can get his powers back?" he asked through a mouth full of food.

"I'm not sure, but it is a start." replied Tyrius.

"Well, what are we waiting for?" asked Rex, finally swallowing his food, excited to hear the good news.

"That's actually why we called you in here. This book recounts the battle of the Mystics and the events surrounding the days leading up to and after the Mystic War. It speaks of a Crystal Cavern that holds magical properties, enhancing objects of magic, and possibly magical people, beyond their original capacity. The description of these caverns sounds remarkably like the caverns the Master Elder transported the King and I to when he rescued us from the palace dungeons. If they are in fact one and the same, then that means they are located in the Birthplace of the World — far to the North." replied Tyrius.

"I see...so you will need to take David there, I presume?" asked General Ryan, still standing politely behind his King.

"Precisely. I believe that is our best chance in helping David rekindle his connection to the orb — something the fate of the world depends on. Without his full might, we cannot possibly hope to defeat the Defiant One." said Tyrius.

"To the North...but that would take us past Eldergate. How do you expect to get past the Defiant

One and his armies unnoticed?" asked General Ryan, always the strategist.

"There might be another way..." replied Rex, running his fingers through his beard – something he tended to do when he was deep in thought. "Long ago, before Ravenfell was founded, there was a great battle within this valley between the Northern and Southern Kingdoms. The Southern King had brought his forces up the southern slopes of the Draconian Mountains through a tunnel leading into the valley. That tunnel still exists today, only it hasn't been kept up with much and the entrance has been blocked by some fallen debris. We could clear the entrance and they could use that tunnel to get around Eldergate and the Defiant One's watchful gaze unnoticed." he said.

"That seems to be a much safer route" replied General Ryan. "Where does it come out at?" he asked Rex.

"It leads to the foothills just south of the Draconian Mountains. In it's prime, there was a bustling mountain village at its mouth that served as a trading post between the Northern and Southern Kingdoms. Now, I'm not too sure – our people don't travel through the tunnel, and we haven't seen any travelers from those parts in years."

"Well, anything can be better than going past Eldergate – we can't risk David being caught by the enemy without having access to his powers. He is our only hope, we must keep him safe until he is ready." replied the General. "The Southern Tunnel may take us the more roundabout route, but it should be much safer and gives us the advantage of secrecy that traveling North wouldn't provide. Do you have any maps from when the tunnel was operational?" he asked.

"Yeah, I think we still have some lying around here somewhere," replied Rex, "Holzer, do you think you can find 'em?"

"Leave it to me, sir!" he replied, and quickly rushed out of the room carrying what remained of his plate of food in one hand and a mug of ale in the other.

"Okay, so that leaves the clearing of the tunnel entrance. Reingard – take some men to the Southern Tunnel entrance and make sure it gets cleared by nightfall. Time is against us, my friend!" said Rex, patting his childhood friend, and now Lieutenant in his army, on the back.

"You got it, boss!" said Reingard, and he too left immediately to carry out his orders, carrying his food and drink with him, its contents sloshing over the rim of his mug as he rushed from the room.

"Right, so who's all going with David on this adventure?" asked Rex, "I would love to go, you know I enjoyed our last one, but my duty lies with my people now. I must stay here to ensure our defenses are ready for when the enemy comes."

"I kind of figured that," said David frowning. He was sorry to hear his friend wouldn't be coming but understood and respected his decision to stay and look after his people. "As it stands now, it will be Tyrius, Erin, and I – we can't risk sending a big party, as that will draw some attention and our success really depends on secrecy. If General Krauss or the Defiant One were to find out we had left

Ravenfell and were out in the wild, they would surely send out the Wolf Guard, or worse, to track us down." said David.

"Yes...that makes sense" said Orin, finally chiming in. "I regret to say, that I, too, will not be going. I think my expertise would best be served here, helping the men prepare their magical defenses. These demons...they aren't just ruthless; they are powerful, and some are gifted with magical powers unlike anything any of you have seen before. I am the only one who has witnessed it firsthand."

With this news, David felt his stomach sink a bit. He had come to rely heavily on Orin and his wisdom over the course of their time together and wasn't sure he was ready to part from the old mage.

He understood why he wanted to stay, but in this moment, he wanted to be selfish and ask him to come along despite his better judgement.

Sensing his internal struggle, Erin grabbed David's hand beneath the table and squeezed before looking him in the eyes. She smiled and David could feel his tension release. He returned the smile in kind, thankful for her understanding and support.

Rex sat across the table, thinking it over for a moment before responding. "I want to send Reingard and Holzer with you. I trust those two with my life, and I would feel better knowing they were by your side on this journey."

"We would be honored" said David, looking at Erin and Tyrius who both nodded in agreement.

"What about you, Ryan" asked Erin, hopeful for her friend and lifelong protector to join their party as well.

He stood behind King Eldergate with a somber expression, silent for a while before he finally responded. "Erin...I've looked after you since you were a young child and have taken a keen interest in your training. You have surprised me in many ways, and I have been honored to be able to play such an integral role in your life. But, this time, I have to let you go without me. I am responsible for my men and their safety now. In the coming days, my men will be looking to me as their leader, to give them hope and direction in their time of need. I can't abandon them now...no matter how much I want to go with you."

Erin could tell those words weighed heavily on the General's heart, and she respected him even more for having the courage to do what he felt was right, over what he wanted.

"I understand" she said, smiling at her friend. "You have always been there for me, looking out for me. Now it is my turn to return the favor. We will get David to these Crystal Caverns safely, and we will restore his connection with the orb so that he can fulfil his destiny and defeat the Defiant One once and for all! You just focus on keeping your men and the King alive, we will take care of the rest!" she said confidently.

They all stood up, feeling the decision was made.

"While my men are clearing the tunnel entrance and getting you the maps, take this time to gather what supplies you need for the coming journey" said Rex, "I will make sure you have whatever you need."

"Thank you, Rex," said David, "I promise I will do everything I can to get back my powers and defeat this threat to your people. You did your part, now it is up to me to do mine."

"May the Creator God be with us in the coming days!" said Orin, to which they all silently nodded and agreed, each wondering within their hearts what chances they truly had of surviving the coming storm.

Chapter III

Octavian Krauss stood silently in the King's chambers of the Royal Palace. He was looking through the outer window and out from the high tower at the shattered earth below, still pouring out an endless supply of demons for his ever-increasing army. An army he would use to expand his kingdom throughout Hurea, exerting his control and dominance on anyone and anything that stood in his way.

His plan had worked marvelously. He had succeeded in luring David right into his trap, giving him the opportunity to turn his Mystic power and its energy into the power source for his spell, unleashing the Defiant One and his endless army of demons into the world of the living.

What a gullible hero they have, he thought to himself.

He turned to leave and nearly jumped in surprise. The Defiant One had appeared behind him and stood silent and expressionless, leaving him with a sense of uneasiness that never seemed to fade, even after having spent several days now working with him, going over their plans for absolute domination.

He was an imposing figure and stark naked, taking the form of a large man. The only indication of his gender was the masculine features of his muscular body. He had no hair on his head or his body, but instead had smooth, flawless skin that seemed to defy the toll of time – appearing to still be in his prime despite being as ancient as the world itself.

His eyes were a milky white, without pupils and devoid of all expression. Despite this, Octavian always knew when those empty eyes were focused intently on him.

"My lord..." said Octavian, bowing low in respect.

"I have been pleased with your loyalty" came the voice of the Defiant One. It rang through the air, seemingly from everywhere at once, or was it just in his mind? He could never tell. One thing he knew for sure, it left him extremely uneasy, even after the past week. Octavian didn't think he would ever get used to it.

"Thank you, my lord. I am your humble servant, as always." he said, still in a bow.

"You may rise" came the voice again. "Tell me, Octavian, what is it that you hope to accomplish?" he asked.

"Only to please you, my lord." replied Octavian.

"Do not make the mistake of taking me for a fool." responded the Defiant One, "I know your deepest desires, I have seen them in my mind. You would be wise to speak plainly, or your usefulness might expire sooner than you might think." he said, threatening Octavian in a calm, collected manner - a manner that left the tyrant king even more uneasy.

"I apologize, my lord. I only meant that your will is my number one priority, but it is as you say...I desire power. The power to seek revenge on those who have humiliated me!" replied Octavian.

"You speak of your former king?" asked the Defiant One.

"Yes...he took me for a fool, and lied to me, keeping my heritage a secret, forcing me to serve the very man who murdered my family. I cannot rest while he lives." said Octavian, rage rising in his chest.

"You will have your revenge. Tell me, how are the raids coming?" asked the Defiant One calmly.

"I am pleased to say that the Outer Woods are finally under our control. The last of the resistance has been squashed. The Northern Kingdom is now yours, my lord." said Octavian proudly.

"Yes...it would seem it is. And how do you think we should proceed now?" asked the Mystic, still keenly focused on the man before him.

"I believe we should send our forces up the mountain pass to Ravenfell, my lord. That is where the remaining forces are gathered, barricading themselves within the mountain valley in a futile effort to stand against your indomitable might." said Octavian, hoping to get approval to begin their expansion South.

"Ahh...but your anger and hatred cloud your vision." replied the Defiant One.

"My lord?" asked Octavian, not following his logic.

"Your hatred of the king is preventing you from seeing the whole picture. The King of Eldergate and the King of Ravenfell, they are not our only enemies. In fact, they are but a fraction of the forces that stand in our way." he replied.

"Do you speak of the Elves, my lord?" asked Octavian, trying to follow along.

"Yes...the Elves, and their brethren, the Dwarves. Do not underestimate the Dwarves. They may be a reclusive people, content to mine away their lives in their hidden chambers but make no mistake – they are a formidable foe once incited to action. You would do well to remember this"

"Yes, my lord." replied Octavian, "What is it that you think we should do, then?" he asked.

"You will order the advance forces to split in two. We will send half to the South to besiege Ravenfell. The other half we will send to the East towards the White City. We will pass by the halls of the Dwarves and leave them be for now. We cannot risk them joining in the fight until the Elves have been handled. Only then will we take the fight to the Dwarves and their Emerald halls." he said, his eyes and expression still unwavering.

When he sensed that Octavian had understood his task, the Defiant One simply nodded slightly and vanished without a trace. Was he ever really there, or was it simply a projection? Octavian never could tell.

Relieved that he was alone once again, the king shook off the lingering uneasiness and immediately started off towards the stairs.

When he reached the bottom and exited into the main corridor leading to the great entrance hall, he was greeted by the general of the Wolf Guard.

"Your majesty. What news do you bring?" he asked in his snarling tongue, stepping in stride with his King.

"The Defiant One has given us new orders, Targon. We are to split our main force in two, sending one to Ravenfell, and the other across Draco's Pass to besiege the White City." he replied, now reaching the main entry hall and stopping before a small company of Wolf Guard who had been waiting for their next assignment.

"And what of the Dwarves? Surely they won't like us passing through their territory." replied Targon.

"Our orders are to leave them be, for now. We must not risk pulling them into this just yet. For now, our focus will be on the Elves and the Humans. With them out of our way, we can then consolidate our remaining forces to take out the Dwarves. Targon, I expect you to lead the forces to the East. As for me, I will personally see to it that our Southern neighbors are extinguished once and for all." said Octavian with a flicker in his eyes.

The company of Wolves bowed to their king before taking off at an incredible pace through the front doors and down the spiral pathway that had been carved into the side of the pillar of rocky earth that the palace now rested upon. They would spread the news to the army of demons and begin their march Eastward, while the remaining forces would prepare for their march south towards the mountain pass.

Octavian couldn't help but smile. His time had finally come to march on Ravenfell – and he couldn't be more eager to begin.

Chapter IV

David and Erin finished packing their bags, finally prepared for the long journey ahead, before sitting down at the foot of David's bed. David wrapped his arms around Erin and pulled her backwards, falling into the soft blankets and cushioned mattress. In that moment, they both cherished the coziness and warmth of the bed – knowing it would be the last time they would enjoy such luxury for a long time. The journey through the wilderness was never a comfortable experience, and they would be heading through unfamiliar and possibly hostile territory. It was going to be a long, hard road ahead of them.

As Erin nestled into the crook of David's arm and lay her head on his chest, she took comfort knowing they would be together through the coming journey. She was confident that no matter what they faced they would be able to overcome it together.

David kissed the top of her head and squeezed her tightly. It was moments like this that he cherished the most. He wished they could just live normal lives together, enjoying each other's company, not worrying about the rest of the world, but he knew that was a fantasy at best. They would never enjoy that kind of peace, not while the Defiant One was still roaming their land, not while his army of demons were still mercilessly killing every living thing they encountered on their march to domination.

He sat up, rubbing his temples. He had been having these horrible headaches ever since his battle with General Krauss. Sometimes they were barely noticeable, while other times it throbbed so painfully that it prevented him from carrying on even simple conversations. Eventually the pain subsided, and he stretched and prepared to get up, knowing that Tyrius and the others were waiting on them.

David gave Erin one last long, passionate kiss before he stood up and helped her to her feet. Then they grabbed their belongings and headed out the door to meet with the others.

They made their way out of the castle and down the road through the bustling mountain city before starting towards the far end of the valley where the Southern Tunnel entrance lay.

Throughout the city the townspeople were busy at work, preparing in any way they could for the coming days. The streets were bustling with activity as carts and wagons full of supplies were pulled by mules towards the castle, stockpiling everything ranging from blankets and clothes, to food and equipment. They had been instructed to help gather as much as they could while they had the chance, knowing that any day now they would be under siege by the hideous creatures that had overrun the Northern Kingdom and caused so many of the refugees that now occupied their houses to flee from their homes in the Outer Woods.

Those who had fled were extremely grateful for the hospitality of the people of Ravenfell. Despite their differences, they had been kind and welcoming – many finding over the past week that they were related and rekindling past familial ties, others quickly developing friendships that would last the ages – if they were so lucky to survive these trying times. The one thing that bound them together most of all and had contributed most to their fast acceptance of one another was the common threat they faced from the Defiant One and his armies. They each knew that their best chance of survival was to work together towards their mutual goals.

As David and Erin walked beyond the city limits and through the valley, they took in the surrounding beauty, knowing it may be the last time they see the valley in such splendor.

The sky was mostly overcast, with a few patches of blue peeking through occasionally as the wind gently moved the cloud cover over their heads, but it only seemed to enhance the natural beauty of the valley. When the sun broke through those openings in the clouds, brilliant shafts of light would pour through, highlighting random patches of rolling hills far below and enhancing the vibrant colors of the changing seasons.

In addition to the visual cues, David could also feel the season shifting towards the cooler fall weather, each passing day growing shorter than the one before and bringing in a cooler northern breeze. The leaves had just recently started to drop their bright vibrant green, being replaced with a slight tinge of orange and brown near the edges indicating the shift in seasons was upon them. On the peaks of the surrounding mountains, snow seemed to be encroaching lower with each passing day, warning of the coming winter that would be upon them in only a few short weeks.

When they finally reached the area before the tunnel, they could see that the clearing operation had been successful.

It had taken Reingard and a crew of roughly twenty men only a few short hours to clear the fallen debris from the entrance into the tunnel, leaving the wide opening into the mountain once again accessible. It was roughly fifteen feet across and twenty or so feet high and was supported by large wooden beams in a rectangular cut, making what resembled a large doorway into the mountain.

Its depths were blacker than night, giving the tunnel a foreboding appearance that nearly made David second guess his chosen route out of the valley. The mountain pass, although hazardous in its own ways and potentially soon to be crawling with demons and undead mages, seemed to look like a much more reasonable approach.

Holzer had been able to sort through the old maps in the record hall and found a map of the tunnel passages along with what was once the Southern Kingdom before he met back up with Tyrius and made his way to the tunnel with his and Reingard's packs. He was standing by Reingard and the others, plotting what David assumed would be their route through the Southern Tunnel and out into the lands beyond.

When David and Erin approached the others, they each prepared to say their goodbyes.

General Ryan seemed to be the most uneasy of the bunch, hesitant to let Erin go off on her own without his watchful eye. He was confident in her ability to take care of herself, but only he and the King knew of her importance to the survival of the Northern Kingdom, and his fear of what might happen to her was beginning to overshadow his duty to his men.

The King put his hand on the General's shoulder and squeezed reassuringly, telling him it was okay and to let her go. With this gesture, the General finally seemed to relax.

He looked to David before speaking, "You make sure you keep a close eye on her, you hear? I know you two have become close, but don't you forget that I've spent my whole adult life watching her grow into the woman she is, and you would do well to make sure she comes back unharmed. You understand?" he said, glaring at David like a father would before letting a young man take his daughter off on a date.

"I understand, General. But honestly, if anything, she'll be the one protecting me. I'm no match for her skills with a bow or blade, and from what I've seen, you'd be hard pressed to find anyone who is!" said David, half-joking and clearly uncomfortable at the sudden intensity of the General's gaze directed at him. He understood the close relationship that General Ryan had with Erin, and noticed it was much like a father to his daughter, and he had felt that intense gaze over the past week more than he would have liked.

"Oh, stop it, you two!" said Erin scolding the two. "Ryan, you know I can take care of myself! And David, you've gotten much better with a sword since our first encounter outside of Eldergate. I am confident you will continue to improve, and will no doubt become a formidable opponent to anyone who stands in your way, orb or not!" she said, smiling.

She wrapped her arms tight around General Ryan, squeezing him and kissing his cheek goodbye.

Orin and Rex took turns saying farewell to David and Erin, and the King wished them all a successful journey before reminding them what was at stake should they fail.

"Trust in the Creator God, He will lead you all to safety and success! Just don't take too long to find it!" he added jokingly, to which they all chuckled nervously. It may have been a joke, but it had a very serious undertone – he was right, if they took too long, there may not be a world left to fight for.

Holzer and Reingard promised Rex they would behave and keep a close eye on David and Erin before they turned and headed into the tunnel entrance, leading the party into the depths of the mountain.

When the last of them disappeared around a bend and out of sight, Rex and the others made their way back to the Castle to discuss the preparations for the defense of the valley.

Rex, Orin, the two Generals, and King Eldergate along with the officers of both armies all took a seat around a large circular table within the war room before spreading a map of the valley out across its surface and beginning their planning.

Rex, having intimate knowledge of the surrounding lands and the defensiveness of the valley, was the first to speak.

"Gentlemen, we find ourselves in a dire situation today and are left with the defensive planning of what will likely become the final stand of men. I cannot say we will make it out of this alive, but I know one thing for sure – we will give these demons one hell of a fight!" he pounded his fist on the table to drive the point home, eliciting a few hearty shouts of agreement throughout the chambers before continuing.

"One of the reasons our forefathers chose this valley for their new home is because of its defensive position within the ring of mountains. The mountains are high and unforgiving, should anyone try to enter the valley through any means other than the narrow pass from the North, or the Southern Tunnel to the South. Knowing this, they built this great city in the valley, depending on its isolation and security to protect our people for generations to come. We will use this to our advantage.

"I propose we build a series of fortifications here, here, and here, behind the mountain pass and before it, along with lookout towers on the northern side to provide ample warning in the event of a pending attack. This will give us foresight on when they are coming and prevent us from being caught off guard."

Everyone around the table nodded in agreement, seeing the logic in the barbarian King's plans.

"We have a vast amount of stone and wood from the valley and from fallen debris that we can use to build several walls leading up the mountain pass on both sides. This will hopefully slow the enemy march once they reach the top of the pass, and the narrow walkway through the mountain will force the enemy, although vast in numbers, to bottleneck and therefore reduce the overall number we must fight at one time."

General Ryan chimed in.

"This is where we must hold them, for if we let them through the passageway into the valley, they will be able to spread out their numbers and we will quickly be overrun. Should this happen, Rex, how long do you suppose we could hold them off within the castle walls?" he asked.

"I'm not sure...it depends on how many of them are left, and how many of us are left at that time too." he said somberly.

Everyone in the room knew that if it came to that, their time would be short-lived at best. The castle was well fortified, but it could only do so much against an army of demons and black mages. Knowing this, they were all the more determined to make sure they held the enemy at the entrance to the valley.

"Orin, what protection will you be able to provide for us against their mages? You proved to be quite a valuable asset during the battle of Eldergate." said General Ryan.

Orin had been standing and pacing back and forth around the room, deep in thought while listening to the strategies being presented.

"Hm? Oh yes...well, I can tell you this much. When the Mystic Wars broke out long ago, there were many more of my kind around to help battle the endless waves of demons and black mages. And even with our numbers, we dwindled away until I was all that was left. The forces we will be up against, they will be ruthless, cunning, and powerful. The mages are humans, or once were before they sold their souls to the Defiant One in exchange for their powers. Now, they are but a shell of what they once were – though no less formidable.

"I will focus my efforts on the mages like you say and do whatever I can to help with the barriers before the enemy arrives. That is all I can do... it is all any of us can do." he said, slowly looking around the room.

Rex nodded in agreement before replying.

"In the meantime, I will instruct my men not tasked on the fortifications to begin preparing for a long siege. We will need an abundance of supplies and food stored away for the men, women, and children. We have already started to increase production as much as possible and the townsfolk have been preparing all produce for long-term storage. Once the siege begins, we won't be able to focus on our farms or livestock – the food will need to be harvested and prepared or risk being soured." said Rex.

"Agreed," said General Ryan before addressing the room.

"I'll have my men help in whatever way possible. We have increased our training exercises to ensure the men are prepared and fit for battle. We will continue to request that any man capable of fighting please step forward and volunteer for service. We have already had several dozen speak up and begin their training, however, we fear it is not enough. We will need every abled bodied man we can get if we are to survive the coming battle." said General Ryan.

"What about the woman and children?" asked the King, concerned for the wellbeing of his people. "Heaven forbid if the demons make it through our defenses and into the valley, we can't ensure the safety of our citizen's if that happens" he said.

"He's right" said Rex, "When the enemy finally comes, we will have all the women and children make their way through the Southern Tunnel, and once we are sure they are all safely through, we will block the entrance once again to prevent any pursuit. It will protect them from the enemy, even if it means locking us inside the valley without a means of escape." said Rex, to which everyone agreed. It would be a necessary sacrifice, even if it meant their own demise – a sacrifice each of them was willing to make to ensure the safety of their families.

With everyone now aware of their task and ready to get to work, the war council set out to put their plans in motion, making sure they used every last minute to prepare for the coming siege, knowing that every moment they had was a blessing not to be wasted.

Chapter V

After trekking for what felt like hours through the unyielding darkness of the Southern Tunnel, David began to wonder if they would ever see the light of day again.

The tunnel seemed to stretch on forever, twisting and turning before branching off in various directions every few hundred feet. It was proving to be a difficult task to track where they were and where they had already been, let alone which direction they were heading.

Fortunately for them, Holzer was a quick study with the map he had found and seemed to be confident in the direction he was leading them.

The only light they had to see by was the light of a few burning torches carried by Reingard and David, and that of Tyrius' staff – which he had somehow magically illuminated to help provide a wider and less blinding light source for the travelers. Eventually the torches burned out, and all the light that remained was from Tyrius, and suddenly David was very thankful he had decided to come along.

They walked on in silence for miles into the depth of the mountains, sometimes traveling downward, other times they took passages that were rising. It was extremely difficult to determine how far they had come, or how much further they seemed to have. All they came to know was the eternal darkness that surrounded them just outside of the circular boundary of light illuminating from Tyrius' staff.

As they walked along through the darkness with little else to look at, David took notice of the textures of the walls. The pathways had apparently been carved out of the mountain itself, hundreds of thousands of chisel marks etched in the rock wall, leaving a disorienting texture that was smooth in some areas, while mostly ridged and rough in others.

As he ran his fingers along the cool, moist stone, he could almost see the images of what must have been hundreds of workers, constantly chipping away at an impossible task for days, weeks, even months on end as they tunneled through the heart of the mountains, never knowing when or even if they would reach the other side.

He imagined the look on the workers faces when they first saw the thin shafts of light peeking through a small hole in the wall as they finally broke through to the other side, signaling the end of their journey had finally come, and the relief that would have flooded through the workers at such a sight. To see the light of day after having endured such infinite darkness would be enough to bring a grown man to tears – and David was eager for the moment when he, too, would see the light of day again.

After what felt like an eternity of hiking through the darkness, they finally decided to stop in a wide natural cavern so they could eat and rest. It seemed to stretch on forever in each direction, opening up into a large chamber filled with great hanging stalactites across the ceiling and enormous stalagmites protruding from the ground all around them. The sound of a steady but distant dripping followed by the distinct plop of impacted water indicated that they were near an underground pond or lake, so Tyrius headed off into the darkness to seek it out.

Erin had set up a small fire to heat up a pot of water and make some tea, while Reingard and Holzer passed around some dried meats and bread for everyone to take and fill their growling bellies.

They suspected the journey to take at least a day or two, maybe more, before they would reach the other side. The only problem was within the depths of the mountain, there were no indications of how much time had passed, and therefore, the party had no real way of measuring how far they had come or how far they still had to go other than markers left on the map and the growing emptiness in their bellies and aching of their limbs.

This cavern was one such marker. It indicated they were nearly halfway through the tunnel. Their next marker would be a large, horse shaped rock formation at which they would have to veer right before reaching their final downward trek through a long corridor that consisted of what was once a vital salt mine for the Southern Kingdom.

Holzer explained that the Southern Kingdom bordered the great South Sea and was littered with similar salt mines – a precious commodity that had become a stable of the once prosperous kingdom.

"What exactly happened to the Southern Kingdom after the war with the North?" asked David, curious to know more about the lands they were headed to.

"Well – we don't know too much since they stopped all trading with Ravenfell nearly ten years ago. At first, we would try to send merchants through these tunnels to commence their trading in the old mining village that rested on the southern side of the mountains, but over time, these trips proved to be more difficult than the bounty was worth, and we shut down the trade route for good." replied Reingard.

"What do you think caused the people to stop trading?" asked David.

"Not sure, really." said Reingard. "The truth is, everyone was kind of wondering the same thing – considering the kingdom had fallen and all. You would have thought they would want to continue trading with us to keep up the supply chain, not shut us out. After all, many of the folk in Ravenfell had come from the Southern Kingdom and still had family who stayed behind, but that communication had eventually stopped as well, but not before the letters started becoming more and more hostile."

"What do you mean, hostile?" asked Erin, helping herself to another small piece of meat.

"Well, people in the South, they started to blame us for their misfortunes, claiming if we hadn't left, the kingdom would have been able to rebound after the wars. That kind of thinking seemed to spread like wildfires down there, and eventually it festered into a kind of hatred towards anyone who lived in Ravenfell or beyond." said Reingard, "My own uncle, whom I had loved and held much respect for, was one of these people. He refused to leave his family farm after the war, and he became bitter with his old age."

Reingard looked down as he finished, clearly still hurt by the past.

"I see..." said Erin, and feeling the topic was a sensitive one, she decided to change the subject.

"So, once we reach the end of the tunnel, what's our next destination?" she asked.

Holzer looked down and examined the map closely before answering, "Well, if the village is still where the map indicates, we should be reaching the small mining outpost of Ashmire.

"It was formed during the First Age when the Southern Kingdom first started its expansion north towards the mountains. Once they discovered the rich mineral wealth within the rock, particularly the salt mines, they established Ashmire and it became a bustling little mining community. It prospered for generations, creating some of the wealthiest families within the Southern Kingdom, although most chose to leave the town for the capital city – leaving the mining businesses to be run and operated by the locals while they benefitted the most from the profits."

"How do you know all of this?" asked David, fascinated by the sudden apparent knowledge of what he had previously misjudged as an uneducated foot soldier.

"I told you, my family is from the South. I know a lot about its history, although most of it is secondhand knowledge passed down by my pa" he answered.

As Holzer finished his explanation, Tyrius finally returned from his exploration and informed the others that there was indeed a large underground freshwater spring not far from their campsite. He led Reingard and Holzer to the waters and had them refill their canisters for the night before rejoining them by the fire and helping himself to some tea, bread, and meat.

When he was finished with his meal, he instructed the companions to rest for the night while he took first watch and they each began setting up their bedrolls.

It wasn't hard for David to fall asleep – the darkness was deep and the silence was even deeper, broken only by the light crackling of the fire and the incessant drip of water from the cave ceiling as it splashed onto the surface of the lake in the distance. No evidence of any life, other than moss and the occasional insect or bat, had been seen or heard throughout their day's journey through the darkness – and this thought was extremely comforting for David as he lay on his back with his eyes closed. It meant no threats would sneak up on them during the night, and he was completely okay with that.

***

David was roused sometime in the early morning, or at least he suspected that was the time, as he had no real idea of what time it actually was. He sat up and stretched before thanking Reingard for the watch and preparing for his hopefully uneventful shift.

As he sat in the dark, watching the embers of the fire slowly dwindle away, his eyes remained watchful towards the outer edges of the illuminated circle. Tyrius had set his staff in the middle of the camp, allowing it to provide a radius of soft mystical light for the others to see while on watch. David wondered what other spells Tyrius might know and told himself to remember to ask him during the coming march to see if he could teach him any potential tricks. With this thought came the sudden painful reminder that his powers had been inaccessible ever since the Defiant One had been released from his prison.

David began to wonder more about the sudden disappearance of his powers, and how it was connected to the return of the Mystic of Destruction. Were they even connected? If so, would he ever get his powers back, or were they gone for good? That thought sent a shiver of fear down his spine and the little hairs on his neck tingling. Without his powers, he wouldn't be able to stop the coming invasion and the world of Hurea would be doomed.

He would be useless, like he had always been, and David was not ready for that feeling to return full-time, not after he had felt the incredible power of the orb and the confidence that came with it.

He decided in that moment, that no matter what happened to his powers, he would never let it determine his own sense of worth again. He knew he was more than just his connection to the orb – after all, the orb had chosen him for a reason before he had its power. He would instead focus his energy on improving his fighting ability, so that orb or not, he would be prepared to fight alongside his friends and able to protect the people he had come to care so much about. People like Erin.

He looked over to where Erin was sleeping and marveled at how peaceful she looked. He longed for a day when they could truly experience peace together without having to carry the weight of the world on their shoulders. A day when they could look to the future with certainty, or as much certainty as anyone could in times of peace. He knew long life was not a sure thing, even without war and threats of extinction on the horizon.

As he dreamed of the possible future he and Erin could have together once the Defiant One was defeated, he noticed the others begin to wake.

Deciding it was time to get up and break camp, he went to fetch some water from the spring in the pot for tea while the others fought off their weariness and began preparing for the long hike ahead of them.

When he returned, everyone was up and enjoying a small helping of biscuits that were starting to slightly harden. Erin tossed him one after he set down the pot and Tyrius got the fire going once again to heat the water and prepare the tea.

When they had all had their share of biscuits and tea, they packed up the rest of their belongings and set off into the darkness, each longing for the moment when they finally reached the end of what they hoped would be the darkest part of the journey to the Birthplace of the World and their magical Crystal Caverns.

Chapter VI

Octavian Krauss stood before his army of demons and undead soldiers at the edge of the Outer Woods, looking out across the fields that were once filled with the green pastures and farmlands leading up to the capital city of Eldergate.

Instead, he now stood before a desolate, war-ravaged landscape leading up to a great canyon of sheer cliffs and unfathomable drops into darkness, broken only by a stone bridge that connected to the jutting rock that now supported the Royal Palace.

The bridge spanned hundreds of feet across the chasm that fell into the Dark Abyss – a land of darkness and doom that had been the prison of the Mystic of Destruction and his army of demons for over a thousand years.

Now that rift was open, giving him access to an army so vast and powerful that all of the free world would soon be trembling before him and his mighty army, making him the most powerful ruler in all of Hurea.

He stood before his army of several hundred thousand demons and undead – all clad for war and ready for their coming march across the Great Plains to the foothills of the Draconian Mountains.

He had been tasked by the Defiant One to personally see to the destruction of the resistance taking shelter within the mountain valley of Ravenfell. With the massive army before him, he knew victory was all but certain. With the barbarians and remaining loyalists finally out of his way, he would be one step closer to his ultimate victory of absolute control of the whole of Hurea – a victory he had been dreaming about ever since he discovered his true heritage.

All that would remain are the wretched Elves and Dwarves – two races that he aimed to extinguish once and for all. None would survive the coming age except for the race of Man – a race he knew well enough were far easier to control, and far less of a threat to his long-term rule.

With the others out of the way, he would move his armies to the Southern Lowlands of his people and bring to them the wealth of the Northern Kingdom coupled with the strength and power of his new army. His people would no longer suffer at the expense of the Northern Kingdom and would instead be free to live as they please – after all, the world would be under his control, and therefore his protection. Any who refused to comply would be eliminated or forced into work camps for the betterment of society. There they would stay until they changed their views or died – either way, he would win.

Octavian Krauss looked out across his army and rose his hand high into the air, releasing a powerful blast of energy high into the sky, exploding in a brilliant display of fire and sparks that fell towards the ground around them. The time had come, they would begin their march towards the mountain.

Immediately, his army began its grueling march down the Great Road towards the Great Plains beyond. He watched as the endless lines of demons and undead stretched on for miles and miles. The ground shook beneath their feet and the air was filled with the booming clatter of endless marching and chanting as they made their way through the corridor of trees near the edge of the Outer Woods and began their long journey along the Great Road towards the foothills of the Draconian Mountains.

A smile stretched across his face as he considered how the barbarians and loyalists would be trembling with fear as they witnessed the largest army on earth march across the plains before them.

This would be an enjoyable victory, he thought. But then again, when was victory anything but sweet?

***

Far across the Great Plains, over the rolling foothills, and up the mountain pass, two men from Eldergate were standing watch for the night and had just started playing their third hand in cards. The cool night air was crisp, and the cold was already starting to seep through their thick outer coats and into their bones, forcing them to continuously breathe into their hands to keep their fingers from going numb.

When the towers and other fortifications had been completed just days ago, Fredrick and Christopher had volunteered to keep watch during the night shifts, a shift that had proven far more difficult than they had imagined. They were no warriors, neither of them had even been in a fight in their whole lives, but they each wanted to do their part, and so they agreed that watch duty played a vital role that they could manage without any prior experience, and they were mostly happy to do it.

The nights were long and often uneventful, the only thing keeping them awake was the bitter cold and the awful realization that if they were to fail in their duties, all of their friends and family, let alone themselves, would be put at risk and potentially die: a weight they did not want on their shoulders.

So instead, they spent their nights playing cards and making bets as to whether or not anything eventful would happen that night. So far, nothing had ever happened, and because of this, they were much more surprised when something caught their attention in the far distance, forcing them to jump to their feet and rush to the edge of their watch tower at the northern edge of the mountain pass.

A bright light had flown high into the air in the distance just before the Royal Palace of Eldergate, it's dreadful presence atop the mighty pillar of rock a constant reminder of their former lives within the bustling capitol – a former life they both suspected they would probably never enjoy again. They watched as the light rose ever higher into the sky before finally bursting in a dazzling explosion, leaving trails of flames plummeting in smoky streaks towards the tops of the trees.

A large dark mass started to seep out of the tree line in the far distance where the Great Road entered the Outer Woods and led to Eldergate.

They shared a silent look of confusion before the realization hit them and they immediately picked up their hammers and started banging incessantly on the warning bells, sending the soldiers below into a frenzy.

The time they were dreading had finally arrived - the demon army was coming.

Chapter VII

Reingard and Holzer led David, Erin, and Tyrius for miles through the eternal darkness of the Southern Tunnels. They would stop occasionally to check the map when passing an unexpected fork in the tunnel or when coming across fallen debris that they would have to clear, but for the most part their journey was unceasing and grueling, leaving the company in horrible spirits.

They had already passed the rock formation that looked like a horse hours prior and had expected to come to the salt mines already, but there had been no indication that they had arrived. The walls were still moist and comprised of what appeared to be some type of limestone, all covered in the same endless chisel mark pattern that they had become familiar with over the past two days.

"Holzer, are you absolutely certain we are headed in the right direction?" asked Tyrius, beginning to get concerned.

"Yes, yes...the map said to take the first right after the Horse Head formation, and that is what we did!" said Holzer adamantly.

"Wait, I thought we took a left?" asked Reingard, alarmed.

"No, it was most certainly a right!" said Holzer, annoyed. "According to the map, we should be reaching the salt mines any moment now!" he reassured them.

"But what about the rubble we had to clear away a while back?" asked David, "Are you sure that didn't open up an alternate path you weren't aware of?" he asked.

"Of course, I'm sure!" replied Holzer angrily, "If this passage wasn't the original one, we wouldn't be seeing these chisel marks all over the walls still!" he said, pointing to the chips in the walls and ceiling.

"Yes...that is, unless they had made multiple tunnels for some reason." interjected Tyrius.

"Why would they do that? And why wouldn't they have a fork in the path showing they made another tunnel?" asked Holzer, looking over the map once again in case he missed anything.

"Look, I'm sure we're heading in the right direction. Nothing on the map indicates distance, remember? It's possible that we just expected the mines to be closer to the formation than they really were." said Erin, tired of hearing the constant bickering between the men.

"She's right. Let's just press on. I'm sure we will reach the mines shortly." said Tyrius, catching the hint.

They continued walking on in silence, knowing that the first one to speak would risk inciting another round of arguments and none of them currently had the patience to deal with that right now. For the time being, all they could think about was getting out of this endless tunnel and into the outer world once again.

David silently wondered how Dwarves would ever be so at home in such a place as beneath the ground. The air was stuffy and damp, the silence deafening, and the smell...well...it kind of smells like...

"The ocean?" asked David aloud.

"What was that?" asked Erin, startled by the seemingly random outburst.

"The ocean! It smells like the ocean!" said David, suddenly catching on to his train of thought.

"Yes! I can smell it too, we must be close to the salt mines!" said Erin, suddenly excited.

David licked his finger and ran it along the walls before sticking it back in his mouth – it tasted of salt!

"I think we *are* in the salt mines!" said David, encouraging the others to do the same.

They all quickly complied and each of them immediately licked their fingers and acknowledged they were in fact in the mines, giving them a much-needed reassurance that they were in fact still headed in the right direction, and would soon be coming to the end of their long, dark road.

It wasn't long before the rocky walls began to show signs of where sconces once held torches along the walls, their rusty iron brackets still protruding intermittently along the tunnel.

The darkness started to become less thick, and the companions could feel the dank, moist air slowly give way to a more fresh, gentle breeze for the first time in what felt like eternity.

As they pressed on, a small light began to shine at the end of the tunnel, indicating they had finally arrived on the other side. The companions rejoiced, knowing they were finally through the mountain and would soon be breathing fresh mountain air and feeling the warmth of the sun on their skin, something they had missed more than anything else.

It didn't take them long before they reached the outer parts of the tunnel and the darkness gave way to the blinding light of the surface world. They each had to shield their eyes to give them time to adjust slowly, but once they did, they were awestruck at the sight before them.

They were high up the side of the mountains and could see miles and miles of winding paths and rolling hills leading up to a vast desert plain. A long snaking river cut through the landscape leading from the mountains to their right and down through the rolling hills and valley floor below, leaving lush vegetation on its borders as far as the eye could see. Far off in the distance, David thought he could almost see the mouth of the river meeting the sparkling blue waters of a vast ocean, with little white sails dotting the horizon.

"That's amazing!" he said out loud, looking out across the landscape.

"It sure is. I've never seen anything like it." said Erin, equally awestruck.

After looking briefly at his map to verify they were in the right location, Holzer pointed off in the distance down the mountain towards a small village, indicating that was Ashmire and their next destination.

They immediately set off down the path, eager to get to a warm bed and a hot bath before the sun found its way across the sky and into the horizon, leaving them once again in darkness.

They reached the outskirts of the village just as the sun was about to set, casting the sky in a pinkish-purple hue. The village had its streets lined with high timbers that held hanging lanterns on their tops, providing ample light throughout the streets for their villagers to safely walk – only, the streets appeared to be empty, despite the lanterns having all been lit.

"That's odd..." said David, looking at the empty streets.

"Yeah, where are all of the people?" asked Erin, catching on to his comment.

"Who cares?" chimed in Reingard, "I'm starving! Let's find the Inn, and chances are, we'll find all of the people!" he said, pushing through the others and heading down the main street towards the center of town.

Tyrius noticed out of the corner of his eyes some of the shutters of the buildings bordering the streets quickly shut by someone unseen from within.

"Keep your eyes sharp, something doesn't seem right." said Tyrius, scanning the streets for any signs of danger.

The others quickly followed behind Reingard, keeping their eyes peeled for any suspicious movement in the shadows beyond the buildings.

They reached what appeared to be the Inn a little while later. The only alarming moment being little more than a scared animal scattering at the sound of their arrival, knocking over a few small crates and causing a ruckus that they feared would wake the entire village. Prior to the racket, the air had been eerily silent for such a decent sized village.

Reingard eagerly pushed open the door, exposing a well-lit dining hall and a bright fire in the hearth across the room. The room was filled with several wooden tables and chairs placed throughout the space, clearly used as a communal dining area for the visitors of the inn. A room that was capable of holding dozens of guests and a lively atmosphere otherwise stood empty and silent.

He walked right in and stood at the main counter by the door, knocking impatiently on the wooden counter to get the innkeeper's attention.

After a few moments of incessant banging, an old man finally appeared from a room behind the counter looking extremely flustered and irritated.

"What is it? What do you want?" he asked with a scowl.

"Isn't it obvious?" replied Reingard, holding his arms out towards his companions. "We are travelers, and we are weary and in need of room and board!" he said bluntly. "Do you have a few rooms and a hot meal to spare?" he added hopefully, feeling his empty stomach rumbling unhappily beneath his shirt.

The old keeper looked the travelers up and down before finally responding, "Yes, yes...but be quick about it. You were out past curfew. That only brings trouble, and I don't want no trouble!" he said, walking back into the room before coming out with a series of small keys.

"Here, these are for a few of the rooms up the stairs and to the hallway on the left. Come back down in a few minutes and I'll have some hot stew and bread for each of you. It's all I can manage with such short notice." he said, before rushing back into the room to heat up their meals.

Reingard turned and looked at his companions, who each shrugged, before heading up the stairs and passing out the keys, one by one.

They each took a key and found their respective rooms before setting down their belongings and preparing for the night.

David's room was furthest down the hall and was small but cozy. It had a soft bed nestled in the corner by a window that overlooked the main street. The sheets were soft and folded neatly and smelled fresh and clean.

Along the wall sat a long, dark walnut dresser with a few small books and a quill and paper stacked on top. It was lined with dust as if it hadn't been wiped clean in weeks. The drawers were all empty, except for one with a change of sheets and an extra blanket in case he got cold.

In the far corner by the window, opposite the bed, sat a rocking chair with a small pillow cushion. David took a seat in it and rocked for a moment, testing its integrity. It held fast and rocked smoothly with barely a noticeable creak – the craftsmanship was excellent, despite the simple design.

After he had taken some time to inspect the rest of the room, including the few paintings on the walls that depicted the town in its bustling prime, a time David assumed had long since passed, David decided it was time to head back down the stairs and into the dining hall to await his hot meal.

When he exited his room, he saw Erin had already made her way halfway down the hallway and was about to head down the stairs. He quickly caught up and followed her down as they made their way to join the others.

They found Tyrius, Reingard, and Holzer already halfway through their bowls of stew, which appeared to consist of chunky beef and vegetables in a thick broth. They had taken a seat close to the fireplace, taking comfort in the warmth that it provided along with the relaxing ambience of the cracking logs.

Shortly after they sat down, the keeper brought out their bowls and mugs before quickly retreating back to his alcove.

"Does anyone else find his behavior...strange?" asked Erin, catching the expression on everyone else's faces.

"Remarkably." replied Tyrius, now finished with his meal and setting down his freshly emptied mug.

"It seems like he's afraid of something. Did you hear what he said about the curfew?" she asked.

David looked back towards the counter to make sure they were alone before answering, "Yeah, he said that we broke the curfew, and that only brings trouble. Trouble from what, or who?" he asked.

Almost as if in response to his question, the door slung open and slammed hard against the wall, nearly knocking it off its hinges.

A group of six rough looking men came barging through the doorway, looking around the room until they found what they were looking for and started walking directly towards David and the others.

They stopped a few feet before their table and just stared silently before the one in the middle, apparently the leader of the bunch, grabbed a nearby chair and pulled it to their table before sitting down on it backwards.

The man had a large, round black hat on his head with a rim that extended far beyond the crown and had shown signs of weathering from years of use. He wore a long, dark leather coat that fell to his calves and matching leather boots with metal bottoms that clinked loudly as he tapped his feet slowly on the wooden floor.

"You must not be from around these parts." he said, spitting a large chunk of brown saliva on the ground at their feet before continuing. "So, I'll tell you just this once. We have a curfew in place, no one goes out after dark. Got it?" he said glaringly.

"A curfew?" asked Tyrius, staring blankly at the man, not at all threatened by his posse. "What on earth for?" he asked calmly.

"It ain't your place to ask what our curfew is for," said the man, "It's only your place to adhere to it. If you don't, you and your little friends here will suffer the consequences."

"And what might those be?" asked Tyrius again.

"Imprisonment, the first time. And if you don't learn from your mistakes and do it again, well..." he said, striking grins and chuckles from his posse before he continued, "let's just say, you won't get to make that mistake twice." he finished, driving home the point by running his finger across his neck.

"I see..." said Tyrius, sharing a look with the others that showed his absolute annoyance with such an obvious bully.

It was clear to him that this goon and his followers were used to people cowering away in fear and getting exactly what they wanted. Tyrius was not one to be taken lightly, and certainly wasn't going to be pushed around by some nobody.

"How about this." said the man, looking around at the companions seated at the table. "I'll let you off with a warning this time since you're new and all. But if we find you roaming about these parts again after nightfall, we won't be too nice about it."

With that, the man stood up and kicked the chair over before walking over to the counter and banging until the old innkeeper came rushing out of his alcove.

It was clear he was even more of a nervous wreck than before.

"Yes, gentlemen. What ca-can I get for you, to-tonight?" he stammered, wringing his hands together nervously.

"You can start with speaking correctly, you ignorant buffoon!" shouted the ringleader, slapping the keeper on the side of his head and sending him falling over onto the counter.

Reingard and Holzer nearly jumped up from their seats in anger, ready to rush the man and his posse, but Tyrius quickly urged them against it, telling them to sit still and be quiet.

They both shared a look so hot it would melt iron, clearly unhappy with being held back from teaching these men a much-needed lesson.

"Then, you can get me and my boys some drinks, on the house." continued the ringleader with a threatening glare.

The old innkeeper stumbled as he quickly rushed to the back to comply as ordered and the man and his posse slowly walked to a nearby table and sat down, waiting on their drinks.

David and the others watched from their table, wondering why on earth anyone would be treating that old man in such a way and how men like these had got along in these parts without being sent to prison for their behavior.

Reingard and Holzer's knuckles were white they were gripping their mugs so hard, trying to contain their rage.

"What do you think their deal is?" asked Erin, looking at the men over her shoulder, trying to distract them.

"Beats me," said David, catching the hint, "But if he smacks that old man again, I'm going to have to have a word with that one." he said, anger rising in his chest too. Erin quickly kicked him in his shin beneath the table as if to say, "you're not helping the situation any", and sent a scathing look his way.

"David, as much as we would all like to knock some sense into that man, I'm afraid I have to advise you against it." said Tyrius. "We don't know anything about these men, or these parts, especially how many they may have in their ranks. We are in no position to confront them." he said, looking sternly at David to make sure his point was clear.

"You're right...it just really hits a nerve with me" said David, reminded of how Tony and Johnny would pick on him and the other orphans on their way home from school.

The old innkeeper came rushing out of his little room carrying a tray of several mugs for the posse, handing them out to each of them before rushing quickly back to his post.

The six men each grabbed their mugs and clashed them together before tilting them back and draining them in full. These men clearly had nothing better to do than sit around and drink while badgering anyone they came in contact with to get them to do their bidding.

Eventually, David and the others grew tired from their long journey and decided to call it a night. Tyrius made sure to remind them each to lock their doors when they got to the rooms, as the men were still downstairs and were getting drunker by the hour. He didn't know what sort of behavior to expect from them and thought it best to prepare for the worst.

When they each made their way to their separate rooms, David lay down in his bed and tried his best to get some sleep over the bantering and laughter that resonated from the group of men downstairs. They were drunk and boisterous, and David suspected they had only just gotten started.

After an excruciating time, exhaustion finally took over and David drifted off to sleep.

Chapter VIII

David woke with the sound of footsteps creaking outside his door. The morning light was shining gently through his window, indicating that it was time for him to wake up and head downstairs to meet the others.

He quickly got dressed and headed downstairs where he found the rest of the group already sitting around a table quietly pouring over the maps while nibbling on a sizeable portion of eggs and bacon.

David took a seat next to Erin who smiled warmly when she noticed he had joined them.

"It's about time, sleepy head!" she teased.

David shrugged, "I had a hard time falling asleep last night with the drunken idiots downstairs. I thought I was never going to get some rest."

"Yeah, I heard them too. Don't worry, you didn't miss anything. We just started going over the maps and trying to chart which course is best for us to take now that we're in unfamiliar territory." she replied.

David listened as Tyrius, Reingard, and Holzer discussed which route they thought was best for them to travel while the Innkeeper brought him a hot plate of eggs and bacon, which he hungrily devoured.

He looked around the empty room, wondering how often the seats and tables around him were actually used. He assumed the inn was built back when the town was more popular, and people were coming and going more frequently than they did now.

He started to wonder to himself what would have caused the trade to stop flowing between Ravenfell and the Southern Kingdom when Tyrius slapped his hands on the table, startling him out of his thoughts.

"If you think you know best, then so be it!" he shouted at Holzer, standing up and walking towards the counter. He quickly pulled out a handful of coins from within a pouch he had been holding and slapped them on the counter for the Innkeeper.

"This should cover us for the two meals and the rooms overnight. Thank you for your hospitality." he said to the man before storming back upstairs to gather his belongings.

"What was that all about?" asked David after sharing a similar look of confusion with Erin.

"Tyrius seems to think we should keep to the hills and away from the towns on our trek north around the mountains, but Holzer and I think the best way to travel is by road. It's an easier route and would give us periodic breaks where we could have a hot meal and a warm bed in the towns along the way." said Reingard.

"Why does Tyrius think we should keep away from the towns?" asked David, confused by the logic. Towns held food and supplies, things they would need for their journey. Thinking of sleeping in the wild for weeks on end did not seem very appealing to him, although he knew at some point they would reach the areas beyond civilization, he just wasn't expecting it to happen so soon after leaving Ravenfell.

"He doesn't like the welcome we got last night with those men. He seems to think something is amiss in the Southern Kingdom and that it could put our mission in jeopardy." said Holzer.

"I can see his point," said Erin, thinking it over. "I'll go talk to him" she said finally before getting up and heading upstairs.

David watched Erin as she walked to the stairs and disappeared. As he was turning back to his companions, his eyes focused on the Innkeeper and noticed he was acting rather strange – more than he had been the night before.

The old man was holding the coins in his hand, inspecting them closely, before his expression changed from curiosity to disgust. He then threw the coins on the ground and stormed out of the building without a word or explanation.

Thinking it strange, he decided to tell Holzer and Reingard, who both agreed it was time to gather their things and get started on the road north. It would be another long day ahead of them, but at least they had the fresh, cool air and shining sun to look forward to, something infinitely better than the damp, stale air and eternal darkness of the tunnels they had trekked through the days before.

As they gathered their belongings and started towards the door, they could hear a commotion just outside the inn. It sounded like a crowd of people shouting and screaming and it was getting closer with each passing moment.

When they opened the door to exit the building, they discovered the source of the noise. A crowd of at least a hundred people, all villagers it appeared, were standing around screaming and yelling at them as they exited.

David didn't understand what they were yelling about, but Reingard and Holzer quickly filled him in.

"I think they know we're Northerners" said Reingard, hearing some of the insults being thrown their way.

"So? Why does that make them so upset?" asked David, still not understanding.

"Not everyone took the defeat very well in the battle of the Northern Pass," explained Holzer. "Many blame the King for the struggles they've had to deal with, what with the crumbling of the kingdom after their king died in battle. His death left a power vacuum within the kingdom, leaving many various factions fighting for control of the land. It was a mess for a while, at least that's what I heard from some of the merchants who used to come through the Southern Tunnel back when it was still operational."

The company tried to press through the thronging crowd, but they were pushed back and prevented from moving forward.

"You ain't going nowhere!" yelled one man with a scowl.

"You're gonna get it!" yelled another, his face distorted in rage.

"Let us pass, we are just on our way out!" yelled Tyrius over the crowd.

Suddenly, the crowd towards the back started to clear and part and the yelling and screaming began dying down, leaving an eerie silence in its wake.

David could see a group of men making their way through the crowd, and suddenly his gut started to warn him something was wrong.

He pulled on Erin's shirt to get her attention, "Erin, I think something is wrong. We need to get out of here fast." he said, alarmed.

"I know, I have a bad feeling too" she replied.

The men finally reached their way to the edge of the crowd and made their way into the opening, stopping just before Tyrius who stood in front of the others protectively.

It was the same man from the night before, along with his friends, only this time, he brought several others with him. Their posse now consisted of fifteen men, each equipped with a short sword in a scabbard on their hips and a mean scowl on their faces. They looked at Tyrius and the others with disgust and anger before their leader finally spoke.

"I knew I didn't like you bunch the second I saw you last night in the Inn" he said. "And now I know why. You're outsiders from the North. I saw your coin – there ain't nobody from here that carries filthy northern money like that."

David could see the Innkeeper slowly wriggle his way to the front of the crowd and stand just behind the posse.

"Is that a problem?" asked Tyrius calmly.

"You're darn right it's a problem!" said the ringleader. "Your kind's been banned from ever coming to our lands again, yet here you are, defying our laws like a bunch of criminals. Now you've left us no choice but to take you in to see the leader. He'll decide what to do with you" he said, smiling threateningly.

"You will do no such thing," said Tyrius forcefully. "Not if you know what's best for you and your men." he said, placing his other hand on his staff and resting it in front of him.

"What, you're gonna whack me with that stick of yours?" said the man, mockingly. "Well, hate to break it to you, but we have more than just sticks and have you outnumbered." he said, before drawing his sword and pointing it at Tyrius. His band of men quickly followed suit, to which David and Erin drew their swords while Holzer and Reingard quickly grabbed their axes off their backs.

They each stood their grounds, prepared to fight their way out if necessary.

The crowd began screaming and yelling, urging on the fight that was about to break loose before them.

"Get 'em!" they heard someone shout from the crowd.

"You have the nerve to stand up to the Guild, old man? So be it!" said the ringleader. Emboldened by the support of the townsfolk and their superior numbers, he quickly lunged at Tyrius, who swiftly deflected the attack and spun around, smacking the leader in the back of his head with his staff, knocking him to the ground.

The others quickly jumped into action when the rest of the Guild rushed into the attack.

The crowd dispersed in a panic at the sudden outbreak, screaming and running towards their homes, giving them full reign of the city streets to branch out and take on their aggressors.

David quickly rushed toward his nearest opponent who unleashed a powerful overhead swing towards David's head. David quickly side-stepped and shoved his shoulder hard into his opponent, knocking him over and giving David the opportunity to take on another man who had been running his way in an attempt to outnumber him.

The man tried swinging his sword wildly at David, but David was too quick, and easily dodged the attacks before parrying and counter attacking with equal ferocity and far more precision. The man was overwhelmed, and David was able to dispatch him with ease, sending him scrambling away with the other man he had knocked over.

David looked over to check on the others, and saw Erin had already taken down two men and was working on another, while Reingard and Holzer were actively chasing down a group of men who had apparently underestimated their opponent's ferocity and instead, decided to turn tail and run.

Tyrius was taking on the leader and had already knocked out several others in his wake, swinging his staff around with the skill and grace of a practiced warrior, landing powerful blows to the man's body before swiftly sweeping him off his feet and pinning him to the ground.

The fight was over in a matter of minutes.

"You're going to regret this, old man!" said the man, blood trickling from the corner of his mouth.

"I would think it wise for you and your men to leave here at once and let us go in peace. I cannot promise you that next time, should you attack us again, you will leave in such good condition" said Tyrius, threateningly.

He lifted the pressure of his staff from the man's chest and the man quickly scrambled to his feet and took off down the street after the rest of his men.

Reingard and Holzer were coming back and passed him on their way up the street towards David and the others, huge grins on both of their faces.

"Did you see those guys run?" asked Reingard, clearly enjoying the victory a little too much.

Everyone chuckled in spite of the dangerous encounter they had just survived before Tyrius brought them back to the task at hand.

"Now do you see why I was so adamant about us traveling *away* from the towns?" he asked, to which Reingard and Holzer both nodded, conceding to Tyrius' suggested route.

With them all finally in agreement and eager to get as far away from the town as possible, they set off into the countryside and rolling foothills of the mountains, traveling Northeast along their base.

They hiked for the remainder of the day before deciding to set up camp for the night as the sky began to darken with the setting sun.

Holzer went out to hunt for some food while the others prepared a small fire for light and warmth to get them through the night.

With the threat of the Guild still fresh on his mind, Tyrius decided it best to set up some traps and alarms in the event they had any intruders in the night, and set about his work, mumbling here and there as he circled the campsite just outside of the ring of light from the fire.

Erin and David prepared their bedrolls and listened to Reingard tell them tales of his youth, where he and Holzer had first met Rex and had determined right from the start that they would cause nothing but trouble together.

He told them of the time they had gotten into his father's stash of ale and had discovered the joys - and potency - of his home brew before rambling around through the town aimlessly looking for young women to court.

Unfortunately for them, the ladies laughed them to scorn when they pointed out they had all pissed themselves and didn't know it.

It was the last time they had decided to drink his father's home brew, deciding it was far too strong for their liking.

When Reingard had finished his story and they all had their fair share of gut-wrenching laughter, Tyrius had already finished his alarms and began explaining that it would produce a loud whistle if anyone were to step through the boundaries, giving them ample time to react to the threat at hand.

In addition to the warning, he had established a barrier that would conceal their camp from view from any unfriendly prying eyes, making their location extremely difficult to find for anyone with the wrong intentions. One would have to be a very keen tracker to follow their footsteps into their camp in the dark of the night.

Shortly after Tyrius sat down, Holzer came back carrying a limp hare in each hand and began quickly preparing the catch for roasting over the fire.

While their food cooked, they sat and talked about the strange behavior of the townsfolk and the members of the Guild attacking them earlier that morning.

"I knew there was some hostility towards the Northern Kingdom after the South fell back in the war, but I never would have guessed that hostility would have endured this long or have grown into such hatred like that" said Holzer, recalling the look in the villager's eyes.

"The Southern Kingdom had fallen over two decades ago. One would think that it would have recovered by now." said Erin, agreeing with Holzer.

"I suspect that there is more to it than meets the eye," said Tyrius, "This Guild has me wondering what kind of government would allow such a band of thugs to enact curfews on their own people. And who exactly was this leader they were going to bring us to anyway?" he asked.

"Who knows," said Reingard, "What I do know is that Innkeeper was fine until he found out where we were from, and that he was scared of those men the night before, but the next morning in the streets, his fear of them seemed to disappear and be replaced by his hatred for us."

Everyone nodded in agreement, recalling the Innkeeper's strange behavior over the course of the night, and following morning.

"I would bet that it was him that went and told the Guild where we were from. I saw him run out of the building looking very angry after Tyrius handed him the coin for our meals and rooms" said David.

"That explains a lot," said Tyrius, "and why they didn't attack us the night before. They didn't know we were from the Northern Kingdom yet. They must have just assumed we were from another village and weren't aware of the curfew." he said.

"Do you think we've seen the last of those guys?" asked David, hopeful but uncertain.

"Something tells me that it's unlikely. But if we can keep to the hills and remain hidden like Tyrius suggested, we may be able to get enough distance between us and them that they give up and don't bother pursuing us." said Reingard.

"I hope you're right..." said David, looking into the fire. "I have a feeling this Guild is a bigger operation than just a handful of inexperienced men. If they get riled up, I'm afraid of what might come our way."

With that, everyone nodded and became lost in their own thoughts and worries until the food was finally ready. They each had their fair share of roasted meat before calling it a night. Tyrius, as usual, elected for the first watch, to which the others happily agreed, eager to get some rest while their bellies were full.

Chapter IX

Jakob Zander was in his mid-twenties with dark skin and jet-black hair that was perpetually dusty and disheveled. His skin was covered in scars from years of tribal combat that earned him the right to lead the northern Guild that overlooked the region spanning from Ashmire, down the rolling foothills to the South, and ending at the coastal city of Brineport.

He was kneeled before the commander of the Southern Wolf Guard, a wolf of incredible strength and stature, even for their kind. His name was Bloodvayne.

The Wolf Guard had fled from the Northern Kingdom after the War of the Mystics had ended ushering in the dawn of the Second Age. They eventually found their way to the Southern Kingdom where they watched from the Lowlands as the kingdom slowly unraveled under the brutal dictatorship of the King, Germone Krauss. They sat back watching and waiting for the perfect opportunity to strike.

After the fall of King Krauss in the Battle of the Northern Pass against King Lionel Eldergate I of the

Northern Kingdom, the Wolf Guard seized their opportunity to fill the power vacuum and took control of the Southern Kingdom with relative ease. The various tribes quickly fell under their control – those who resisted were slaughtered and eaten in front of their brethren, a strong reminder of what would happen if anyone else decided to resist.

In place of the former government, the Wolf Guard set up a caste system with their kind being at the top of the hierarchy and the former citizens making up the bottom – most being forced into slavery and manual labor, with only a select few making their way into a position of influence – mostly the business owners who ran the fisheries, shipyard, and mines, and some of the more talented armorers and other specialists of various useful occupations.

They separated the kingdom into four regions, each area covered one of the four cardinal directions: North, South, East, and West – with the Wolf Guard being in control of the overall operation of each region and their militia-like overlords.

These overlords became known as the Guild – a tribal-like military that controlled the population through fear tactics and bribery. The Guild mostly consisted of orphans that were handpicked off the streets by the Wolves and trained and manipulated into doing their dirty work.

They had no loyalty to the people, as they had been abandoned by their own kind, forced to live off the streets while begging and sometimes being chased away and beaten by local business owners for stealing from their stores.

"My lord, I've received news from my brother in Ashmire. As you had suspected, he came across some travelers from the Northern Kingdom. They must have reopened the Southern Tunnel" said Jakob Zander.

The deep growling voice of the wolf echoed his displeasure from his great stone throne. "Where are they now?" he asked impatiently.

"They got away, my lord, fleeing to the North along the foothills." replied Jakob, lowering his eyes.

"Your brother's incompetence displeases me, Jakob." replied Bloodvayne. "My master has a way of dealing with those who displease him. Fortunately for you, I am a little more forgiving than my master. I will give you one more chance to find these travelers and bring them to me, but this time, you are to personally lead the men. My master tells me they are with a boy of great importance to him. He wants the boy alive, the others you can kill." said the wolf.

"What will come of my brother, my lord?" Jakob dared to ask.

The large wolf growled deeply, indicating his displeasure at being asked a question that was clearly not his place to ask.

"Your brother will be given the same punishment as any other who would fail me. He will be fed to my brethren as an important reminder to all who should think of failing me again." he growled.

Jakob bowed his head, clenching his teeth in anger. His brother had always had a way of screwing up, and now it had cost him his life. Jakob vowed right then and there that he would make the ones responsible pay with their lives if it were the last thing he did.

The large commander of the Southern Wolf Guard stood from his throne and slowly walked towards Jakob, stopping merely inches from his face. He could feel the hot breath of the beast on his face but dared not move for fear of offending him by showing any sign of weakness – the wolves despised weakness.

Bloodvayne pulled something small and round out of the cloth around his waist, handing it to Jakob.

"What is this?" asked Jakob.

"This is an artifact of my people imbued with dark magic. It will bring you back to Brineport quickly when you find the boy, no matter the distance. You need only break it when you have him in your grasp, and it's magic will do the rest." he growled.

"Thank you, my lord." replied Jakob, as he stood and turned to walk away, placing the small glass ball in his pocket.

"And Jakob, I've always took pride in you, ever since the beginning. But should you fail me, don't expect any special treatment." snarled Bloodvayne.

Jakob stopped for a brief moment. "Yes, my lord. Your favor will not go unrewarded." he replied, and he swiftly exited the room.

Jakob made his way through the pyramid-shaped desert palace to his men who were gathered outside in the courtyard. When they saw their leader alive and well, they all let out a collective sigh of relief.

The last Guild leader who had a faction under his control that failed to carry out his task never made it to an explanation. Bloodvayne simply lunged from his throne and bit off his head in one fell swoop. The rest of his body was tossed to the other wolves and was quickly devoured. All that remained were the bones which were tossed aside for the vultures to carry away and pick clean.

Jakob looked around the courtyard at his men, and they all gathered around to hear their leader, eagerly awaiting their next assignment.

"We are to hunt down the scum from Ashmire and bring back the boy. The one with the tattoo on his hand. He is to be brought back alive. The others we have been ordered to kill." he shouted loudly, to which the men all cheered.

They lived for assignments such as this. They paid better, and they satisfied their need to kill – a need they had been trained to fulfill since they had been taken from their lives of begging and scavenging the streets as children.

The Guild had given them all a sense of purpose that left their bellies full and their purses fat. Being in the Guild was a privilege for those who lived in the sprawling desert city of Brineport. It gave them power and purpose and the promise of a better life – something they never would have had otherwise.

To those who weren't fortunate enough to end up in the Guild, the city had little to offer but a meager life under constant threat from the wolves. Their wages were taxed heavily, leaving them with very little reward from their own labor. Those who tried to pack up and leave were never heard from again – the Guild made sure of that. Everyone knew that leaving was suicide, so no one dared attempt it.

Brineport wasn't always this way. It was once a sprawling metropolis, the center of commerce in the ancient world of men, but that was before the end of the war and before the Wolf Guard had arrived.

Brineport was a city located on the great Southern River that flows from the Draconian mountains down to the South Sea, providing the area with lush vegetation in an otherwise dry, desert climate. It also provided access to an abundance of fish in the South Sea and a means of traveling quickly from the most Southern parts of the kingdom to the most Northern parts by way of sailboat. It was how the Guild moved so quickly throughout the kingdom and how they kept control of the population – as only the Guild members were allowed to travel by boat, just another means of control over the less fortunate.

Jakob and the northern Guild members quickly gathered their gear and prepared the ships to set sail up the river towards the old mining community of Ashmire.

When he reached the ships, he made his way to the Captain's cabin where he set down his pack before greeting the rest of his crew who had been waiting on deck, keeping watch to make sure no one tried any funny business while they were in port.

The city was not only filled with worthless slaves, but it also was sprawling with thieves, and Jakob never took any chances when it came to his things – he knew better than that.

Once they were all on board and the dock lines had all been released and stowed away, the Captain gave the order for the fleet to set sail and they began their voyage upstream.

With the wind rushing through his hair, Jakob finally allowed himself to relax for the first time since they docked. He knew his luck had run out with his brother's failure to capture the travelers the first time. That failure had cost his brother his life, but fortunately he had been spared due to his position of favor with Bloodvayne.

This time he would not return empty handed, for he knew that if he did, it would be the end of his wretched life.

Chapter X

The alarm bells rang throughout the cold, cloudless night, as the soldiers of Ravenfell scrambled to finalize their preparations on the frontline fortifications.

With the demon army amassing in the Great Plains far below, they knew it would only be a matter of a few days at best before the enemy was at their gates. It would be their duty to fend them off for as long as they could, and they knew they were going to be in for the fight of their lives.

"How are the preparations coming along, Captain?" asked General Ryan.

"The walls have been built and reinforced, General. We have prepared the boulders at the top of the walls and doubled the archers on patrol. We will be ready when they come, sir!" replied the young Captain – a man from Eldergate who had fought with General Ryan and Erin during the battle to take back the city and stop General Krauss.

"And what of the men, how do they fare?" asked the General, concerned of their morale as the demon army grew ever nearer.

"They are well, General. My men know what they are facing and are prepared to give their lives for the protection of their families." said the Captain proudly.

"Good. See to it that the men are rotated so they get enough rest in between shifts. Once the battle begins, we will need all the strength we can muster, and there won't be any time for breaks I'm afraid." said General Ryan.

"Yes sir!" said the Captain.

"And Captain," said the General.

"Sir?" asked the Captain, turning back to his General.

"Make sure you get some rest, too. You can't lead your men if you're too tired to think straight." said General Ryan, concern etched across his face.

"Yes, Sir! I will sir!" said the Captain, clapping his fist to his chest before returning to his duties.

General Ryan had been overseeing the defensive fortifications for the past few days while they were being built. He knew that the walls would be their first line of defense and made sure there would be no gaps in their lines that could be exploited by the enemy.

So far, they had completed the front gate and walls which were several feet thick and nearly twice as tall. They were built from the same hard stone of the mountain and put together skillfully by the local builders in the valley. It had taken them nearly half of the time Ryan had expected, which was a tribute to their superb skill and expertise in their field.

Once the outer wall was completed, they had begun construction of several similar walls that served as additional barriers in the event the first would fail.

All together, they would have a total of three major fortifications for the enemy to overcome before they reached the mountain pass. Each wall would be topped with mounted ballista's and catapults, and hundreds of archers and soldiers, ready to rain down volley after volley of arrows and rock from above.

Behind the fortifications would be the bulk of their army, ready for the moment when the integrity of the walls would fall, and the demon army would break through. The natural canyon between the two rock faces would serve as a funnel, preventing the whole force from attacking at once, and improving their odds of holding off the demons.

If the enemy forces broke through these defenses, they would have to overcome a series of wooden, maze-like barriers filled with protruding spikes and barricades that narrowed down into a single, six-foot wide opening into the valley.

The men would fall back through the opening and again use the narrow doorway as a funnel, hoping it would slow the approaching army enough to render their overwhelming numbers useless.

So far, two of the three walls had been fully constructed, and the final wall and wooden barricades would be ready before the army reached their doorstep.

If all went according to plan, General Ryan felt they actually had a chance in surviving the coming siege, albeit a smaller chance than he would have liked.

When he was satisfied with the progress of their defenses, General Ryan made his way back down the winding valley road through the city and toward the castle of Ravenfell to meet with the others and give his report. He ran into General Owen along the way who had been tasked to check on the townspeople and their preparations for the pending exodus through the Southern Tunnel.

Ever since the watchmen had sounded the signal, the townsfolk had been in an uproar, rushing everywhere back and forth trying to deliver their final shipments to the keep before frantically packing their own belongings for their journey through the Southern Tunnel.

When the two Generals reached the castle gates, the large iron portcullis slowly rose and came to a grinding halt.

Inside the courtyard, Rex and Orin were waiting for them, eager to hear the news of their findings.

As they walked together through the main double doors and towards the war room, he told them of the progress that had been made since his last inspection and assured them the defenses would soon be completed.

"Those men are something else," said General Ryan, speaking of the builders. "I've never seen anything like it!"

"Yeah, they are skilled with stone and mortar, having worked with it most of their lives here in the valley. I couldn't be prouder of those men and I am sure they are happy to help with such an important task." replied Rex, beaming with pride.

"How are the townsfolk faring? It seemed like the whole city was in an uproar since the sighting of the enemy forces" asked Rex as they made their way up the large stairway leading to the second floor.

"As good as can be expected, considering the circumstances. It seemed most of them were preparing for their journey through the Southern Tunnel and had already finished delivering their final cart of supplies to the storehouse." replied General Owen.

General Owen was the head of Ravenfell's army and had been promoted to his new rank back when Rex took control of the kingdom after his uncle's defeat. He had served with Rex during the siege of Eldergate and had proved to be a loyal friend and a valuable asset to the kingdom.

"That's good to hear. It won't be long before the fight is brought to our doorstep. We need to ensure the people are ready and safe from harm before that day comes." said Rex.

"Agreed. We will ensure they are ready; you can count on it!" replied General Owen.

They reached the war room where King Eldergate and several officers were awaiting their arrival with a series of finger foods to fend off the hunger while they finalized their plans for the coming battle.

They all stood as Rex and the others entered, showing their respect for the king of Ravenfell. When he seated, the rest followed, and they wasted no time in assessing the situation.

"We have a combined might of roughly twenty thousand strong, including roughly five hundred archers, fifty ballistae and catapult support each," began one of the officers. "With the reports coming in from the men standing watch, the enemy has a force of several times that, and it's still growing. Each hour more and more demons are pouring into the plains" he said somberly.

The room was silent, each knowing they were facing insurmountable odds, but nonetheless ready to fight to the death if fate required it.

The officer continued, "When the enemy strikes, their numbers won't matter as much given the narrow pass up the mountain, let alone the pass through the rockface, if they get to it. My worry lies with the fact that their sheer advantage in numbers provides them with the opportunity to lay an endless siege on our fortifications, without worry of ever running low on men...or in this case...demons. Our biggest concern will be fatigue." he said, looking around the room.

Everyone seemed to catch on to what he was saying. With such a huge disadvantage in numbers alone, even with their fortifications, their men would eventually tire and need to be replaced by fresh troops. Eventually, this cycle would begin to get strained as they lost more and more men, leaving less and less time for each successive wave to rest between fighting. If the battle waged on long enough, it would only be a matter of time before their fatigue would overcome them and sloppy mistakes would start being made. The kind of mistakes that lose a war.

"There is one thing that I can do that may help," chimed in Orin, to which all heads turned his way. The old mage stood up and addressed the room of kings and generals with a confidence that only comes with age and vast experience.

"There's an elixir that can be made, if done properly and mixed with the right level of skill, that can enhance a person's ability to focus – giving them increased sensory stimulation that can last for hours on end." he said, to which several officers immediately went into hushed conversations with their neighbors.

"But there's a catch." he continued, "Like all magic, there's a price to pay. When the effects start to wear off, the fatigue that ensues comes tenfold – all of the exhaustion postponed over the duration of the elixir will come crashing down on the user like a boulder, effectively rendering them useless until they get at least half a day's rest."

"This elixir, can it be made in bulk?" asked Rex, clearly aware of the usefulness of such an elixir if the timing were right.

"Yes, theoretically it can be done. But I would need time, and a lot of materials" replied Orin, thinking it over.

"General Owen, see to it that Orin gets everything he needs to make this elixir. Time is of the essence!" said Rex to his General.

"I'm on it, sir!" said General Owen before marching out of the room with Orin in tow, meticulously listing all of the materials and ingredients he would need to complete the elixir.

"All right, men." said Rex, turning to the others. "We know what must be done, and we know the enemy we are about to face. Some of you weren't there for the battle of Eldergate to witness first-hand the abominations that poured out from the Dark Abyss that day, but most of you have heard by now the accounts of those of us who were. I am here to tell you, none of them were exaggerated.

"Our enemy is fierce. They are fueled by a hatred for humanity that dates back over a thousand years to the Mystic War of our forefathers. It was that war that left them imprisoned in the Dark Abyss, and now I fear they are ripe for revenge.

"It is our duty, our privilege, to ensure they don't get it!" he finished.

"Some of these demons are almost dog-like, crawling on all fours with vicious teeth and fangs and powerful legs that allow them to run at incredible speeds and jump to incredible heights. These beasts will most likely be toward the front of their lines and will try to scale our fortifications to get behind our lines. We must ensure that doesn't happen!" said General Ryan.

"Others are winged bat-like creatures that are as big as a horse. They will be one of our greatest threats at first and it will be up to our archers to ensure they do not get beyond our walls to wreak havoc on our forces.

"Their foot soldiers are much like the undead, they are easily dispatched, but are merciless and unyielding. They have no worry for their wellbeing. They do not feel the blade or the arrow, nor do they fear being sent back to the Abyss from whence they came. The best way to dispatch these warriors is to attack at the limbs and joints and sever the head. Without a head, they drop to the ground. Without legs and arms, they are immobile and pose no threat.

Do not waste your efforts on these with jabs and slashes – remember this and you will fare well against this enemy." said General Ryan, looking at all of his men.

Some who he knew had been with him during the battle of Eldergate were nodding, remembering all too well the monstrosities of that fateful battle, and acknowledging his tactics. Others who had not witnessed first-hand the battles, stood wide-eyed and horrified at the descriptions they were being given, afraid of the enemy they would soon be facing.

"It is important to know, too, that we may not yet know all of what the enemy forces possess. We have never truly battled against such foes in our times and have only our history to teach us what may come. This is why it is important to be prepared for anything that comes our way, and to adjust as you see fit on the battlefield. If you see that a tactic isn't working, try another. If you come across a new enemy and find a way to take it down, spread the word as best you can." continued Rex.

"Communication will be our lifeline, men. We must ensure that our lines are not broken no matter the cost. If we can't communicate with one another, then all will be lost. Understood?" he asked, to which everyone nodded in agreement.

"Good! Now let's get to training. Spread the word to your men so they are prepared for the coming days. Ensure they are well rested and trained up. I fear that our time of waiting will soon be coming to an end."

With that, the meeting finished, and the officers all went their separate ways, each going to their own division to disseminate the information given to them by their leaders.

Rex and the King went to see to the preparation of the town's folk to ensure they were prepared for their long march through the Southern Tunnel.

When they reached the city, nearly everyone had already abandoned their homes and businesses and only a few last stragglers remained behind, packing up their final items before rushing out of the door and down the valley towards the tunnel in a hurry.

The crescent moon was shining bright in the cloudless sky, and the stars were blazing brilliantly in the velvet blanket beyond, twinkling in an endless multitude that dotted the sky in every direction.

A gentle breeze was rustling the fallen leaves and had scattered a few forgotten sheets of paper across the abandoned street, presumably that had fallen from one of the villager's packs as they made their hasty escape from the doomed city.

They made their way through the now desolate and littered streets and across the dimly lit valley as they went over their battle plans once again, making sure there weren't any important items they forgot to address.

When they arrived at the southern wall of the valley, a massive crowd of villagers and refugees were gathered together, embracing their loved ones that were staying behind to fight in an emotional scene of heartfelt goodbyes. Some held it together, their pride keeping back the tears, while others freely wept, not knowing if they would ever see their husbands, fathers, or sons again.

When they finally determined they could wait no longer, the group of young soldiers who had been selected to lead the citizens to safety rounded up the last of the group and began reluctantly leading them into the Southern Tunnel before disappearing behind the bend.

When the last of them had vanished from sight and the valley was once again silent, apart from the gentle rustling of the wind through the barren trees and the endless construction of the final fortifications in the distance, those soldiers who had been left behind got to work blocking the passageway once again.

When the final boulder was set in place and the entrance was completely obscured from the unknowing eye, the two kings and their soldiers solemnly made their way across the valley and back towards their respective positions. Each in their own way, solemnly wondering what fate awaited them in the coming days.

Chapter XI

W "ake up!" whispered Reingard, shaking David roughly.

He slowly rolled over on his bedroll, trying to shake off the sudden intrusion. He had been in a deep sleep and was having a wonderful dream. But Reingard was persistent.

"David, you have to wake up, now! We think they've been tracking us and have found our camp!" said Reingard, a sense of urgency in his voice.

With this, David opened his eyes and looked around, trying to take in his surroundings.

It was still dark, sometime in the middle of the night he assumed, given the position of the moon still high in the starry sky. The air was cool and clear, and the bitterness of the cold left his limbs stiff and somewhat uncooperative as he tried to stand up.

He could see the others had already woken and were frantically moving about, gathering their things, and packing their bags as quickly as they could without making too much sound that would give away their position.

David's mind began to clear, and he focused on Reingard who was holding his finger up to his mouth.

"Hush, lad. Gather your things quickly, we gotta get going before –" he was swiftly cut off when the unmistakable sound of a loud whistle shot out through the air.

It was the alarm Tyrius had set up, and it meant they were about to have company.

Immediately, David could see the outline of several dark figures creeping their way into the outskirts of the brush around their campsite. They were crouched down low, looking around at each other, trying to figure out which idiot had let out the loud whistle.

David quickly gathered his wits about him and began packing his things as quietly as he could. He watched as Erin silently moved across the camp toward his location and crouched by his side.

"I've counted at least a dozen. I think it's the men from Ashmire, the ones we encountered outside of the inn," she whispered. "They just don't know when to give up, do they?" she asked, shaking her head in disbelief.

"Why do you think they're following us?" David asked, confused why these men would take such a keen interest in them.

"I have no idea – but I don't think we should sit around to find out." whispered Erin. "Did you get all of your things?" she asked, looking at the pack by David's side.

He nodded in confirmation.

"Good, let's go!" she said, pulling his hand and, crouching low, swiftly crossed the campsite to where the others had gathered behind a small bundle of bushes.

They each greeted David and made sure they had gathered everything before creeping away into the night. They headed north along the foothills of the mountain and continued until the moon had set and the sun was high in the sky.

They rested for a brief meal before setting back out at a steady pace until night had fallen once again and the moon began to rise above the mountains on its journey across the deep dark sky.

When camp was made and Tyrius had once again set up his alarm system and spell of concealment, they lit a small fire, sitting around talking while Reingard prepared their supper.

"Do you think they're still following us?" asked David, a hint of concern in his voice. They had been running nearly nonstop all day, and he was not sure how long he could go on this way without a decent night's rest. He knew the other's felt the same – they all looked just as exhausted as he felt.

"I'm not sure..." replied Tyrius, "but something tells me we should expect the worst."

"Why are they so intent on following us?" asked Erin, "It's not like we have stores of treasure enticing them to keep up their pursuit."

"Yeah, seriously...they need to give it a rest now, so *we* can get some rest!" said Holzer, rubbing his bare feet. They were rough and calloused from a lifetime in the rough terrain of the mountains, but something told David he wasn't accustomed to

97

cross-country running. He sympathized with him – David wasn't accustomed to it either and he just knew if he looked, his feet would be covered in blisters. This world had been extremely rough on his body – and he didn't know if he would ever get used to the constant battering he had been taking since he arrived.

"We will have two people on watch tonight, just in case. I don't think we should take any chances with the luck we've been having." said Tyrius, looking into the fire.

He looked old and ragged, even more than he had before. The past few days on the run had been taking its toll on the Elder – he wasn't nearly as old as the Master Elder was, or even the other Elders, having been the last apprentice chosen to take on the sacred responsibility of protecting the orb, but ever since the Defiant One had returned through the breach in the seal he had felt like his powers were wearing thin with each passing day. Those powers are what allowed the Elders to age beyond any normal man – the Mystic magic within them causing their bodies to remain preserved in a way, giving them a deeper strength and resilience that a normal man his age couldn't possibly possess.

Before the other Elder's had passed on, they had given up what remained of their powers into the last remaining Mystic Crystal. It was a tradition that had been repeated several times throughout the past couple thousand years and one that gave Tyrius full responsibility of the task of choosing and training the next five Elder's. When chosen, he would pass the powers given to him into his new apprentices, one by one, until their ranks were complete once again, one Elder for each of the six Mystics of Creation.

Unfortunately, with the Defiant One back in the world of the living, the powers within the Crystal had all but dwindled away, thereby rendering his mission obsolete. For the moment, he was the sole protector of the Orb, and the final Elder. If he were to die, the legacy of the Elders would die along with him.

"I'll volunteer first watch." David and Erin said simultaneously. They looked at each other and smiled. They must have both noticed how weary Tyrius had looked and decided he needed the rest more than any of them.

Much to their surprise, Tyrius didn't object, but instead nodded silently and continued prodding the fire with a stick, lost deep in thought and exhausted from their flight through the night and ensuing day.

It wasn't long after they finished dinner that the others had fallen asleep, leaving David and Erin alone for the first time since they had left Ravenfell.

David sat down on a nearby hill overlooking the camp and Erin came and sat beside him, leaning her head on his shoulder affectionately. He looked up at the sky and the endless array of tiny stars dotting the deep velvety blanket above, wondering if these were the same stars he used to watch as a child outside the orphanage. He didn't recognize any of the formations, but he also knew from his studies in school that those same stars would look different depending on where you were located in the galaxy.

He assumed he would never truly know, and instead decided to focus on the area around them, scanning for any signs of a threat.

As they sat there together on the hilltop, hand in hand, David could almost forget the troubles of the world. He admired how peaceful the countryside seemed, despite knowing there were dangers lurking somewhere in the darkness.

"What are you thinking about?" asked Erin, breaking the silence, but still keeping her head on David's shoulder.

"I was just thinking about how beautiful this world is, and how simple life could be here if it weren't for everything else going on." he replied.

"Yeah...it is beautiful." agreed Erin, looking out at the rolling hills. She squeezed David's hand gently, sitting silent once again.

"Do you think we will ever be free from the Defiant One?" asked David, doubt reflecting in his voice.

Erin lifted her head from his shoulder and looked at the boy beside her that over the course of just a few shorts weeks, had been growing into a man before her eyes.

She thought about how feeble and scared he had looked when she first found him in the temple. Since then, he had saved her life on many occasions, risked his life for near strangers, and faced off with the most powerful man in the world – General Krauss, who possessed terrifying black magic. She had never known someone so brave and selfless as David had been. In the face of absolute danger, he had gone running into the fray, prepared to lay down his life for a world he had never even known existed until a few short weeks ago.

Her time with David had proven beyond a doubt in her mind that he had what it takes to make a real difference in this war. She believed in him, and she had come to love him deeply, not because of his heroism, but because of his kindness and willingness to help those around him.

"David, the prophecy foretold your coming, and here you are. The prophecy also foretold that you would be the one who would bind the darkness away for good. You are the one from prophecy, there isn't a doubt in my mind. But more than that, I believe in you, and so does everyone else. Not just because of what the prophecy says, but because of what we have seen you do." she said gently.

"You choose to fight when others would have run. You choose to stand up for our world when others would have walked away. Your spirit is strong, stronger than you give yourself credit for. If anyone can stop the Defiant One, it's you." Erin finished with a warm smile and a gentle kiss on his cheek before settling back into her position with her head resting on his shoulder, looking out at the scene around them.

The light from the moon was reflecting off the rolling hills, covering the landscape in a blanket of gentle silver. The hills extended far into the distance to the north, and some ways to the east before dropping into vast flat plains dotted with trees. Far into the distance the trees became thicker and seemed to dominate the landscape.

They sat there together for some time in silence, just enjoying each other's company. When the moon reached its apex in the sky, they decided to head back down to camp to get some rest and change out their shift with Holzer and Reingard.

As they made their way down the gentle slope, David's eye caught some movement in the shadows just south of the camp. He quickly stopped and notified Erin, pointing in the direction of the movement.

As they peered into the night, the shadows once again moved with the malicious intent of a stalker. There were dozens of them, and they were moving more quickly as they approached the campsite. Moonlight briefly reflected off something metallic – it was unmistakably a sword. Despite the spell of concealment, and their furious flight through the previous night and day, their pursuers had found them!

Knowing time was running out, David and Erin sprinted as fast as they could down the hill towards the camp in a race to get to the others before the gang breached the alarms and sent them into a frenzy.

As soon as they reached the camp, the alarm went off, sending a shrilling whistle through the air followed by the yells of men running into battle – this time, they recognized the sound for what it was and were determined to prevent their victims from escaping.

Tyrius and the others quickly jumped up from their positions, struggling to shake of their sleep and grasping for their weapons while David and Erin rushed toward the incoming enemy with their blades drawn, hoping to give their companions enough time to prepare for the battle.

When the men left the shadows of the trees they had been creeping around and the light from the moon revealed their true numbers, David's heart sank to his stomach. There was more than just a dozen – there were at least three times that, maybe more, and they were coming at them like a horde of raging pirates.

Prepared to stand their ground and fight to the death, David and Erin planted their feet and swung with all their might as the crowd of men crashed into them.

The majority of the men flew past them towards the camp, while a couple met their blades with equal ferocity, clashing steel against steel and forcing David and Erin on their heels.

Fortunately, they were becoming more seasoned fighters and they quickly deflected their charging opponent's attacks, each breaking off into their own isolated battles while hoping their friends had had sufficient time to wake up and prepare for the incoming attack.

The sound of screams and a sudden intense flash of fire erupting through the darkness told Erin that Tyrius had successfully prepared for the attack and had cast a fury of powerful spells towards the aggressors. Several of the men caught fire and started running wildly into the darkness, weapons and anger forgotten once the flames began licking their flesh.

As she fought back her opponent, she heard the unmistakable roar of her barbarian friends as they ran into battle and a smile flashed across her face – they, too, were ready – the fight was on.

She quickly ducked under an attack that left her opponent's right side open, giving her ample time to stab her dagger deep into the man's ribs before she kicked him hard in the chest, knocking him to the ground.

She pulled back her dagger and threw it hard into an incoming man's chest, dropping him instantly to the ground.

No time to spare, she lifted up her sword to deflect an incoming attack, blocking it and deflecting it back into the air before ramming her pommel hard into the face of her newest victim, sending a spray of blood from his mouth and nose before dropping him with a swift and fatal cut to his throat.

Meanwhile, David was locked in combat with a man he recognized all too well – it was one of the men from Ashmire.

The man was a fierce opponent and attacked relentlessly and with abandon, leaving David little time to react between each blow.

As he dodged the endless fray of attacks, he quickly focused on trying to find an opening that would allow him to catch his opponent off guard and give him the chance he needed to turn the tides and go on the offensive.

That moment finally came.

The man put all his weight into an overhead swing, hoping it would knock David down when he tried to block – instead, he side-stepped out of the way, causing the man to stumble forward with the unexpected lack of resistance. David used this to his advantage and twirled around, arcing his blade outward towards the man's exposed back. It made contact, slicing a deep gash across his upper back, and forcing him to turn around with the blow.

David didn't let up, knowing doing so could cause him to lose the advantage. He followed with a series of swift jabs and cuts, which the man just barely blocked. David could see the man was starting to tire, his movements were becoming slower and his breath more labored. He was losing a lot of blood, and soon he would become too weak to fight any longer.

Knowing this, David pressed on even harder, until the opening he was waiting for finally came. The man had anticipated a high cut, leaving his lower half unguarded. David quickly diverted his attack into a low sweep with his leg, taking out the man's legs from beneath him, sending him landing hard on the ground. David quickly plunged his sword into the man's stomach with a finishing blow before running off toward the camp to help his friends.

When he arrived, he could see they were still vastly outnumbered, but all of them were still alive and seemingly unharmed.

"David! You okay mate?" asked Reingard through the chaos as he felled another man with his battle axe.

"Yeah, how're we looking?" David asked over the roar of the battle. He could tell they still had a lot of work ahead of them.

"Not good mate, not good. There's too many of them!" he screamed, ducking under another blow, and sending his attacker flying with a powerful kick to his chest.

"We have to run!" yelled Tyrius, still sending showers of fire into the endless stream of attackers. It was enough to keep some of the men at bay, but others would simply just run around the patches of fire and join the conflict from a different angle. Eventually, they would become surrounded and their chance of escape would drop to zero.

Knowing this, the companions decided to cut their losses and make a run for it.

Tyrius gathered his energy and unleashed a great torrent of wind towards the flames, enraging them and causing them to rise high into the sky, creating a wall of flame to escape behind.

When the flames finally subsided enough for their pursuers to see they had escaped, they jumped over the line of fire and followed hot in pursuit.

David and the others knew they couldn't outrun them. They were still worn out from the previous day's journey and the lack of sleep the night before. It wouldn't be long before their reserves were depleted, and they would be too exhausted to go on.

They only had a few hundred yards between them and their pursuers and the gap was closing with each passing moment.

Just as they felt they could go on no longer, the unimaginable happened – the earth opened its mouth and swallowed them whole into the darkness.

They fell into the ground and landed hard on a smooth rocky bottom several feet below the surface where they just stood. The barbarians were the first to gather their wits and jumped up, looking around for their pursuers.

They found themselves in a dark tunnel several feet beneath the surface, a narrow shaft of moonlight pouring in from the hole above where they had fallen through. Apparently, the tunnel was close to the surface and had eroded too much to support their weight, causing the ground to cave in.

They brushed off the dirt and dust from their clothes before checking to make sure the others were okay.

David had suffered a slight blow to the head and was slowing getting up, rubbing his head, and cursing under his breath.

Erin was now up and was working on getting Tyrius on his feet – he seemed to be struggling the most out of the group, but given his old age, that seemed reasonable enough.

When they had all brushed off the fall, they heard the yelling of their pursuers and the thumping of dozens of feet approaching the area above them. The earth shook and dirt and debris fell from the ceiling of the tunnel as they approached.

They each hid in the shadows away from the shaft of moonlight, hoping they would pass on by.

Erin held her breath as the men neared. She knew if they found the hole that they would follow them inside. They would probably follow them to the ends of the earth if they could.

As she listened intently, the footsteps began to slow before suddenly speeding up again, eventually fading away into the distance.

They hadn't seen the hole!

They each let out an audible sigh of relief, happy to finally be free from the pursuit of the blood-thirsty bandits.

They looked around to assess their new surroundings. They had fallen too far from the surface to be able to climb back up the way they came. The walls were too slick and smooth, and the opening was too high above their heads to try to lift each other out. Their only option was to try to find a way out of the dark tunnel they now found themselves in.

With no maps, and no earthly idea of where it would take them, Tyrius lit the orb on the crest of his staff with a simple wave of his hand and began leading them into the darkness.

Chapter XII

D avid and the others walked in near total darkness for what felt like hours. Without an end in sight and completely exhausted from the constant pursuit and threat of danger over the past couple of days, the party finally stopped to rest.

They had no wood for a fire and in the rocky tunnels there were no other fuel sources, so the companions had to make do with the light from Tyrius' staff to set up their bedrolls before enduring the cool dampness of the cave as they rested their weary limbs.

Each took a watch throughout the night while the others slept, but nothing eventful occurred in any of their shifts. It seemed as if they were alone in the vast underground cave system, each silently wondering whether they would ever find an end to the seemingly infinite network of tunnels.

When they had all finally rested and had a bite to eat from what remained of their supplies, they continued on their miserable journey through the dark.

They went on like this for what seemed like an eternity until they came to an area where the rough stone floor and walls had changed. They changed from a natural, rocky look into an obvious man-made texture that showed evidence of weathering on the floor from years of foot traffic and countless chisel marks on the walls and ceiling. Eventually the tunnel led them to an intersection that was unmistakably a mineshaft.

The ceiling and walls were supported by great timber beams that were spaced evenly in both directions and stretching as far as they could see into the darkness. The companions looked at each other with expressions of relief, overjoyed to have finally reached an area of the tunnels that showed signs of life after such a long, dark expanse of endless trekking through the uncharted caves.

"Now the question is, which way do we go?" said David, speaking aloud the question they had all been silently wondering themselves.

"Good question..." replied Tyrius, examining the passageways and clearly deep in thought.

David started to mindlessly rub his hands along the wall, feeling the carefully cut stone. He felt a warm breeze gently caress his neck and his eyes shot open.

"This way! We have to go this way!" said David, rubbing the chills from the back of his neck.

"What? How do you know?" asked Tyrius, confused how David had come to such a conclusion.

"I felt a warm breeze on the back of my neck, and it came from this direction" said David, pointing down the dark corridor.

"Are you sure? I didn't feel anything" said Erin, the others each nodding in agreement.

110

"Yes, I'm positive!" said David. "Come on, let's go!" he said, and he started down the dark tunnel in the direction of the warm breeze with the others following in pursuit.

It wasn't long before they discovered David had been correct. They reached another intersection that branched off in two opposite directions with the ground having metal tracks running in both directions. Along the walls were old iron sconces that once held torches and countless years' worth of soot still stained the ceiling and walls above them.

Just as David was getting a feel for which direction to go, the sound of screeching metal and squeaking wheels came echoing off the walls, faint at first, but quickly getting louder with each passing moment. Whatever it was, it was heading their way, and quickly!

The companions promptly jumped off the tracks and into the dark hallway they had just come from. In a matter of seconds, a minecart came crashing through the intersection at incredible speeds. It went by so fast they could hardly tell what it was, but they did notice one thing – the cart wasn't empty. Inside had been two bearded Dwarves, each carrying a lantern and a pickaxe!

"Hey!" shouted David as loud as he could after the passing cart.

Suddenly, a horrendous high-pitched screeching filled the tunnels, forcing them all to cover their ears. Sparks flew wildly in the distance behind the cart as it screeched to a halt.

Then, just as soon as the screeching stopped, they could hear a grunt and a series of heavy footsteps quickly slapping against the ground – the lantern light growing brighter and brighter as the Dwarves ran quickly their way.

The Dwarves finally reached the intersection and stopped a few feet from the companions, holding up their lanterns and pickaxes to see who had called out to them while making sure they weren't a threat.

"Oy! What're you lot doing down here?" asked the Dwarf in the front when he finished sizing them up. He was short but stocky, with huge arms and legs that were built from a lifetime of mining and hauling away rock. His chest was as large as a barrel and his brown bushy beard had a few tinges of gray and flowed down to his shiny belt buckle.

***

Once the Dwarves were sufficiently convinced that David and the others meant no harm and had in fact actually been lost for days in the tunnels, the Dwarves took them into the cart and said they would bring them along to the city.

As they sped along the tunnels, wind flapping wildly through their hair as they raced along the tracks, the companions were excited for the first time since getting out of the Southern Tunnel. They were headed to a place no mortal man had ever been before – the great Dwarven city of Emerald Keep.

The city was the stuff of legend and was the home that the Dwarves had been actively building and developing since the dawn of time. It was said to be filled with massive buildings and structures spanning miles beneath the Draconian Mountains in every direction and possessed an abundance of treasure so vast that it could fill the entire Mystic Mountain from top to bottom!

It was common knowledge in Hurea that the Dwarves were masters of their craft – mining precious metals from the earth and forging them into masterfully crafted jewelry and splendid sets of armor, but they were also master builders and ingenious engineers.

When the cart started to slow from that of a charging horse to a more comfortable speed for the companions, they came around a bend and for the first time caught sight of the city.

Everyone in the cart was silent and awestruck as the tunnel opened up into a cavern so vast it could have fit all of Eldergate within it and still have plenty of room to spare. There was a network of crisscrossing, arched stone bridges that spanned taller than the highest towers, some simply serving as roads and walkways, while others serving as railways for mine carts and supplies to be loaded and transported throughout the city, each with dozens of little carts flying back and forth carrying an assortment of goods and supplies throughout the network.

The bridges weaved in and out between massive buildings that varied in shape and size – the one commonality between them all is that their walls were made out of pure emerald crystal.

"So that's why they call it Emerald Keep" said David, completely dazzled by the brilliant green city.

"Aye – she's a beauty, ain't she?" said one of the Dwarves, seeing the look of shock on their faces. "It never gets old, coming home" he said, and they could believe it.

They traveled along the rails through the city, passing hundreds of Dwarves busy at work. Most were simply loading or unloading the carts before sending them back on their way into the mines, while others were getting on or off the carts to start or finish their shift, carrying pickaxes or shovels on their shoulders. The ones getting off were covered in sparkling dirt and were filthy, but despite their scowling faces, they seemed happy in their own way.

At last they found themselves headed towards a large building in the center of the city. It stretched so high it strained their necks when they tried to see to the top. The closer they got, the more they realized how large it truly was – it was like a mountain within the mountain!

When their cart finally came to a grinding halt before the large courtyard leading up the gigantic building, the Dwarves jumped out and helped their passengers disembark before the cart magically sped off on its own back down the tracks.

"How does it do that?" asked Erin in awe.

"Why, magic of course!" replied one of the Dwarves matter-of-factly, before leading the way towards the entrance to the building as if that were all that was needed to be said about it.

Erin laughed and, grabbing David's hand, walked with him and the others towards the building, following the two Dwarves.

When they reached the steps leading up to the building, two large and elaborate shiny metal doors slowly opened revealing a sizeable antechamber filled with bustling Dwarves moving about every which way.

As they entered, all of their heads turned, watching the humans enter the chamber as they went on about their business. None of them said a word, and they weren't rude about it, but it was clear they were surprised at what they were witnessing. David realized this was the first time any of these Dwarves had ever had a human visitor within their city and it must have been a strange sight to see.

When the two Dwarves reached a large central marble counter behind which dozens of very old looking Dwarves were seated, some taking paperwork from Dwarves as they came from their shifts, while others handing out new forms for the ones leaving, one of the older looking Dwarves stopped looking over his paperwork and nearly fell out of his seat.

When he finally composed himself and remembered his manners, he quickly, but politely, asked what in the world these humans were doing in the city.

The Dwarves quickly took turns explaining the circumstances behind their encounter with the humans and what led them to bring them here, before the old Dwarf looked up at David and the others and waved his hand for them to approach the counter.

Tyrius was the first to speak.

"We are humbled by your kindness and hospitality, great sir. My name is Tyrius Vanderbolt. I am the last of the Elders of Eldergate, and I beg your assistance for myself and my companions in this troubling predicament we find ourselves in." he said politely, bowing low, to which the others followed suit, not quite sure what the custom was in such situations.

"Tyrius Vanderbolt you say?" said the elderly Dwarf behind the counter, looking over Tyrius and the others. "What is it, I may ask, that brought you to our lands so far East of your own?" he said.

"Have you not heard?" asked Tyrius, surprised.

"Heard of what, dear fellow?" asked the Dwarf sincerely.

Tyrius turned back to look at the others, surprised that the news hadn't traveled to the Dwarven city yet. The Dwarves had always been a reclusive bunch, but something as significant as the coup in Eldergate, followed by the breach of the Dark Abyss and the release of the Defiant One and his minions surely should have traveled to their city by now, he thought. They each shrugged before he turned back to the counter.

"The Defiant One has returned, and he has overtaken Eldergate along with all of the Outer Woods region." said Tyrius, matter-of-factly.

It took a moment for the news to sink in, but David was quite sure that it hit home when the Dwarf's expression changed from that of mixed curiosity and humor, to the pale horror one would expect to see on someone who had just seen a ghost.

The Dwarf's expression quickly recovered and changed to one of utmost irritation as he dismissed the claim with the wave of his hands.

"That is impossible, Mr. Vanderbolt! The Defiant One has been locked away in the Dark Abyss for over a thousand years! The Mystics sealed him away, along with his dark army, at the end of the Battle of Salvation – I saw it with my own eyes! There is no way he could have escaped that place, not in a million years!" said the Dwarf loudly, to which all of the others quickly stopped their tasks to see what was causing all the ruckus.

The overall buzz in the air had dropped at this point to a deafening silence, so quiet it was that the drop of a pin could be heard from across the room.

David and the others looked around at their faces, uncomfortable at the sudden influx of attention now focused on them.

But Tyrius didn't seem to notice, or at least to not mind. He continued his plea, now with even more vigor than before.

"I know the history, Master Dwarf, but you must believe me, it is the truth! General Krauss of the Royal Guard has been manipulated and twisted into doing the Defiant One's bidding for some time now. Ever since he started secretly dabbling in the dark arts of the Order of the Abyss, hoping to gain the power needed to overthrow the kingdom, the Defiant One has had his grasp on the General – silently manipulating him, pulling his strings to lead him to do his bidding, until finally, just a few weeks ago, the unimaginable happened. He used one of the last remaining Mystic Crystals to harness enough power during the summer solstice to perform the ritual and unleash the Defiant One from his prison. I saw it for myself, we all did!" finished Tyrius, a look of horror in his eyes as he recalled the events from that day. Everyone nodded in agreement.

"But how did he gain such power? It would require an immense amount of Mystic energy to break the barrier." replied the Dwarf, now starting to see this wasn't some bad joke.

"It was my fault..." said David, chiming in and stepping forward to the counter.

At this point, the group was completely encircled with Dwarves, all listening in to what the humans had to say about the return of the Defiant One. Some of them seemed to not believe the words they were hearing, shaking their heads in disbelief, and whispering to one another, but others apparently did believe it. Their faces were white as snow as they were hanging on their every word.

"What do you mean, it was your fault?" asked the Dwarf, raising his white bushy eyebrows skeptically at the young man standing before him.

"My name is David Bishop – and I am the bearer of the Orb of Power." he said, holding out his hand and getting to the point.

This drew audible gasps from everyone crowded around them, each trying to peak around those in front of them to get a clearer look at the boy who claimed to wield the orb of legends past.

"I was trying to stop him – we all were – but he outmaneuvered us. He used my powers against me and harnessed them into the Mystic Crystal, using it to power his spell. I should have seen it coming...I should have connected the dots, but I failed..." said David, hanging his head low.

Erin came up behind him and put her hand on his shoulder, trying to console him.

"You see...what Tyrius says is true." said Erin, looking at the Dwarves crowded around them. "The Defiant One *has* returned, and we could use all the help we could get on our mission to try and stop him." she said.

Seeing the reaction of the Dwarves crowded around, the old Dwarf at the counter realized he was losing control of the situation. Some of the Dwarves were whispering frantically within the ranks, looks of fear on their faces, others looked angry at the claims the newcomers were making – they didn't want to believe the Defiant One had returned, knowing such a truth would surely pull them away from their families and lives of isolation and back into the world above, just as it had done so long ago.

Quickly assessing the situation, the old Dwarf made up his mind. He had to get things back under control, and fast.

"This is nonsense! I will not have you come barging into our halls and inciting a panic with these unfounded claims!" he said, pounding his hammer forcefully on the counter. Immediately, everyone in the room hushed once again, their focus intent on the Master Dwarf.

"It's not nonsense!" replied Erin quickly, but the Dwarf was done listening to their story and was instead looking over their heads towards the group of Dwarves standing around them.

"Take them away for the time being. I will speak with the King and see what he wishes to do with them. I suspect he will not be thrilled to hear what has transpired today – we can't just take their word on something this important and risk inciting a riot! But alas, it is up to King Tybrin to decide, not us, on what needs to be done." said the Dwarf.

With this, several Dwarves that appeared to be soldiers came from behind the crowd and grabbed David and the others, leading them swiftly out of the chamber.

Knowing that to struggle would only make things worse, the companions all complied and let the Dwarves lead them out of the building, back towards the railway passing in front of the courtyard. They could hear the murmurs of the crowd as they were taken away.

It seemed as if the ploy mostly worked, as the majority of the Dwarves dispersed and went back to their work, but a few stayed behind in small tight groups, discussing what had just transpired quietly among one another, occasionally looking up at the prisoners as they were led to the carts.

When they arrived at the carts and climbed in, it quickly sped off down the rails towards a tunnel leading deeper into the mountain. It wasn't long before the glorious emerald buildings quickly faded out of view and were replaced once again by darkness, broken only by the occasional torchlight as they flew quickly past.

Eventually they reached a dead end and were instructed to exit the cart before being led to a doorway into another chamber that held a series of isolated cells. Their weapons were confiscated and placed in a small holding area before they were each put into separate rooms. The thick metal doors now closed and locked behind them, they were once again left alone and in the dark, each wondering how in the world they were going to get out of this one.

Chapter XIII

It wasn't long before the Dwarves returned, this time carrying dishes of wonderful smelling food for them to enjoy while waiting for their meeting with the King.

David's mouth began watering as soon as he smelled the food, suddenly much more aware of how long it had been since he had eaten a savory meal and eager to fill his empty stomach with warmth once again.

One of the guards named Gavin apologized for the way they had been treated. Having been a friend of one of the Dwarves who had been in close proximity when the news was shared in the great hall, he had heard all about it and he and his friends believed their account to be true.

He explained that the councilmen had only been doing what he felt was best to avoid a panic and had intended to get permission from the King for them to have a private audience so they could tell him their story first-hand without risking the news spreading uncontrolled and uncorroborated.

The Dwarves had always been allies to the humans, even fighting with them in the War of

Salvation to fight back the Defiant One's army, but they were also a private folk – happy to keep to themselves and not too eager to get involved in the affairs of the surface world. When something came along that risked that peace and security, it tended to cause problems within the ranks, and therefore, the kingdom's security. Trying to quell a bunch of angry, panicking Dwarves was no small feat!

David and the others took the news well and acknowledged that their intrusion could have had unintended consequences they didn't consider at the time, but also expressed their sense of urgency in getting out of their cells and getting back to their mission – with or without the help of the Dwarves.

After they had all finished their meals and their plates had been taken away, another Dwarf came to their cells and informed them that they would have to stay here for the night, but first thing in the morning they were to speak with the King regarding their claims.

With this, they each settled down on the bedding provided in their respective cells and decided to take the time to rest, knowing that such security was a thing of luxury when it came to being on the road and on the run.

As David lay in his bed, he tried to brush off the events of the past several weeks as he mindlessly counted the bricks in the ceiling above his bed. He had been in Hurea for nearly two months by now, and so much had happened in such a short time that even he had a hard time believing it. Eventually he became too tired to think straight and slowly drifted off into a deep and restful sleep.

***

David awoke to the sound of keys rattling and his cell door squeaking open.

"Oy, it's time to see the King" said the guard. It was Gavin again.

David rubbed the sleep from his eyes before stretching and heading out of his cell as instructed.

When he exited, he could see that Erin, Tyrius, Reingard, and Holzer were all waiting for him at the exit near the cart that would take them back to the city.

The ride from the jail was more enjoyable now that he knew they weren't in any real trouble. He felt like he was on a rollercoaster, speeding around the twists and turns in the track, watching the torches appear in the distance then quickly fly by just to disappear again behind them. It didn't take them long to reach the opening into the vast chamber, once again bringing the emerald city into view.

David was amazed at how skilled the Dwarves were to have built such an incredible city out of crystal and stone. It was unlike anything he had ever seen.

As they raced past the central building from the day before, they continued onward through the heart of the city and into a long section of climbing spiral railways leading to the upper levels of the chamber. By the time they reached the top of the spiral, they were high above the majority of the city and could see across the entire cavern.

It was even bigger than he had first thought, this new perspective giving him the whole view of the city in one large panorama that left them all speechless.

They finally came to a stop in front of a long walkway that led to a great palace overlooking the city and were instructed to exit.

Two Dwarves decked out in magnificent gold-plated armor and carrying long gold-plated halberds waited by the front door of the palace. They looked straight ahead as the company approached as if they were statues, but David had no doubt that if a threat were to present itself, they would be more than ready and capable of handling it.

Once they entered through the palace doors, they came into a large, vaulted room with polished floors of sparkling white stone with silver veins running like rivers throughout. The ceiling was supported by massive columns of the same material that were several feet wide and hundreds of feet tall, towering above them like giant trees.

The room was adorned with colorful tapestries and banners hanging on the walls and was lined with soldiers all standing guard in the same decorative armor as the two sentries from before.

At the end of the room stood a massive staircase that rose several flights before tapering off at the top level where a large metal door opened up into a throne room where the King awaited their arrival.

David could see him, sitting on his elegant throne of crystal, the light reflecting off in thousands of refracted beams. He looked majestic and powerful.

The guards led them up the staircase and into the throne room, instructing them to stop several feet before the few carpeted steps leading up to the King.

King Tybrin Hammerclaw sat on his throne, waiting patiently for his audience as they took a knee and bowed respectfully before him. He was large for a Dwarf, and thick. David could see his bulging muscles even beneath his flowing robes.

His fingers were encrusted with lavish rings of various metals and gemstones, and the crown on his head was made of thick bands of gold and silver, skillfully twisted around each other in a spiral fashion that made it look as if it had grown together naturally, like a vine does with a tree, rather than crafted by hand. When he finally spoke, his voice boomed like thunder and echoed throughout the polished chamber.

"I hear ye caused quite a bit o' trouble in me halls yesterday" said Tybrin, looking down at the group before him.

"So, ye claim the Defiant One has returned, is tha' so?" he asked in his thick accent.

"It is, your majesty" replied Tyrius, taking the lead. "And it is also true"

"So, I hear..." replied Tybrin. "May I see the boy?" he asked, holding out his hand for David to come closer.

David looked over at Tyrius and the guards beside them, who each nodded in approval, before he started slowly up the stairs. When he reached the King, he slowly held out his hand for the King to inspect the image of the orb. It was glowing faintly as it always seemed to be, a former shadow of its once more vibrant self.

King Tybrin inspected his hand, turning it over as he carefully examined the markings.

"So, what ye say is true. At least the part about the orb bearer." said Tybrin at last, releasing David's hand and sitting back in his throne.

"But what proof do ye have of the return o' the Defiant One?" he asked, looking down from his throne at each of them in turn.

"Proof? We have no proof that we can give right now, your majesty. But if it is proof that you seek, you can find it simply by sending scouts to the surface and looking towards Eldergate." said Tyrius. "The city has all but fallen into the chasm of the Dark Abyss, and the Royal Palace has been lifted high into the sky on a black rock that rose from the depths from whence an army of Demons came, along with the Defiant One himself. There is no disputing it, he *has* returned, and his numbers are only growing each day. It is only a matter of time before they march on Ravenfell, and even your own lands."

Tybrin Hammerclaw sat for a moment processing the information Tyrius provided, running his thick sausage-like fingers through his great beard as he thought.

"Very well. This is a simple thing ye ask, and one we can easily prove in a matter o' a day or two. I will send some scouts to the surface at Draco's Pass and have them take a look. If it is as ye say, we are in some troubling times indeed. If it isn't...well, it is a serious crime lying to the King. You'll be punished according to our laws and customs. What say ye?" he asked.

Tyrius looked around at the others who were all in agreement before he said that they agreed to his terms.

"Good. In the meantime, I'm sure ye are all starving! I will treat ye as our guests o' honor until we have more information. Ye can stay here in me palace in the guest's chambers – they haven't been used in ages. We will have a feast to celebrate yer arrival, but I warn ye, no talk of the Defiant One outside o' these chambers – I will not risk a panic rising in me halls!" said Tybrin sternly.

They all agreed and immediately were taken to their new temporary quarters, which were far more lavish and welcoming than the cells they had stayed in the night before.

Seamstresses had come and measured each of them quickly and efficiently before speeding off to their workshops and returning surprisingly quickly with brand new outfits for each of them to wear for their time in the city. They were bright and festive and went well with the attire that most of the Dwarves in the city seemed to be wearing.

They were instructed to get washed up and changed into the clothes that were provided, then were told they could roam around the city and explore as they wished until the feast was prepared.

Once they had each washed and changed, they met in front of the palace and made their way to the carts that would take them down to the main parts of the city.

"Well, where would ye like to go?" asked the Dwarf in the car who was instructed to take them around the city and keep an eye on them.

His name was Darryn Faircloth, and he was a very nice Dwarf, well-mannered and down to earth like the majority of them were. He wore a bright blue outfit with brown boots and trousers that went up to his round belly and were held in place by bright red suspenders. His face was plump with rosy cheeks and his beard was brown and well groomed, only hanging just below his neckline with little braids on the ends.

After little debate, the group decided they wanted to see the business district of the city so they could tour the shops and businesses and get a better idea of what life was like in the great Dwarven city of Emerald Keep.

This seemed to really excite Darryn – he really enjoyed shopping and mentioned his cousin Gerryn owned and operated the most popular fine metal and gemstones shop in all the kingdom dubbed "The Sparkling Hammer". Darryn explained his cousin came up with the name because of how at the end of the day, his tools would all be covered in a fine, sparkling dust from all of the hammering and chiseling he did throughout the day with the precious metals and gemstones.

Darryn took them down the spiraling tracks and into the bustling business district then led them the rest of the way on foot.

The walkways were sprawling with Dwarves of all shapes, sizes, and ages. David realized his initial impression of Dwarves was completely wrong – they were just as diverse as humans were in all of the same ways: fashion, height, weight, skin complexion, hair color, and even accents.

David noticed as they walked that some of the Dwarves had thicker accents, sounding like the king missing some of the ending sounds to words, while others spoke more clearly, pronouncing all of the syllables with crystal clarity. Darryn explained it was mostly due to their profession and lineage – those who were what he called "traditionalists" tended to stick to the traditional professions of the Dwarves – mining, smithing, crafting, and building had maintained the traditional accent, mostly staying underground, while the less traditional folk tended to the more "civilized" professions that sprouted up after their time spent among the humans and Elves – those tended to work in banking and currency exchange, and trading on the surface world where they had adopted more of the common tongue so they could better communicate with the other races.

David was amazed at everything he was experiencing, and he was thrilled to see that Erin and the others were just as stunned, which was a first. He always seemed to be the one gawking at everything, being from another world, but this time, they were all equally entranced with the Emerald city and its rich culture.

It wasn't long before they reached "The Sparkling Hammer". It was a relatively small building within the business district and sat between what they were told was a large bank to the right – an enormous sprawling structure that seemed to have several floors and took up the majority of the block – and a jewelry store to the left – a more modest building with great big windows in the front filled with displays of dazzling jewelry of all sorts and sizes.

As they were heading into the stop, they were stopped by a highly dressed Dwarf wearing a gold-embroidered scarf and a gold-plated walking stick. He wore a top hat and a solid black jacket over his shirt with a jeweled pocket watch hanging by a thin gold chain from his chest pocket.

Although he was short in stature and relatively thinner than most Dwarves David had seen, he held himself in such a manner that screamed wealth and power. His snow-white hair and beard were immaculately trimmed and manicured, and his piercing eyes were a crystal blue like sapphires.

"So, these are the wonderful newcomers I've been hearing all about?" said the Dwarf, taking each of their hands and stopping briefly to kiss Erin's. "I heard you caused quite a racket in the Great Hall yesterday evening" he said with a twinkle in his eye.

"'ello Manny! Aye, these are the ones" confirmed Darryn. "But it's being settled, and they are our guests now. I've been given the great pleasure o' taking 'em around myself. Was just about to take 'em to my cousin's shop." he said.

"So, it would seem" said Manny. "If you wish, I could take you around the bank and show you the...more sophisticated side of the city, once you're finished touring with Darryn, of course." he said with a smile.

David noticed Darryn shifting uncomfortably under Manny's gaze and quickly realized that this

Manny character was not the kind of Dwarf he would like to hang around.

"No, thanks." he said, "I think we've only got enough time to see a few places before we have to get back to our quarters. We're expected at the King's feast tonight." said David, emphasizing the last part.

With this Manny's mouth slightly twitched at the corner and his smile faded just enough for David to notice his displeasure. David assumed he was not invited to this feast, and that must have struck a nerve with the Dwarf who was most likely accustomed to such honorary invitations.

"I see." said Manny, slightly bowing. "Well, if you happen to find yourselves in the area again, please do stop on by. You'll come to find there's another side to Emerald Keep that caters to those who prefer a more...classy atmosphere."

With that he took his leave and headed up the stone steps and through the large double doors into the bank's lobby.

David watched with displeasure as the Dwarf disappeared from sight before turning to the others.

"Something about that guy really set me on edge" he said.

"Aye, you oughtta look out for that one. He inherited the business from his father and has gained a lot o' reputation in these parts as a crook and a cheat, but he's the one who controls the trade. If anyone wants to sell their goods on the surface, they have to go through him. When he took over, he upped the charges for using his routes – making it cost twice as much as before for him to sell yer goods, claiming it's because o' the increased distance his boys have to travel to make a sale, and the increased dangers on the surface. But everyone knows it's just to line his pockets with more gold." explained Darryn.

"Why do people still go through him then?" asked Erin, not understanding what would stop them from selling their goods on the surface on their own.

"Most people are afraid o' the surface. They like the underground, and the stories o' Dwarves trying their luck themselves and never returning – those are enough to keep anyone from trying again. That's why he's so popular – he's got the routes secured and his boys are seasoned enough to know where to go, when to go, and how to avoid trouble up there." said Darryn. "But that's enough o' that! Let's go meet me cousin Gerryn!" said Darryn, his expression cheerful again at the thought of showing off his cousin's skills.

Darryn was right to be proud. His cousin's skills with the hammer and chisel were unlike anything any of them had seen before. His shop was lined with exquisitely crafted metal pieces and jewelry ready to be capped with precious gems and stones that were perfectly cut in thousands of unique shapes and sizes.

Once the stones were set in the pieces, he would give them to the jewelry store next door to sell, where he would earn a percentage of the sale, giving a sizeable amount to the owner. He explained his cousin was not interested in the sales aspect and would rather spend all of his time on the crafting and forging of the items, leaving the sales and customer interactions to his partner next door.

After they had been introduced to Gerryn and were given a quick tour of the business and some of the other local stores, David and the others had decided to head back to the palace to prepare for the feast.

They made their way back to the cart and took off down the tracks and up the spiral railway before heading off to their separate rooms to prepare for the coming feast, something they were each eagerly awaiting.

Chapter XIV

Manny quickly made his way through the interior of the bank, gesturing for his two most trusted advisors – Glenn and Glynn – to follow him to his office.

Glenn and Glynn were brothers, and they were built big and sturdy like most Dwarves. When Manny had taken over the business from his father, he hired them as his own personal bodyguards. He also used them to run his little errands. Errands like making sure anyone who tried to sell goods on the surface never found their way back to Emerald Keep. It was a nasty business trying to remain on top, Manny had always told them.

When they entered and shut the door, and he was certain no one else was close enough to listen in on their conversation, Manny quietly but urgently began explaining what must be done.

"Word has reached me of the King's plan to send a small scouting party to the surface. He wants to verify the human's claims that the Defiant One has returned." began Manny, looking at the two large Dwarves.

"It is your job to make sure that this news does not reach the King. You have whatever resources you need to make this happen. Do you understand?" he asked, looking sternly at Glenn and Glynn.

They both shook their heads in unison.

"Good. If word gets out that the Defiant One and his armies have indeed returned, no one will risk sending their goods to the surface to trade, and therefore, no one will come to me for my services. The bank will lose its most lucrative business, and with all of the money I've already committed to keeping my insiders quiet and on the prowl, I'd lose more than I can bear." he said, pacing back and forth. "We must not let this happen...whatever the cost, do you hear me?" he reiterated.

"Sir, you can rest assured we will take care of this quickly and quietly." said Glynn after sharing a look of understanding with Glenn.

"But we will need a considerable amount of gold to convince the scouts to give a false report – they won't risk lying to the King without a big incentive."

"Yes, yes, take whatever you need from the vaults. If we don't get them on our side, our business is doomed anyway!" said Manny frantically. "We can replenish the funds later. Right now, our only focus is in keeping the truth from the King! Now be off, there's no time to waste!" he said, pointing to the door.

Glenn and Glynn quickly walked out of the room. When it came to finding the weakest link in an organization, there were none better.

They had been the ones who found out that the King's personal accountant had been stealing little by little from the King's treasury over the years. Now, he was giving them insider information in order to keep them from spilling his little secret.

They were also the ones responsible for finding the guard who patrolled the palace who was facing financial uncertainties due to his gambling addition – now he was doing quite well, and only had to pay the price of his loyalty to the King to gain back his losses. That and his promise to keep tabs on the whereabouts of the soldiers patrolling the city so they could plot out the best places and times to carry out their more lucrative deals in privacy, without the risk of interference.

Yes, their boss had given them many assignments indeed, and they had been very busy buying off the weak and feeble-minded ones wherever they could be found.

Because of this, they knew just where to go to carry out their latest assignment.

Glenn and Glynn made their way through the city proper and up the higher walkways of the upper-class district. After several long paths and quite a few turns, they found their way to the Office of the Guard Patrol who's ranking officer had recently been caught in a compromising situation, one that would have left his wife quite disappointed in him were she to find out.

Fortunately for him, Glenn and Glynn knew how to make secrets disappear, but they always had a price. Today, that price was to be paid by getting him to choose his two newest recruits for the King's assignment – recruits he knew could be manipulated if offered a vast amount of coin to keep quiet certain details of their report.

They quickly dropped off the large bag filled with gold coins and explained their terms to the ranking officer, terms which he quickly agreed to after a small reminder of why he was doing their bidding.

"For your troubles" said Glynn, handing over a smaller bag of coin to the officer, to which he smiled and eagerly slid into his pocket.

"Thank you, sirs. Always a pleasure doing business," said the officer.

With their business settled, Glenn and Glynn made their way out of the Office of the Guard Patrol and headed to the lower district for a celebratory drink. They loved their job, and they were very, very good at it.

Chapter XV

The feast turned out to be better than any of them could have imagined. It was held in a great dining hall filled with several long wooden tables that spanned across the room from wall to wall.

King Tybrin had spared no expense when it came to the food. There were all kinds of roasted game ranging from boar, turkey, venison, all the way down to what David was told was duck. In addition to the meats, there were countless varieties of salads, vegetables, and fruit bowls on every table.

The popular drink of choice was a dark, amber ale that the Dwarves took great pride in and was brewed within their caverns by the hundreds of gallons. It had somewhat of a spicy note, with hints of cinnamon and vanilla. Darryn told them that the spice came from a local pepper that grew in the dark caverns near the city and was extremely spicy if eaten raw but toned down quite a bit during the brewing process.

The King had also requested an assortment of live music and entertainers to attend the feast, singing heroic tales in song form of ages past and ballads of long-lost lovers, while others performed juggling acts and reenacted plays of historic battles and other important events.

Eventually, enough drink had been consumed that several Dwarves began jumping up on the tables and dancing to the music, swinging arm in arm and knocking over several mugs and dishes in the act. Some of the patrons that were less intoxicated didn't take too kindly to their meals being kicked to the floor and began shouting at the hooligans, trying to get them down from the tables. Others simply decided to join them and before you knew it, nearly all of the tables were filled with dancing Dwarves!

Reingard and Holzer, feeling much more at home in this environment than David, Erin, and Tyrius would have liked, jumped up on the table and joined in the merrymaking, laughing and trying their best to sing along and keep up with the footwork of the Dwarves.

Overall, the evening was quite enjoyable and was filled with joy and laughter. It was a nice break from the hard, and sometimes dangerous journey thus far from Ravenfell. It allowed them to forget the woes of the world above them and focus instead on the moment, basking in it for as long as they could. After all, the companions knew in the back of their minds that the festive mood would be short lived at best, soon to be broken by the harsh reality that lay awaiting on the surface world.

As the evening grew later and later the crowds began to disperse and the staff started clearing off the tables, signaling that it was time for the party to end and for the companions to call it a night.

David escorted Erin back to her room and gave her a long kiss goodnight before she playfully pushed him away and told him to go to bed, shutting the door gently behind her.

David stumbled through the hallway, feeling quite high on life, eventually making his way to his room before flopping down on his bed. The mattress was soft and molded to his form, swallowing him in a gentle cushion of warmth in which he quickly drifted off to sleep.

***

The next morning came faster than he would have liked, and far less enjoyable than the previous night had ended.

He awoke to a loud banging on his door before it was violently flung open. In came two Dwarves decked in the armor of the Guard. They promptly placed him under arrest and escorted him out of his room.

Still half asleep and at this point completely confused, David did his best to catch his feet up with the swiftly moving guards that were practically dragging him through the hallway. It took him a few moments before he finally gathered the awareness to speak.

"What's going on?" he asked the guards, "Why am I under arrest?"

"It's not for us to ask questions. We were instructed to gather you and your friends up and take you to the King at once. I expect you'll find out soon enough." said one of the guards grimly, never missing a beat.

It wasn't long before they led David to the large, vaulted entryway and he caught sight of Erin and the others for the first time. They too were being escorted by armored guards and looked just as shocked as he was.

He could hear Tyrius demanding the same explanation David had asked for. Clearly none of them knew what was going on!

They were all led to the throne room and forced to kneel before the King, who was waiting patiently on his throne. He looked extremely disappointed.

"When we spoke yesterday, I mentioned to ye that if ye were lying to me, ye would be punished. Yet ye still insisted, and even had the nerve to join me feast, drink me ale, and eat me food as if ye were worthy of such things!" spat Tybrin, furious.

"What are you saying?" asked Tyrius, confused by King Tybrin's accusation. "Have the scouts returned already? Surely they would have told you the news!" he pleaded.

"Aye, they told me the news! They said there was nothing out o' place at Eldergate from what they could tell. No army of Demons, no giant outcrop of rock! How do ye suppose I should take that?" asked Tybrin, glaring fiercely at his captives.

"No.... that can't be!" said Tyrius, "We saw it for ourselves, we were there when it happened. The scouts, they must be lying to you!"

"And why would they lie to me?" asked Tybrin, "What would they have to gain but a swift trial and severe punishment?"

"I don't know, but there has to be an explanation! Send another scout party, I beg of you. You will see - " started Tyrius, but Tybrin swiftly cut him off.

"I will not send another scout party! What I will do, is promptly schedule a trial for ye all to answer to yer crimes! Ye will no longer be welcome in me house. Ye will stay in yer cells until the evenin' when we can hear the case against ye. I will have Darryn represent ye, since he's the one who was with ye the most and will be most inclined to speak honestly for yer cause. Now, be off! I want ye out o' me sight!" said Tybrin, waving his hand for the guards to take them away.

"Your majesty, please, you must believe us!" shouted Tyrius as he was dragged away.

The guards escorted them out of the palace and back to the carts where they were promptly taken back to the cells they had occupied after their initial arrival.

They were not allowed to talk during the cart ride, however, once they were securely locked in their cells, Darryn came promptly to the prison to speak with them and discern what had happened.

He went to Tyrius' cell, which was in the middle of the hallway, so everyone could hear what was being said.

"Tell me it ain't so." said Darryn to Tyrius through the bars in the door.

"It's a complete fabrication!" whispered Tyrius angrily. "I don't understand why the scouts would lie."

"I don't either," replied Darryn, "But if we don't find out why by tonight, you'll all be spendin' a whole lott'a time in these cells." he said seriously.

"I know...I know...we must find out who the scouts were. If we can do that, we can determine why they would have lied, what incentive they would have had in keeping the truth from the King. That has to be our focus." said Tyrius, to which everyone agreed.

"Right, I'll see what I can find out and come back as soon as I have some news." replied Darryn, and he quickly took off down the hallway and sped off in the cart back to the city.

***

The hours passed by slowly as they waited in their cells for the hour of their trial. They were given a meager meal for breakfast, then lunch, and then finally dinner, before the guards came at last to get them for their hearing.

When they each were taken from their cell and escorted to the cart that would take them back to the city, they all shared worried looks, wondering where Darryn was and if he had ultimately decided to abandon their cause.

They sped off down the railways to the city, the dark tunnels suddenly feeling very confining and miserable in light of their increasingly bleak situation.

Chapter XVI

It was early morning, and the mist was still hanging thick in the air over the Great Plains between the southern bend of the Draconian Mountains and the Outer Woods. The men of Ravenfell were waiting atop their great towers at the top of the mountain pass. All they could do was watch helplessly as the Great Plains continued to swell with endless masses of Demons preparing their march toward Ravenfell.

Their ranks looked like a great black flood, slowly taking over the green grasslands and flowing over the rolling hills like a great wave of death. Thousands of banners were reaching into the sky throughout their ranks, bearing the black Raven in front of a blood red circle – the insignia of the Southern Kingdom that General Krauss had adopted when he took over Eldergate and what remained of the Royal Guard.

Although the distance between the soldiers and the incoming army was still great, they could feel the vibration of hundreds of thousands of marching feet, pounding away on the ground as they made their way down the Great Road, and it left the men restless. They had prepared for this fight for several days now, anticipating its arrival, but the sight of such a vast army was unsettling and left the men chilled from more than just the cool mountain air.

Rex and Orin were standing together with the King and General Ryan on the first of the high walls to catch a glimpse of the enemy they would soon be facing.

"And so, it begins" said King Eldergate somberly, peering out across the vast plains at the enemy force. He had a fierce look of determination mixed with overwhelming sadness for the countless lives he knew would soon be lost in the fighting.

"Aye. We are as ready as we will ever be," said Rex, confident they had done everything they could in the two short weeks they had had to prepare since David's departure. "Let's just hope it is enough." he said, peering out into the plains below at the marching army.

Their fortifications had been completed in the night, leaving the valley protected by a series of high stone walls with crenelations spaced evenly throughout. They would provide cover for their archers to rain fire from above and hopefully slow down the enemy advancement. Behind the fortified walls were a series of wooden barricades, cut to sharp points facing outward, that were set up in a way that would force the enemy to zigzag through the maze-like barriers before reaching the second, and eventually third, walls.

On top of the walls were ballistae to hold off the flying demons, and catapults to fire large tar-filled pots that would be lit and fired, exploding upon impact.

If the enemy forces were able to breach the final wall, they would be faced with the full combined might of the armies of Ravenfell and Eldergate that would be waiting for them should they get that far – and there was no doubt that they eventually would.

The last of the walls was about halfway through the narrow mountain pass, meaning the enemy would still be forced into smaller numbers as they faced off against the two armies, giving the defenders of Ravenfell a better chance at holding the enemy horde than they would have had in a more open setting.

"Orin how are we looking with the magical preparations?" asked Rex, looking over at the old mage.

"The barriers are in place along the outskirts of the valley and before each wall, as well as around the castle should we need to fall back. It won't hold the ground forces forever, but it will hold them long enough to keep the flying ones at bay and from flying over our defenses. They won't be able to attack from above, at least. The barrier won't let them pass and from my experience with the flying demons, they aren't very powerful – at least not powerful enough to break through my barriers." said Orin confidently.

"The spell will help strengthen the physical defenses significantly, allowing them to withstand far more of a beating before giving way than they would have otherwise, however, the ground demons are strong, and they are relentless. I am sure they will have made siege equipment that will help them get through any obstacles we present them. It is only a matter of time before they are able to scale the walls or batter their way through. We will just have to focus on defeating as many enemies as we can while they concentrate on the walls. That will at least help even the odds once they eventually do get through." finished the mage.

"Very good, Orin, thank you." said Rex.

"Sir, we have our most skilled archers in place along the battlements and a sizeable number ready on top of the castle walls should we need to retreat to the castle for a final stand. We also have our most experienced fighters towards the front of the defenses, manning the tops of the walls as well as the head of our forces behind the walls. They will know what to do when the forces break through and will have the courage to face the enemy." said General Ryan, finishing his report.

"Very well, thank you General" said King Eldergate, dismissing the General to get back to checking on his men and the defenses.

The three continued to watch as the enemy forces slowly made their way across the Great Plains. By this time, the mist had started to clear, and the true size of the enemy forces was even more visible.

They could now see the great flying beasts slowly circling the main army high above, keeping pace with them as they marched. Their sheer numbers seemed to block out the grey Autumn sky wherever they flew. They could also make out a group of larger demons that towered above the rest. They were large and bulky, several times taller than the main forces, and appeared to be carrying large timbers the size of trees as clubs.

These would certainly pose more of a threat to the barriers and walls and would need to be taken down quickly to prevent them from breaking through. Orin said these forces had been a major problem back in the Mystic War, but their hides, though strong, had a weak spot at the neck and armpits that could be exploited by skilled archers and warriors. He made sure to pass the information on to the officers to relay to their men. They would know what to do when the time came.

They knew it would only be a matter of a day or two before the first of the enemy lines reached their doorstep. They were prepared and ready. It would be a battle that would go down in history as did the last Great War between the forces of good and evil. That is if they survived to tell the story.

They were determined to make sure that they did, knowing the fate of the world rested squarely on their shoulders.

Chapter XVII

Darryn had been frantically searching the city for any clues as to who the scouts were and why they had given the King a false report, but he was unsuccessful no matter where he searched and who he asked for information.

No one seemed to know anything about this mission, not even the guards in the patrol office.

Knowing his time was running short, he decided to make a bold move – he quickly gathered what supplies he could, including a medium sized battle hammer that his great grandfather had passed down for generations from his time in the Mystic War, and began his long journey through the dark tunnels leading to the surface near Draco's Pass.

The rails would take him to the beginning of the tunnel that would lead to the surface. Once there, he would be able to see for himself if his friends had been telling the truth or not. He suspected that they were, why else would they have fabricated such a story in light of the punishments? They had nothing to gain in lying, and his time spent with the humans, no matter how short it had been, led him to believe they were an honest bunch and had good intentions.

As he made his way through the dark tunnels, the wind rushing past him as he urged the cart onward beyond its normal safe speeds, he noticed the air began to cool and the dark seemed to be less intense between the areas lit by torchlight.

In just a couple of hours he reached his destination, and he quickly hurled himself out of the cart and began racing as fast as his legs would carry him to the end of the tunnel. The light began to change from the artificial glow of fire, flickering on and off as he rushed past the torches, to the brighter natural light of the surface world that Darryn's eyes were not accustomed to seeing.

As he neared the exit, his eyes burned with the intensity of the light and his legs felt like giving up, but he pressed onward, knowing what was at stake if he should fail. The fate of the world depended on David's mission. Should he fail in his, the world would be doomed.

When he finally breached the tunnel and entered for the first time in his life into the wide-open air of the surface world, he had to cover his eyes to slowly let them adjust a little at a time.

He could feel the cool mountain air rushing past him through the narrow mountain pass. Little speckles of cold gently brushed his skin. It was snowing!

When his eyes finally adjusted, he looked around and dropped his hammer to the ground in complete awe. The surface world was more beautiful than he had ever imagined!

The snow had covered the rocky landscape in a light blanket of white. It was cold and wet at the same time, and its fluffy texture left him delighted every time he brushed his hand through its powdery surface.

Suddenly remembering why he had come here in the first place, he shook off his amazement and quickly ran to the edge of the cliff that faced West towards the Great Plains and Eldergate. When he crested the ridge and looked out beyond the mountains to the great expanse Westward, his stomach dropped, and he nearly lost his breath.

The entire plains were filled with a vast army stretching as far as the eye could see – a large faction of it was heading to the West towards where he knew Ravenfell was located, the other half was heading directly towards his position – towards Draco's Pass. There was a giant rocky outcrop rising from the Outer Woods where Eldergate was supposed to be according to the maps he had brought with him. Instead, what he saw was the great palace of Eldergate lifted high above the canopy of the forest, just as his friends had said.

They hadn't been lying – it was true, the Defiant One had indeed returned, and war was coming to their doorstep.

***

The cart had finally reached the stop before the King's palace and David and the others were instructed to exit the cart. They were led to the large, vaulted antechamber of the palace then up the stairs and into the large throne room.

King Tybrin Hammerclaw was seated atop his throne, but now before the steps leading to his throne stood a large wooden counter with several official looking Dwarves seated behind it. The Dwarf in the middle was the same elderly Dwarf they had encountered on their first day in Emerald Keep – the one who had sent them off to their cells the first time.

"Hello again." he said to them with a slight smile.

Something told David he didn't really like humans, a feeling that didn't make him feel any better given the circumstances they found themselves in. He assumed these other Dwarves were part of a council that would be trying them for their crime of lying to the King.

Once all of them had been brought before the counter, they were all chained together by a great chain that was latched to each of their handcuffs. The other end was securely fastened to a great eye hook on the far end of the room. When they were securely fastened in place, one of the Dwarves at the counter stood up and began the proceedings.

"Today we have brought before us a group of humans who have come to our lands unannounced and with the malintent of inciting a riot through their lies and propaganda." said the Dwarf, reading from a scroll set on the counter before him.

"Their crimes – lying to the King. How do you plead?" he asked, looking at David and the others.

Each of them vehemently pleaded not guilty, to which the council members all shook their head silently in disgust.

"So be it. And where is your council?" asked the lead Dwarf behind the counter, looking around the chambers. "Where is Darryn?" he asked them with raised eyebrows.

"Sir, we do not know where Darryn is. We spoke with him last night but have not seen him since" replied Tyrius solemnly. "It appears he may have abandoned us."

"Master Dwarf, can we represent ourselves?" asked Erin quickly, hoping to be able to stall long enough to give their friend a chance to show up.

She knew he said he was going to search for the answers needed to prove their innocence. Maybe he was still out there, working his way through the city, trying to get to them with the evidence needed to set them free.

The council members quietly murmured among each other for a moment before the head council member stood again and spoke.

"It is not the traditional way of Dwarves to represent themselves, however, we will give you the exception considering the unusual circumstance you find yourselves in while lacking your own representative. We will have to address a grievance against Darryn Faircloth for abandoning his responsibilities to the accused." said the Dwarf writing down the record as the others nodded in agreement.

"I am sure he has his reasons for not being here today" said Erin, speaking loudly for all to hear. "Before he left us, Darryn told us he would be seeking the truth. He left to find out who the scouts were that were sent by the King to gather evidence to our claims of the Defiant One returning. We have no direct evidence ourselves, but we know the integrity of our claims, as we witnessed his return first-hand. What we don't know is what incentive these Dwarves would have to lie to their King and give a false report!"

With this, the council erupted in outrage over Erin's accusations.

"You stand before us, accused of lying to the King, and choose to use your time to make even more baseless accusations?" asked the lead Dwarf. "Have you no honor?" he asked.

"I might ask the council the same question!" shouted Erin, "Do we not have the right to stand before our accusers, to question the ones who claim they went to the surface and saw evidence contradicting our claims?" she asked defiantly.

Tyrius couldn't help but smile beside Erin, despite the dire circumstances they were in. He had trained Erin well for her eventual responsibilities, he thought, and he took great pride in watching her grow into such a strong and remarkable young woman.

The council members quietly spoke amongst themselves again, determining whether or not she could request such a thing under the circumstances. After some time, they conceded and granted her request, having the guards bring forth the two scouts who had been sent to the surface to see first-hand if their reports were in fact true.

The two Dwarves walked up to the front of the group of prisoners while looking around the room nervously. They stopped just before the council members, awaiting their questions.

"So, you are the Dwarves responsible for our sudden imprisonment?" asked Erin, eyeing the two young Dwarves up and down with a scolding look.

They shuffled uncomfortably beneath her gaze. Erin knew they had lied, but she didn't yet know why, and that was what she needed to prove in order to get her and her friends off the hook.

"Tell me, how did you two get chosen for such a task?" she asked.

The Dwarf on the left spoke first. He was the shorter of the two, and stockier, leaving him with the appearance of what David compared to a garden gnome back home. His attire was that customary of the Guard, but not the ornate armor that the King's Guard wore, instead it was a more bland, reflective armor with chainmail underneath, adorned over a basic leather brown tunic and trousers that were held up by a wide black belt with a gold-plated buckle.

"We were chosen for the task by our commander." he replied in a gruff voice that was customary to the Dwarves.

"And did he say what you were supposed to find?" she asked.

"Yes. He said we were to go to the surface and look to the West towards Eldergate to verify if the palace were in fact raised into the air by a giant black rock." he replied smugly.

"And did you actually *go* to the surface?" asked Erin, incredulously.

"Of course, we did!" replied the Dwarf defensively.

"Then you would have seen that we were telling the truth!" shouted Erin suddenly, making the two Dwarves jump in surprise. "Isn't that so?" she asked, "When you reached Draco's Pass and you peered across the Great Plains, did you not see the palace of Eldergate on the same rock you just described? Did you not see a great army of demons amassing at its feet, preparing for war?" asked Erin, gazing intently at the Dwarf, gauging his reaction.

The Dwarf started to show signs of perspiration beading up on his forehead. He was nervous, she could tell. Either this Dwarf was lying about what he saw, or he never even made his way to the surface to begin with.

"No! No, we didn't!" shouted the Dwarf. "It is as we reported. No such things were seen by our eyes!" shouted the Dwarf.

"Liar!" shouted Erin, trying to lunge at the Dwarves but falling to the ground as the chains pulled her hands down, preventing her from reaching her intended victims.

"Enough!" shouted the head council Dwarf. "Without evidence of your claims, we will not allow you to stand here and accuse our honorable guard members of dishonesty!" he said. "Now, if you have no further words, I suggest you –"

Suddenly, his words were cut off by the sound of the great throne room doors bursting open and quick, heavy footsteps slapping the stone floor.

David and the others quickly turned to see the source of the commotion and saw that it was Darryn! He had come back for them!

He was filthy from head to toe and covered in sweat. Barely able to breath, he quickly made his way across the great room, stopping just shy of the stairs to the King.

He stood for a moment, trying to catch his breath, bracing his hands on his knees.

Finally, after a few moments, the head council Dwarf spoke up.

"Darryn, so nice of you to finally join us." he said in mocking pleasantries. "But unless you have evidence of your friend's innocence, they will be sentenced to six months in a cell." he said matter-of-factly, having felt the conviction was all but certain at this point.

"No! They are innocent!" said Darryn between great, heaving breaths. "I saw it with me own eyes!" he said.

"What do you mean?" asked the council member. He knew Darryn hadn't been to the surface world, he had always been afraid of the surface. What could have possibly convinced him to say such absurd things, then?

"I went to the surface, and I saw the truth, just as they said! Eldergate is in ruins, its palace perched atop a high rocky cliff. And the demon army. It's real too. Splitting its forces between Ravenfell, while the other half is heading our way! We must prepare for war!" shouted Darryn, panic rising in his voice.

With his last words, the council erupted, each member seemed to be conflicted internally between the reports from the patrol and the report from Darryn. Some seemed to believe the patrol, while others believed Darryn because of his convincing look of panic and his good standing within the city. Both sides were arguing loudly, pointing fingers and shouting, until finally the King had had enough.

"SILENCE!" he shouted at the top of his lungs, his booming voice echoing off the marble walls and throughout the chamber.

David and Erin exchanged a look of relief, feeling like their luck had finally changed for the better.

"Darryn, if what ye say is true, why is it these two have reported otherwise?" asked Tybrin, looking down at the two Dwarves still standing before the council.

They both exchanged quick looks before bolting towards the exit. The guards by the door quickly barred their escape and retained them, bringing them reluctantly back to stand before the council, this time in chains of their own.

"What is the meaning of this?" demanded King Tybrin, outraged at the events that were transpiring before him. "You two dare betray your King?" he asked, anger rising in his voice.

"Yer Majesty, please forgive us! It wasn't our idea. It was Glenn and Glynn! They paid us a large bag of coin to lie about our reports. Please, yer highness, have mercy. We have families to feed!" said the taller Dwarf, speaking for the first time.

The shorter Dwarf to his left elbowed him harshly before the guard brought him back under control.

"I see..." said Tybrin thoughtfully, "Guards. I think ye know what to do. Release the humans. It appears we were mistaken, after all." he said.

"As for those two, I want them out of my sight. And someone bring me Glenn and Glynn immediately! And while yer at it, bring me their good fer nothin' boss, Manny!" shouted Tybrin.

With their chains removed and their charges dropped, David and the others walked up to Darryn and each thanked him immensely for his loyalty.

The Dwarf's cheeks went rosy red when Erin kissed him on his cheek, and everyone burst into laughter, relieved to finally be free from this fiasco and happy to have won the trust of the King once again.

It wasn't long before the guards returned with Manny, Glenn, and Glynn. They were bound in chains and being dragged across the floor, fighting every step of the way. The once calm and collected Manny looked enraged, his hair and clothes disheveled from his scuffle with the Guard.

When his eyes caught David and the others, standing free before the council beside Darryn, his eyes narrowed, and he spit on the floor towards them. The Guards holding him whacked him across the back of his head, "Try that again and I'll break your teeth in." said the one on his left with a severe look.

Manny immediately stopped resisting, knowing the threat from the Guard was not to be taken lightly.

The guards brought the three to rest just shy of the wooden counter, each hanging their head low in shame. They knew their time had finally come and their reign of fear and corruption was toppling down around them.

One of the guards walked up to the King and handed him a large stack of leather-bound pages that looked like a journal of some kind. He spent a few moments looking through them and the longer he spent reading, the more his face distorted in disgust.

"What do ye have to say for yerselves?" asked the King, finally looking down at the banker.

"Your Majesty, I swear – I had no idea these two were conspiring behind your back!" pleaded Manny.

Both Glenn and Glynn quickly turned to their boss with glaring looks that could kill.

"They were acting on their own accord, I assure you!" said Manny.

"Is that so?" asked King Tybrin skeptically. "Then tell me, Manny, why me men found these in yer quarters?" he said, holding up the ledgers.

They were the bank ledgers, and it had meticulously documented years of corrupt bargains and bribes with some of the highest-ranking members of society. Each transaction had a note to the side, describing the blackmail Manny was holding against the members, and the payment that he had made for their services throughout the years.

Manny, seeing what was in the King's hands, quickly turned pale. He knew he was caught and there was no amount of smooth talking that would get him out of this one.

"That's what I thought," said the King with a scowl, "Guards, take them away. And please, make sure that our friend Manny is placed in a cell along with his two conspirers. I'm sure they would love to reward him for his loyalty."

Hearing this, both Glenn and Glynn smiled from ear to ear. They would have their revenge in the end.

"No! Your Majesty, please! You can't do this!" begged Manny, knowing his punishment would be far worse at the hands of his two cronies than simply spending his sentence in isolation.

"Oh, but I can, and I have!" replied the King, signaling for his men to take them away.

The guards quickly began escorting the men out of the building. Manny was kicking and screaming the whole way to the carts. They heard his screams slowly fading, even as they disappeared into the tunnels towards the prison.

"Well, that was quite the spectacle!" said Tyrius, laughing.

"And to think, just the other day he seemed untouchable!" said Erin, smiling at the irony. "Serves him right!"

The King stepped down from his throne and around the council before standing humbly in front of David and the others.

"It would seem I owe ye an apology." he said, holding his crown in his hand.

"I have dishonored me guests with me rash judgements, and therefore, have dishonored meself. How can I make it up to ye?" he asked eagerly.

"Great King Tybrin, you humble us with your apology, but it is neither warranted nor needed. You were doing what you felt was right for your kingdom and your people and were acting on the information you were provided. Please, do not fret. No harm has come from it, thanks to our dear friend Darryn." said Tyrius, gesturing towards the Dwarf, who had finally caught his breath and was settled back down once again.

His cheeks blushed bright red.

"A debt I will pay him personally!" replied the King looking over at the plump Dwarf. "How would you like to take over the bank in Manny's absence, Darryn?" he asked, to which Darryn nearly fell over in surprise.

The bank was one of the most profitable and highest esteemed organizations in the entire kingdom. To be the owner would be one of the greatest honors, and of course, he graciously accepted.

"Thank you, yer majesty. I am honored to serve yer people and will do so with honor and integrity." replied Darryn, bowing so low his nose touched the floor.

"Indeed, ye will" replied the King, smiling.

Once Darryn graciously accepted the offer, bounding off to his cousins' shop to tell him the good news, King Tybrin turned to the others.

He promised to give them whatever supplies they needed in order to continue their journey North to the Birthplace of the World. As a token of his appreciation and their newfound friendship, he gave them each a parting gift and promised that he would send his armies to the surface to help fight back the demon army and play their part in the coming battles.

They each received a custom-made set of chainmail – as light as a feather, but as strong as stone – that they could wear beneath their outer garments, along with new traveling clothes that were better equipped for the cold they would be enduring on their journey to the North.

They stayed for one last big feast that night, and the next morning said their goodbyes to King Tybrin Hammerclaw, their friend Darryn, and his cousin Gerryn, before taking in their last sights of Emerald Keep.

When they were packed and ready to go, they hopped in the cart and headed down the rails at breakneck speeds, out of the massive caverns and into the winding tunnels towards the upper passages leading to Draco's Pass.

It wasn't long before they reached the end of the track and exited the cart, each of them excited to see the light of day once again, but sad to say goodbye to Darryn and the beautiful city of Emerald Keep. They vowed that they would return once again to visit if they ever found a way to defeat the Defiant One and lived to tell the tale.

After walking a short way down the tunnel, the small opening at the end began to grow larger and larger while the light increased in intensity as they neared the exit. Finally, after roughly a week in the enclosed caverns of the inner mountain, the close quarters of the tunnel gave way to the wide-open air of the mountain pass as they returned to the surface world.

The cool breeze whipped through Erin's hair as she took in her first deep breath of the fresh mountain air. The coolness burnt her lungs, but she savored it. She could feel the small little kisses of snowflakes as they landed on her face, sending bumps down her arms and legs, and racing down her back. They had finally made it to Draco's Pass.

She looked and saw David and the others were standing near the edge of the ridge looking West towards Eldergate. When she reached the edge, she stopped by David and grabbed his hand.

The Great Plains were covered in a large dark mass of soldiers and demons, each marching slowly across the plains in their direction. Another large mass was breaking away far off in the distance, heading the opposite direction towards Ravenfell.

It was worse than they had imagined.

With so much time wasted from getting lost in the mountain tunnels, along with their rendezvous with the Dwarves, they had lost nearly a week of travel that they knew would cost the lives of thousands. The armies would be on Ravenfell any day now, if they hadn't made it there already, and they were still a great distance away from their destination where they hoped David would be able to restore his connection to the orb and the source of the nearly limitless power it possessed.

Without it, all would be lost. Unless David regained his powers, they had no real chance of winning against the Defiant One and his incredible power of destruction.

Time was running out.

Chapter XVIII

Jakob Zander and his crew of misfits searched for hours into the night after the trail went cold. He couldn't understand how all of a sudden they had just vanished in thin air. His trackers were some of the best in the Southern Kingdom, and he was outraged that they had lost the tracks of the boy and his companions after the brief skirmish at their campsite.

It was as if they had just disappeared, and that thought left him extremely on edge. Maybe they possessed some dark magic he wasn't aware of? he thought.

He knew what was on the line if he were to return to Brineport and confront Bloodvayne empty-handed. Failure was not an option.

He gathered up his resolve and urged his companions onward. They would search the foothills for as long as it took to find the trail once again, even if it took weeks, months, or even years. His only hope of keeping his good standing with the Guild, no... his life, was to succeed, and that thought alone fueled his endless drive to find the boy and bring him back to Brineport.

After several fruitless days of searching, the party reached the road that spanned between Draco's Pass to the West, and the Land of the Immortals to the East. He knew that if the boy was trying to get back to the Great Plains, he would have to take Draco's Pass, and there was no evidence of any foot traffic headed that way from what his trackers could see.

If he were traveling East on the road it would take him to the Forest of the Immortals – a forbidden forest that was protected by the Woodland Elves. They were unforgiving to any mortal who dared enter their domain uninvited, and no mortal had ever been invited, so he knew that couldn't be their destination.

Without any indication showing that the area had seen any travelers recently, he decided that they must have somehow traveled ahead of the boy and his companions, and so they decided to set up camp and wait.

Fortunately, they only had to camp out in the small cave near the base of the mountain pass for one more day before he finally got word from his scouts that the boy and his friends had been spotted once again.

They were coming down from Draco's Pass, of all places, and heading in their direction.

"Sir, I don't know how they managed to get all the way up there, but they should be passing our location just before nightfall." said one of his men who had been scouting the area.

"They must have found a way through the mountains. I don't remember seeing any caves along the way, do you?" asked one of the other men.

"Silence, you insolent fools! What does it matter how they got there? What matters now is that they did, and now they are headed our way! We will sit and wait for their arrival, and once they get close enough, we'll take them by surprise!" said Jakob, his hands clasping together like a cat catching a mouse.

This thought seemed to really excite his men. They had been out in the wild for days without any real excitement. Some of the men had even resorted to senselessly killing the local game for fun to satisfy their twisted need for killing. They had been trained to kill since they were young, learning to steal and kill, for the alternative was to be robbed and killed themselves. It was a hard life growing up in Brineport, but if you were good enough at what you did, you were rewarded for it through selection into the Guild.

It was something all the young boys and girls dreamed of. They took their selection with pride and arrogance, seeing it as their proof of superiority over the lesser qualified citizens. Because of this system of rewarding the strong and, often more violent, children over their weaker counterparts, each new generation of members became increasingly more violent and uncontrollable than the last, knowing it would earn their favor in the ranks faster than their predecessors.

Over the years, Brineport became a cesspool of thugs and hooligans at the expense of the more civilized families, and in turn, became a more dangerous place to live. Living in those kinds of conditions led people to one of two things: leaving for the hope of a better, safer life elsewhere to raise their families, or giving in to the constant demands of the Guild and putting up with a life of crushing poverty and hopelessness. Most chose to stay, as to attempt to leave put their families at risk of being captured and killed in a bloody public execution – something the citizens had come to enjoy immensely.

Seeing their opportunity for a bit of fun, the men quickly devised a plan and got into their positions. They would wait for just the right moment when the boy and his companions would reach the part of the road that would take them between two large outcrops of jutting rock, creating a sort of natural tunnel. Once they entered, a small group of men would block the entrance behind the company, forcing them to run toward the exit. Just as they were about to get away, the rest of the men would jump out and block their escape, taking them by surprise and blocking them in the tunnel. It was all planned out. Now all they had to do was wait.

By the time the sun had become nearly completely obscured by the peaks of the mountains to the West, the boy and his company were spotted coming around the bend in the road just before the outcrop into the tunnel.

It was time.

The men crouched in position just off the road behind a few fallen boulders, waiting for the time to strike. They could hear the sound of laughter and voices talking and they were getting closer with each passing moment. The men were nearly beside themselves with anticipation.

Finally, the time had come. The last of their small group had entered the tunnel. The men quickly jumped out from behind the boulders and sprinted towards the boy, screaming wildly in an attempt to intimidate them into running frantically towards the other end.

Just as they suspected, the group started running towards the exit in an attempt to escape. As they neared the exit, the rest of the gang jumped into the opening from the rock above, blocking their escape.

Jakob stepped in front of his men towards the boy with the tattoo on his hand, slowly clapping his hands.

"You pulled a fast one on us back in the foothills. You even managed to kill a few of my men. Bravo!" he said, mocking applause.

The boy and his companions stood silently, weapons drawn and in the ready. Jakob thought something looked different about their appearance. Their clothing looked... strange, but he couldn't figure it out in the near darkness of the coming night.

"What do you want with us?" the boy finally asked bravely. "Who are you?"

"I'm glad you asked!" said Jakob. "My name is Jakob Zander, and these are my men. We're of the Northern Guild. You ran into a few of us back in Ashmire if you recall?" asked Jakob.

"Yeah, we remember" replied one of the men standing behind the boy. He was lean and muscular and was carrying a battle axe while sporting a determined scowl on his face.

"Well, because of your little stunt in front of the inn, and his failure to bring you into custody, my brother is now dead. I intend to return the favor" said Jakob glaringly. "Get the boy!" he yelled.

He jumped into action, drawing his blade and swinging it violently at the man with the axe, but was pushed backward by a furious counterattack. They quickly began trading blows back and forth, attacking and deflecting each other's blows with skilled precision.

The man grabbed hold of Jakob's sword arm and swiftly jammed his fist into Jakob's stomach, knocking the breath out of his lungs before hurling him through the air and out of the fight.

Jakob quickly recovered but it was too late, the boy and his friends had already fought their way through his men and were frantically running down the path down the mountain side towards the Forest of the Immortals!

"How do they keep getting away!" yelled Jakob frustrated, before picking up his sword and yelling for his men to go after them.

Jakob and his men started running full throttle after the boy and his companions, gaining on them slowly but steadily.

They finally caught up to them just as they broke through the edge of the plains and into the thick, ancient cluster of trees.

"Gotcha!" yelled Jakob as he grabbed a hold of the boy's cloak, yanking him backward hard enough to knock him off his feet.

He put his sword to the boy's throat in a threatening gesture, and his companions immediately stopped fighting, afraid of what would come if they pressed on.

"Drop your weapons! Now!" yelled Jakob, tired of the games.

They each dropped their weapons and the sound of metal clanging on the ground rang through the cool night air.

"Good! Now, tie them up! We are going to bring them all back to Brineport so they can suffer the wrath of the Wolf Guard. I hear they love eating their captives alive." said Jakob, as his men finished securing the captives' hands with rope.

"You'll pay for this with your life!" spat the old man, after which one of Jakob's men swiftly struck him in the back of the head, knocking him to the ground.

"You'll do well to shut up and only speak when you're spoken to, old man!" said Jakob threateningly.

One of his men caught sight of the girl. She was pretty, with fair skin and dark hair and had a fierce look about her that betrayed her battle-hardiness. She had been responsible for the death of several of his men, and it was time for her to pay.

"Eh boss, what say we have a little fun with this one before we go? After all, we have been away from home for a while. We could all use a little fun!" he said, licking his lips and reaching for the girl.

"Leave me alone!" screamed the girl, wriggling to try to get free from the rope, but it was useless. The rope was too tight, and the knot was tied skillfully and wouldn't budge.

The man slowly started towards her, eager to reach his prize. His eyes were blazing like a wolf before he reached his prey.

"You touch her, and I'll kill you!" shouted the boy, anger rising in his chest. He couldn't bear to see Erin hurt, and he knew these men had the worst of intentions.

"Don't worry, boy. We'll be gentle." said the man, licking his lips as he grabbed Erin and lifted her up to take her further into the woods away from the others. This brought a booming laughter from the group of men – they knew they had no such intentions.

As soon as the words left his lips, the tip of an arrow exploded through his forehead, dropping him to the ground like a sack of potatoes.

The girl fell hard on the ground, shocked as the wind rushed from her chest.

What just happened? she wondered as she struggled to catch her breath, the feel of hot blood dripping down the side of her face where the man's blood had suddenly splattered.

Immediately, a flurry of arrows shot through the air, each landing securely in the chest, back, head, arm, neck of each of his men, dropping them all instantly. Jakob looked around into the dark recesses of trees and suddenly remembered where he was – they were in the forbidden Forest of Immortals.

He suddenly dropped into a crouch and, dragging the boy behind him, started running towards the edge of the forest. It was only a few yards away. If he could just get to the edge, he would be free from the enchanted woods and could use his transport ball to get back to Brineport.

He could hear arrows whizzing past his head as he zig-zagged frantically from left to right to avoid being struck by the projectiles. He could hear the loud thud and crack as some the arrows struck deep into the trunks of the trees all around him, cracking the wood and just barely missing their mark.

Finally, he reached the edge of the trees. Free from their magical enchantment, he threw down the small glass ball that Bloodvayne had given him for when he captured the boy, his heart racing wildly in his chest.

It shattered as it struck the ground and immediately a thick smoke erupted from the ball. The thick, swirling fog surrounded them and masked their forms from the archers in the woods. The arrows whizzed and whirred through the smoke, sending curling trails in their wake. Fortunately, they all missed their mark.

When the smoke cleared, both Jakob Zander and the boy were gone.

Chapter XIX

Erin watched helplessly as David was hauled away by Jakob Zander. The men around her were quickly dropping like flies as the mysterious attackers were rushing from tree to tree, firing projectiles faster than anything she had ever seen.

She could hear the arrows whiz past her head as they flew through the air and penetrated deeply into the flesh of the men of the Guild. She lay low and looked around to make sure Tyrius and the others were okay. They were each down on the ground, keeping their heads low to avoid being hit by the incoming projectiles. None of them appeared to be hurt. While the majority of the hidden attackers took care of the rest of the Guild, a few other shadowy figures flew through the moonlit forest after Jakob as he pulled David back towards the plains.

Suddenly, she could see Jakob pulling something from his pocket before throwing it to the ground. A great fog began to rise from the earth and obscure their forms from her view.

"David!" she screamed after him, "David!"

But no response came. She began to fear even more for her friend, wondering if he had been hit by one of the arrows.

As the smoke began to clear, she gasped in shock – Jakob and David were nowhere to be found. They had just vanished, as if they were never there!

Suddenly, Erin felt a strong grip on the ropes around her arms as she was lifted into the air and planted firmly on the ground. She turned around to see who had picked her up, and a wave of relief flooded through her.

It was the elves!

"Oh, thank the Creator!" she said to the Elf. "You've come just in time! Those men, they were about to kill us!" she said, panting. "Our friend, David. You have to go help him! He's just been taken, that way!" she said, nodding her head over towards the edge of the forest where Jakob had taken David.

But the elf just looked at her silently and without expression before roughly shoving her towards the others. They were all still bound and being led single file by a few other elves. She didn't recognize any of them, but knew they had to be of the Woodland Elves, and therefore, under the rule of Prince Gilric Ellisar

"Hey, what are you doing? Why aren't you untying us?" asked Erin, outraged at the treatment they were getting and the fact that they weren't going after David.

"You have to help our friend; he's been taken away!" she shouted.

"Erin, they don't care about David," said Tyrius calmly, "They are taking us prisoner. We have violated their laws with our presence. These woods are the Forest of Immortals. It is forbidden for mortals to set foot on its sacred soil." he said as the elf behind him shoved him and told him to keep moving and to be quiet.

But Erin couldn't accept this, "Why are you doing this? We aren't your enemy, we fought with you at the battle of Eldergate against the true enemy, General Krauss!" she cried, but the elf leading her wouldn't hear any of it and had finally had enough. He turned around and quickly shoved a cloth in her mouth then grabbed her and forcefully slung her over his shoulder.

Erin kicked and screamed, but the cloth held fast and muffled the strength in her voice. Finally, seeing her resistance was futile and was getting her nowhere but even more exhausted, she gave up fighting and lay there motionless while the elf carried her deeper into the forest.

***

It was sometime early in the morning when they finally reached the outskirts of what she assumed was the White City.

Erin couldn't see much from her perspective, still being carried over the shoulder of her captor, but she could tell from the way the ground had transitioned from the untamed forest floor to the nicely trimmed and manicured lawn of civilization that she was no longer in the outlying forest.

The grassy path eventually changed into a mossy stone walkway and she could see randomly scattered beams of sunlight lighting up the ground as they walked.

The sounds of the forest were vibrant and lively, birds cooing and singing everywhere around her along with a symphony of other creatures calling through the air. It was a beautiful and peaceful sound that almost put her to sleep had she not been so uncomfortable in her current position. Her head was dizzy from being carried upside down for so long, the blood having mostly rushed to her head, and her legs were numb and tingling.

As she turned her head from side to side, bouncing ever so slightly with each soft step, she could see the faces of little children staring at her, trying to keep pace with the longer strides of her captor. They were laughing and smiling, as if it were a silly thing to see a young woman being carried in such a way – *it kind of was*, she thought to herself.

She wished now that she hadn't fought so hard. She would have saved herself a lot of discomfort over the past few hours!

Eventually the company came to a stop and the elf that was carrying Erin casually swung her off his shoulder and placed her firmly on the ground, facing him. She nearly fell over, her legs not anticipating the sudden requirement to stand on their own again, but the Elf kept her steady so she wouldn't fall.

He had bright blue eyes and golden hair that framed his soft-featured face. He was extremely beautiful for a male, she thought, even for an elf.

He held her gaze for a long moment, as if to say, "If you behave, I will set you free."

She nodded her head, and he seemed to understand what she meant, because he immediately took the cloth from her mouth and unfastened her ropes from around her midsection.

She rubbed her arms where the rope had been rubbing her skin raw, inspecting the red, chaffed skin, and wincing slightly at the pain that ensued.

"Thank you," she said finally to the elf, who just stared at her blankly before nodding behind her, indicating that she needed to turn around.

When she did, she noticed the others were also unbound and were standing before a small group of elves who were all clad in similar attire as the one who had been carrying her.

They were standing before a great white oak tree that looked to be as ancient as the world itself. Its trunk was as thick as a building, with giant roots digging deep into the earth for what must have been miles to support its great height and stature. Its thick, twisting branches reached high into the canopy and stretched far and wide in every direction, with large golden-colored leaves that provided a huge blanket of amber-colored shade under which they now stood.

High above them in the canopy of the tree was a great city, built on the wide branches and apparently made of the same white wood. It had a variety of bridges connecting the gaps between the thickest branches, forming what made up a network of interconnected walkways and stairs for the citizens to move around the canopy by. Its design and intricate carvings must have taken centuries to plan and build, she thought, staring up at the city.

Erin never realized that the White City was actually built atop an ancient tree!

Looking back at the elves, she noticed that each wore a dark brown tunic with lighter trousers and a dark brown belt at the waist that blended in perfectly with the natural color of the woods around them.

On their backs, each had a quiver full of arrows with white feathers protruding at the ends, shaped in such a way to make the arrow fly perfectly through the air towards its target. Over each of their shoulders rested a long bow made of yew, each polished to a mirror shine and sported elegant carvings on the riser and grip. Although they each had the same overall design, each bow was slightly different than the other – something she assumed was a custom marking for each warrior that helped them indicate which weapon was theirs.

At their waist, their belts held decorative scabbards made of a hard leather and sported gold-plated mouth pieces. Inside each scabbard rested the gold-and-silver-plated hilt of a masterfully crafted sword sitting firmly in its sheath.

Each elf had long, golden hair that flowed from their heads and bright blue or grey eyes she noticed. Some had their hair braided and pulled back, while others wore it straight, letting it fall past the middle of their backs.

She slowly and cautiously walked over to the others and stood silently, waiting for an indication as to what was coming next.

The elf who had been carrying her walked up to the others and stood in the middle. He seemed to be the leader of the group, or at least slightly elevated in class – if there were such a thing with the elves. He definitely held his head a little higher than the others, and carried himself with a sense of nobility, she noticed.

At last, he spoke – a voice like that of a song, or what one would expect from an angel, ringing from his parted lips.

"I suppose this is where you explain yourselves." he said simply, looking over the four companions standing before him.

Erin looked over to Tyrius and the others. Reingard and Holzer were looking to Tyrius too, expecting him to speak for the group. When Tyrius noticed the others' eyes squarely focused on him, he sighed ever so slightly and began explaining the events that had transpired leading them up to their unfortunate circumstances the night before.

When he had finally finished his retelling of the events since their departure from Ravenfell, the elves patiently waiting without interrupting a single time, the head elf stood silently. He was apparently thinking over the details of the story, dissecting them to discern if there were any traces of dishonesty within their narrative.

At last, apparently satisfied that the story had, in fact, been truthful, he once again spoke.

"Very well, but this does not change the fact that you were found trespassing on our lands. It is forbidden for any mortal to set foot within the boundary of the forest. Normally, such individuals found violating our sacred lands would be killed on the spot. However, since you were found bound already, and clearly posed no threat to us, we thought it wouldn't be prudent to take your lives in such a state. Instead, we will take you below and let our Prince decide your fate." he said, and with a casual flick of his hand, he signaled that the conversation was over and the other elves quickly walked up to Erin and the others and began leading them towards the great white tree.

As they neared its trunk, she could see that it opened up into a large hollow area that had steps protruding up into the trunk to the left or down into the earth in a spiral fashion to the right. They took the stairs to the right.

Along the interior of the stairwell were lanterns fixed securely to the walls that were glowing within from some unknown light source. It was a gentle kind of light, but bright enough to let them see the steps winding ever deeper into the ground as they made their way down the stairway into the cool earth.

When they finally reached the end of the staircase, they entered into a wide-open chamber that branched off into a series of long, round hallways leading in various directions like burrows through the ground. They appeared to be carved right out of the roots of the tree and created a vast tunnel system by which the elves moved about. Erin could see that these areas were mostly used for storage of foods and other supplies, the coolness of the underground providing the perfect condition for long-term storage.

As they walked, she could see some round openings that led to large rooms that held countless wooden barrels she assumed were filled with drink of various kind, maybe wine or ale, she thought.

They were led down one of the long hallways which turned sharply at the end before reaching a dead end with a great wooden door that had metal braces for increased durability.

The leading elf opened the door, which was locked, and led them inside.

Inside was a large room that housed several cells behind thick metal bars. Each cell contained a small, clean bed and a fountain sprouting crystal clear water from a spicket in the wall that flowed into a little pool in the corner of each room. The rooms were small, but they were big enough for a single occupant and were surprisingly nice for a prison.

The elf led them each into their own cells before locking the doors behind them and closing the large door as he exited.

A single elf remained behind and sat casually behind a desk, with his feet propped up as he prepared to take a nap.

"Excuse me" said Tyrius to the elf, which the elf blatantly ignored.

He tried again, "Excuse me, sir," much louder this time.

The elf gave him an annoyed look before turning the other way and closing his eyes once again.

"I would like to speak with Gilric Ellisar" said Tyrius.

At this, the elf opened his eyes and turned to Tyrius. "How do you know that name?" he asked, surprised a human seemed to know of his Prince.

"He's a friend of mine," replied Tyrius, glad to have finally gotten the attention of the elf.

"Oh, really?" asked the elf, skeptically. "And how did you meet him?" he asked, as if he didn't expect a logical response and were simply entertaining himself to pass the time.

Detecting his reluctance, Tyrius made sure to be as specific as possible with his response.

"We met in the Outer Woods during his campaign to find the lost villagers who had been kidnapped by the Wolf Guard. He thought we had been the ones who had taken the villagers, but when we told him it was General Krauss and his loyalists that had taken over Eldergate by force and were responsible for the kidnappings, we helped him, along with a great army of soldiers from Ravenfell, to take back Eldergate in hopes of finding the missing villagers. Unfortunately, we were too late... not a single elf was found, and shortly after the city crumbled and fell into the Dark Abyss." said Tyrius solemnly, remembering that fateful day all too well.

It was the day the Defiant One had been set free along with his endless horde of demons.

The elf's eyes were wide with shock and he sat up straight, eyes glancing back and forth between Tyrius and the door leaving the chamber and into the halls.

"See, as I said. I am a friend of Gilric Ellisar's, and I would like to speak with him immediately." replied Tyrius, sternly but politely.

"I see...um...excuse me, while I go and inform my captain." said the elf urgently, as he stumbled out of his chair and quickly exited the room.

Tyrius could hear his footsteps rapidly disappearing down the hall until they were too distant to detect.

He smiled in spite of their situation. If anything, he at least created a smidgen of doubt in their captor's mind about whether or not they should, in fact, be held captive.

At most, he would get to speak with Gilric and they would be set free and be on their way once again, this time, headed back South towards Brineport to rescue David from whatever torture and torment he would be forced to endure there.

How did *they keep finding themselves in such predicaments?* he silently wondered to himself.

It wasn't long before more footsteps could be heard coming back down the hallway, this time there seemed to be more than just a single person.

When the door opened again, in walked Gilric Ellisar, dressed as fine as ever, followed closely by the elf who had left the room earlier. His eyes were focusing on the ground before him as if he had received a very heavy scolding.

"Tyrius, my friend," said Gilric when he saw Tyrius standing patiently in the cell. "Please accept my sincerest apologies. We never can be too careful when it comes to protecting our lands from outsiders." he said, bowing slightly.

"Not a problem, dear friend," replied Tyrius, smiling, as their cages were unlocked and opened one by one by the elf, still refusing to lock eyes with any of the captives.

They each walked out of their cells, happy to be free once again. They seemed to be making a habit of getting locked away, Erin mused, and she wasn't sure she liked the new trend.

"Please, come with me. I am sure you are all famished. We have a feast being prepared as we speak in the Great Hall above." said Gilric, motioning for the others to follow as he turned and headed back out of the room and down the hall.

He led them through the hallway and back up the large spiral staircase rising up the trunk of the great white tree. Erin couldn't help but marvel at how large the tree truly was and noticed that throughout the inner walls were intricate little carvings spiraling up and down the trunk. They were beautiful and unpredictable, almost the way the wind soars through the air, billowing and twisting about freely like a dancer.

As they made their way up the spiraling stairwell, Erin traced her fingers along its intricate carvings as they passed the entrance and continued upward for several minutes. Their legs began to ache with the strain of the ascent, until finally, after countless floors, they reached a landing somewhere around the middle of the trunk that branched off through a wide opening in the side of the tree and led out onto one of its enormous branches.

A smooth walkway had been carved into the top of the branch, making for a nice even path that followed the curving limb. They had also built in highly decorative rails that served to prevent anyone from accidentally falling off the edges – a fall that would surely end in death at this height.

Erin tried her best to look down as they walked, but the height was staggering and she was experiencing a severe sense of vertigo, so instead she focused on the areas around them at the same level plane. She couldn't believe how much the elves had built within the branches of the tree.

It was an entire city of buildings built throughout the canopy like a great tree house. There were great, arching bridges all over the place, spanning between the largest branches and providing access throughout the massive tree canopy for all to enjoy.

In addition to the main central staircase moving up and down the tree trunk, there were several staircases throughout the canopy that allowed for easy access between each level of the city. All of the buildings seemed to be built from the same white wood of the tree, giving the city a bright white appearance while also a gentle, natural feel that was peaceful and transcendental.

There were several different species of birds and butterflies, flying and flittering throughout the air, each visiting the endless variety of flowers that were growing nearly everywhere Erin looked.

She could see squirrels and chipmunks and other woodland creatures scattering about the rails and staircases, jumping across great distances as they ran about, playing like little children.

It was the most remarkable thing she had ever seen, and that was saying a lot after having just visited the great Dwarven city of Emerald Keep!

As Gilric led them throughout the ever-winding complex, they eventually reached a large structure that was beautifully crafted with large, vaulted ceilings and intricate carvings around the outside of the building. The carvings looked like flowering vines cut into the large pillars supporting the balcony before the main entrance, its roof reaching high above their heads and sporting great timber beams that would arc back and forth throughout the structure of the ceiling.

When they entered the room, they could see it was furnished with dozens of long tables fit for dining and hosting a large gathering.

The tables were already prepared with silver dishes filled with wonderful smelling foods of all kinds. Nearly all of the dishes sported some type of grilled or roasted fish, coupled with garden vegetables, nuts, and salads with a sweet, berry vinaigrette that looked delightful.

Gilric led them to a large table positioned at the front of the great dining hall and beckoned for them to take the seats next to his. The elves all turned to watch the humans entering their halls and being seated next to their Prince.

Prince Gilric addressed the crowd, seeing their curiosity.

"My dear brethren. Today we will host our most esteemed guests." he said, introducing each of them by name starting with Tyrius and working his way down to Reingard and Holzer.

"They have come a long way and been through a great ordeal. Please join me in making them feel at home." he finished, to which a gentle round of applause echoed throughout the chamber.

After his introductions, they all sat down to a wonderful meal. After some time when they had each finished eating and their bellies were full of food and wine and their spirits were bolstered, they sat and spoke about their adventures since the battle of Eldergate.

They caught Gilric up on the purpose of their quest from Ravenfell. How they had trekked through the Southern Tunnel into Ashmire where they were chased by the Guild before falling into the Dwarven tunnels. They told him of their time spent in Emerald Keep and their legal battle with the King, and finally how they had ultimately ended up captured by the elves down at the edge of the forest when they had been ambushed by Jakob and his Guild once again. All the while, Prince Gilric sat patiently listening to their tales and saying very little but nodding his head as the story unfolded to acknowledge that he was following along.

When they finished, he seemed very troubled by the capture of David. He knew that David played a key role in the prophecies related to taking down the Defiant One and his demon army, and because of this, he pledged his support for their mission in getting him back. If David were to fail in his mission, the elves would have a much greater threat at their doorsteps that would threaten their peace for generations to come. Possibly even their survival. That was a risk he was not willing to take.

At last, when the night was growing late and their eyes could hardly stay open any longer, the companions expressed their gratitude to Gilric for his kindness and hospitality.

He had one of the housekeeping elves, fair as ever with very obvious feminine features, prepare them each a room for the night with the promise of catching up in the morning to see them off on their journey. He said their bags would be waiting for them, restocked with some additional surprises, when they awoke the next morning. They each wondered what the surprises could possibly be, but he would only smile and tell them to wait and see in the light of the morning.

That night, Gilric had the smithies up all night, preparing for his guests a set of magically enhanced blades fitting for each of their preferred combat styles.

For Erin, he had crafted a lightweight, curved blade that would easily compliment her smaller frame – its weight balanced perfectly to match her dance-like fighting style. Its edge was thin and sharp like a razor, but strong as the hardest steel. It would never dull and would cut through anything unfortunate enough to feel its sting as easily as a hot knife cuts through butter.

He also crafted her a bow such as the ones the elves had carried. They were particularly effective against the undead and demons, as their arrows were made from the wood of the great white tree and would have devastating effect on anything dark and unholy.

For Reingard and Holzer he had crafted great twin battle axes – their pommels shaped with a spike at the end for an extra means of defense. They were imbued with a spell that would enhance the strength of their wielders, given them super-human strength to take down their enemies and incite a fear in the hearts of anyone who would stand in their way.

For Tyrius, he had crafted a twisted staff cut from the heart of the ancient white tree itself. Its magical properties would enhance his skills tenfold, giving his powers increased vitality and taking much less of a toll on his body and mind with each casting. It was impossible to break and would never show signs of wearing.

Finally, he crafted one final blade for David, for when they found him once again. It was a long blade, lightweight and curved like Erin's, but it had the emblem of the orb engraved on each side of the blade, with ancient ruins of power dedicated to the bearer of the Orb of Power. Its pommel was elaborately decorated and capped with a jewel that sparkled with the brilliance of a million stars. The blade was foretold in legends that were passed down by the Elves for centuries, and now with David's appearance, it was time for the weapon of legend to be forged into reality.

Each of these weapons would serve them well in the coming battles, having been forged precisely for the purpose of combating demons and other creatures from the depths of the Dark Abyss – their powers rendering such foes obsolete. In all the lands there were no better forgers than the elves when it came to weapons. The Dwarves were masters of armor, true, but the elves were masters of war.

Chapter XX

The next morning Erin and the others awoke with the early rays of the sun shining through their windows. It was a gentle waking, something they had each missed dearly and had been rare since they left Ravenfell.

Their last good night's sleep was spent in the halls of the Dwarven city of Emerald Keep when they were staying in King Tybrin's quarters, however, the light there was not natural, having only been provided by artificial means, being underground and deep within the mountains.

There was nothing more natural than being woken by the gentle light of the morning sun shining through the canopy of the great tree above while listening to the morning song of the birds.

When they each got up, at the foot of each of their beds were their packs, just as Gilric had promised. They were each full to the brim with clean bedding and fresh food that would last them weeks in the wilderness.

Aside each of the packs lay their newly forged weapons glittering in the morning sun like precious artifacts found within a king's treasure room.

They each slowly walked to their individual weapons in awe, inspecting them up and down and running their fingers along their expertly crafted surfaces.

Erin lifted her blade and gave it a few practice swings, marveling at how light the blade sat in her hand and how perfectly it fit her grip. It whizzed through the air as she spun it around in an arcing circle, feeling as if the blade were cutting the air itself.

She placed it back in its scabbard, which was also finely decorated in precious gold and silver designs running up and down its front, before securing it to her belt at her hip.

She then went to her bow and ran her fingers down its spine, gently testing the pull of the string. It hummed in a deep vibration as she released the tension, returning the string to its original position. She could feel the power of the bow and knew it would serve her well in the coming days.

After everyone had taken a few moments to get acquainted with their new weapons, they headed down to the forest floor where Gilric had told them he would be waiting in the morning.

When he saw the looks on their faces, each still in awe at their gifts, he smiled, happy to see they liked their surprise.

"I see you've become well acquainted with your new weapons, they look good on each of you." he said, smiling.

They each nodded and thanked him in return, to which he waved his hand, shrugging off the gesture.

"It is the least I could do, after your most horrendous treatment by my brethren." he said.

As he finished speaking, another elf came running up to his side before whispering something urgent in his ear, too quietly for the others to hear.

Gilric nodded and said "I see" before the messenger ran urgently into the White City and disappeared from sight.

Gilric, seeing the concern on his friends faces, said "It seems the scouts have reported sighting of a large army of demons heading through Draco's Pass. It would seem the battle is coming to our doorstep, now rather than later."

"We saw them coming from the Western ridge just a couple of days ago, before we were ambushed by Jakob and his clan. Was there any word of Ravenfell?" asked Erin, holding her hand to her mouth in fear for her friends back at the Barbarian city-kingdom. She remembered seeing the large mass heading in that direction and knew that they were in for the fight of their lives once they arrived.

"No, no... I do not believe that they have yet reached the barbarian city. The reports stated they saw an equally large mass still headed in that direction, towards the mountain pass, but no indication that they had reached the city. It would seem they intend on attacking both fronts simultaneously. Not a bad strategy... it keeps us divided. It would seem the Defiant One remembers the strength of our people when we were all united together against him, and that he would prefer to not experience that again." said Gilric, smiling arrogantly.

"It is unfortunate, but I must cut our goodbyes short and see to the preparations." he said, turning to leave. He stopped in his tracks and turned back, looking at his friends. "Would any of you care to join me?" he asked, turning his head slightly.

Erin and Tyrius both quickly shook their head, knowing their efforts must be focused on getting back David safely so they could continue North to the Birthplace of the World, but Reingard and Holzer both hesitated before looking to Tyrius and Erin.

"You wish to go with him, don't you?" asked Tyrius, understanding their dilemma. Their King and their family and friends were all in Ravenfell. They had only agreed to go with David and the others because Rex himself couldn't go and had to stay and lead his people in the coming fight. They did it as a personal favor to their friend and King. But Tyrius and Erin knew their hearts were always with their people.

If they were able to help the elves take on the coming army, they would then be able to press on to help the others in Ravenfell against the enemy forces heading their way. They could come up from the rear and break them into two fronts. It could make all the difference for their hometown.

"If we go with you, and we win, would you then do us the honor of bringing the fight to the other front?" asked Holzer, speaking aloud what they were both thinking.

"It would be my greatest honor to accompany you both in such a noble feat." said Gilric, bowing his head again.

Reingard and Holzer both shared an equal look of determination before nodding.

"Then we will go, and we will fight!" they said together.

At this, Gilric Ellisar, Reingard, and Holzer each said their farewell to Tyrius and Erin. Gilric was generous enough to offer them both a horse to take on their journey South, telling them it would serve them well and would help speed along their journey to Brineport.

They said their thanks and after being accompanied to the edge of the Forest of Immortals by Gilric and the others, they sped off into the open fields hoping they would be able to reach David in time before something horrible happened to him.

Behind them, an enormous army of elves, led by Gilric Ellisar, Reingard, and Holzer, began their march toward the foothills of the Draconian Mountains to meet the demon army head on.

War was coming and the fate of the Land of the Immortals and all its magical creatures was hanging in the balance.

Chapter XXI

Night had fallen and Christopher and Fredrick were once again back on the watch tower keeping an eye on the demon army in the foothills below. They had appeared to stop just short of the path leading up the mountain and this was troubling news indeed.

"What do you think they're waiting for?" asked Christopher, his breath leaving a cloud of vapor as he spoke in the cool mountain air.

"I dunno, but if you ask me, it ain't good. Not one bit!" replied Fredrick, rubbing his hands together to stave off the cold.

They had been watching the army grow larger and larger with each consecutive night of their shift. Each night revealing the expansion of the enemy forces from the previous day, and so far, it seemed their forces were growing by the tens of thousands – a bad omen for the battle that was to come.

Besides their growing numbers, it left them uneasy seeing the army just sitting there camped out day after day. It was as if they were waiting on something spectacular to happen that would indicate it was the right time for them to begin their long descent up the pass towards Ravenfell.

"You up for a game of cards?" asked Christopher, satisfied the army wasn't going anywhere fast and eager to pass the time in a more entertaining manner.

"Not until you hand over your copper piece you owe me!" said Fredrick, punching Christopher's arm playfully.

They had made a bet each night as to whether or not the army would reach them by their next shift. Last shift, seeing how close the army was and that they had been camped out for several days, Fredrick had finally decided to bet against the odds and say that they would remain camped for the day. A bet he had apparently won.

"Fine, fine," said Christopher, reaching into his pocket and pulling out a few small copper coins and handing one over to Fred.

Just as he did, a high-pitched whistle came flying through the air and an arrow stuck through his outstretched hand. Blood splattered over their faces and the impact of the blow sent Christopher twirling around before he fell to the ground, gripping his hand in pain.

Fredrick, completely caught off guard, quickly shook off the surprise and ran to the bell, ringing it hard while screaming "The enemy has come! The enemy has come!" as a volley of arrows flew over the walls striking several men who had jumped up to prepare for the coming attack.

General Ryan, hearing the alarm bells at the front tower, quickly jumped out of his bed in the encampment behind the final walls, got dressed, and ran as fast as he could to the front lines to meet with the officer on duty.

Soldiers were running everywhere, scrambling to get into their positions. Men were screaming and being carried away with arrows protruding from various places. By the time General Ryan had arrived at the front, blood was pooling up in a few areas on the walls where a high number of men had been struck and long streaks of blood could be seen where the men had been dragged away to safety before being lifted and carried to the infirmary.

"Captain, report" said General Ryan, to the captain on duty.

He was a young man with brown hair and green eyes. He had been in the battle of Eldergate, so he had seen his fair share of battle, but tonight he looked deathly afraid.

"Captain, I said report!" said General Ryan, snapping the young soldier out of it.

"Sir! It seems the enemy has snuck up the side of the mountain pass on a series of ladders with a smaller group of archers to avoid our detection. We never saw them coming, but we don't think it's the main force just yet. No casualties so far, but a few men have suffered wounds that will keep them out of the fight." he said, quickly gathering his wits.

"Thank you, Captain!" said General Ryan. "How many do you think there are? How are our archers doing?" he asked.

"A few dozen, maybe? It's hard to tell in the darkness, sir. Our archers are doing the best they can. I ordered them to return fire but, again, it's hard to tell how effective their firing is. Without the moonlight, it's a dark night, sir." said the Captain.

"Understood, thank you, Captain." said General Ryan, dismissing the soldier to return to his post.

He looked out from the barricades, careful to not let too much of his body be exposed to the incoming arrows. The captain was right, it was near impossible to see anything further than the light from the torches.

Every now and then they could catch a few glimpses of the enemy here and there when the cloud cover would open up enough of the sky to let the starlight reveal more of the landscape. That is how they were able to spot the ladders and the men climbing up the mountain side in the first place. But those breaks in coverage were far and in between.

As he peered through the darkness, a loud horn blew somewhere far off down the mountain followed by the unmistakable roar of thousands upon thousands of demons and men still loyal to General Krauss. Slowly a line of torchlight began marching up the mountain pass.

It had finally begun.

Fortunately, the losses from the surprise attack had been minimal, and had done no real damage to their fortifications or preparedness.

The General ran up and down the walls, yelling to his men to make sure they were ready for the coming battle.

The hours passed by as if they were minutes and soon the main force could be seen coming up the final bend of the switchback pass. Torches stretched as far as the eye could see down the mountain road, revealing the true size of the army to all who watched from the ramparts of the fortifications.

Since the initial firing had stopped from the enemy's surprise ambush the spectators watched in awe, fighting back their internal urges to run. The men had to suppress their fear and remind themselves of what they were fighting for. It was either kill or be killed. Victory or absolute annihilation.

General Ryan stood at the front of the wall by his men, looking out across the expanse of empty road between his position and the coming army. They were roughly a few hundred yards out when they suddenly stopped.

The night was still and silent. It was the calm before the storm.

The General looked down his line of defenses one more time. He could see the rows of archers standing at the ready, arrows notched and prepared to fire at his command.

The soldiers behind them stood prepared to take out any siege ladders that landed on their walls – instructed to knock them back and push them away as quickly as they could and to fight back anything that crawled over.

He could see Orin in the distance on one of the towers on the second wall, prepared to send flaming balls of fire towards any flying beast that got through the archers' volleys, and Rex was standing at the opposite end from General Ryan, giving a final inspirational speech to his men before the battle began in full force.

He could hear him through the chilling silence, screaming at the top of his lungs.

"This is it men! Tonight, the battle for Ravenfell begins. These demons and traitors come to our lands with the intention of taking it for themselves! They come here looking for a fight, I say, LETS GIVE IT TO THEM!" he screamed.

Behind him, the deafening roar of thousands of men rang through the air, the strength of it vibrating the air like a great wave shaking the very ground beneath their feet.

Immediately, as if in response to his invitation, the demon army began their charge. The earth shook under the hammering of their feet and the sound of their roar.

The mass of blackness swept across the distance between them and the fortifications at incredible speeds. The front lines were filled with thousands of undead soldiers mixed with demons of various shapes and sizes. Some were carrying large ladders for scaling the walls, others were carrying long throwing spears and were launching them with inhuman strength across impossible distances. One such spear flew over the ramparts and struck a soldier standing near General Ryan, flinging him backwards and over the other side of the wall. He fell with a scream before landing below with a sickening thud.

"Fire!" screamed General Ryan, and volley after volley of arrows flew from the walls around him and behind him into the dark massive army charging towards them.

When the demons were struck, they stumbled, some falling and getting trampled by the horde behind them. But the undead continued on, unphased by the impact of the arrows, many sticking out from various places as the army continued moving forward.

They reached the walls and started slinging up ladders, some already starting to climb them with unnatural speed, but the defenders were prepared for this and quickly dispatched the ladders, only for more to replace them. Some of the demons were able to climb the walls independently, using their powerful claws to cling onto the imperfections in the stone and scale it at incredible speeds. These seemed to be the most problematic, as there were hundreds of them climbing at once.

The defenders on the wall were slashing them down as soon as they would crest the top of the walls, but just as one fell, another would take its place. The fighting became intense and bloody, every man for himself as they fought back the demon horde.

Through the fighting, Rex saw in the distance one of the larger demons making his way through the crowd, stomping on anything that got in his way so he could reach the wall. Several dozen demons fell under his powerful feet before they got the hint and moved out of his way, leaving a great divide between him and the defenses.

Rex, seeing the threat he posed to their defenses, immediately ordered the archers and ballistae to begin firing everything they had at the great brute. Volley after volley of arrows flew towards the target, striking him all over his body to no avail. Enraged, he began charging full speed at the gate with his tree-sized club preparing to crash into the barrier.

One, then two, then three large projectiles fired from the ballistae, striking him in his chest mere feet before he reached the gate. He stumbled from the impact and fell to the ground lifeless, crushing several demons under the weight of his giant body.

"That was too close!" yelled Rex, to which the others agreed vehemently. "We have to watch out for those big ones, or our defenses are going to get smashed to pieces!" he yelled over the roar of the battle.

The archers and men manning the ballistae seemed to understand, because the next ones didn't get nearly as close as the first – but instead were taken out at the legs before they could reach within fifty yards of the gate.

The constant assault continued on for some time until at last the wall was breached. Too many demons had crested the walls for the men to push them back any longer and the fighting that ensued was ferocious.

Men and demons alike screamed with rage and pain, falling left and right under the flurry of attacks. The enemy came over the wall wave after wave, breaking on the defenses like an endless surge of ocean tides falling on the face of the wall, only to regroup and come back again in full force.

As the men started to show signs of fatigue, more fresh soldiers were brought in to replace them while the wounded were carried off to be tended to.

The sun began to break in the East over the Draconian Mountains, and Captain Ryan said a silent prayer to the Creator God for the much-needed light.

Their archers were now able to spot the demons better and started shooting with more accuracy and precision, taking down more and more demons with each shot fired and now avoiding the undead all together. The winged creatures were trying their best to pick off the archers from the wall. Some were successful, but most were being shot out of the sky before they could reach the defenders on the wall and towers. The barriers Orin had placed were proving to be extremely effective in keeping the winged beasts from flying over the fortifications and getting behind their forces.

Captain Ryan could see balls of fire, flying past his head and arching over the walls, catching beasts and undead afire after exploding on the ground. Each great blast would send flaming rocks and debris in all directions, catching everything in its path on fire and sending demons flailing violently through the masses. It was causing chaos in their ranks, but because of their incredible numbers, it didn't seem to slow them down one bit.

Orin continued casting left and right relentlessly at incredible speeds, sending flaming spheres into the air at the flying beasts and into the rushing enemy lines, causing huge explosions that would send enemies flying into the air and off the cliffside.

Large catapults were also sending an endless rain of combustible pots filled with ignited oil, each exploding upon impact and creating large swaths of flame that would send the enemy screaming and flailing off the cliffs. But no matter how much destruction and carnage they inflicted on the enemy forces, they seemed to just keep coming. More and more demon soldiers would take their place, filling the voids like water fills an area scooped away by a bucket.

Meanwhile, Rex was busy swinging his double-sided battle axe with terrifying effectiveness. Anything that met his blade fell under its deadly strike. He roared with rage as he kicked another ladder from the walls, sending its occupants scrambling before falling backward into the mass of bodies below.

Seeing an undead soldier climbing over the wall in the distance, he quickly ran to confront him and fill the gap where the previous soldier had been wounded and was being taken away. He swung his axe and lopped off the head of the incoming soldier, his body falling to the side in a lifeless heap, only to have another take his place. The bodies were beginning to stack up into enormous piles of stinking flesh leaning against the walls. The enemy began using these mounds as ramps, climbing up the dead to get to the top of the walls much quicker and in greater numbers.

Rex saw General Owen in the distance making his way to him, blood streaked across his face. It wasn't human blood – but the black sticky ichor that spilled from the demons and undead. Rex could barely make him out from behind the mask.

"My King! They are breaking over the West wall!" he screamed, kicking over another ladder as soon as it landed on the walls.

Rex looked around, his men were being overwhelmed, but they were doing their best to hold the line. Despite their valor, he knew it was only a matter of time before their line would break and they would have to retreat to the inner walls.

"Lead the way!" screamed Rex, and they quickly ran off down the wall towards the area getting overrun. Rex wasn't about to let those demons through just yet, not on his watch.

Chapter XXII

How much longer until we get to the surface?" asked King Tybrin Hammerclaw.

The dwarven army was making its way up the foot paths towards the opening at Draco's Pass. There weren't enough carts to efficiently transport the entire Dwarven army to the surface, so instead they had to take the route less traveled by foot, and Tybrin, or any dwarf for that matter, was not very patient.

They had been walking for several hours and he was eager to get to the surface for a good fight. He hadn't been in one since the last great battles of the Mystic Wars where he had fought alongside his grandfather and father, both of which had perished in the conflict, leaving him king of the Dwarven Empire.

He remembered his oath that day. He had promised to avenge their deaths by destroying any demon to ever set foot on the surface again – and he held true to that promise. He had been responsible for sending thousands of demons back to the depths from whence they came by the time the war had ended. And he was eager to do it once again.

At last, the bright light began to shine through the darkness of the tunnel system, revealing they had finally reached the last stretch before the end.

Tybrin could feel the rush of air from the mountains blowing through the tunnel. It felt good on his skin and even better in his lungs as he filled them with the cool, fresh air.

When they reached the secondary opening, they came out a couple hundred feet above Draco's Pass and their eyes opened wide at the sight beneath them.

Thousands of demons were marching through the snow littered pass, led by a company of few hundred Wolf Guard. They were winding up the mountain road through Draco's Pass and headed towards the Land of the Immortals.

To the East in the distance down the mountain they could see a huge mass of figures in shining armor headed their way – it was the elves, and they were clad for battle, headed to the pass to meet the enemy head on!

Tybrin Hammerclaw looked at his brethren, lifted up his battle hammer and screamed at the top of his lungs, "CHARGE!" before running full speed down the side of the mountain and clashing into the flank of the completely surprised demons, breaking the enemy forces in two.

He swung his massive battle hammer around his head like a twirling baton, knocking enemies to the ground and smashing their skulls under the weight of his mighty blows. The rest of the dwarves began picking off the demons, one by one, scattering them into a frenzied mass, completely unprepared for the ferocity of the unsuspected attack.

The enemy finally gathered their composure and attacked with renewed ferocity, tearing into the flesh of the Dwarves with their sharp teeth and claws and swinging wildly at them with their jagged weapons. The Dwarves fell by the hundreds, but not without taking out ten times as many demons.

Darryn Faircloth was one of the dwarves who had volunteered to join the army on their march to the surface. He wasn't skilled in battle, but like all Dwarves, it was in his blood to fight such vile creatures.

When he reached the opening and saw the demon army marching below, something within his blood boiled and a righteous rage flowed through his veins.

He watched as his mighty King plowed into the flank of the enemy roaring like a lion, and he rushed after his King and brethren, eager to join the fight.

When he got to the level ground of Draco's Pass and joined into the fray, he was confronted with a group of snarling demons with great fangs and piercing claws. For a moment, his heart dropped as he second guessed his decision to join in the battle, but then he remembered his friends and what he was fighting for, and his confidence returned full force.

"Bring it on ye stinky bastards!" he yelled, much to his own surprise – he was always such a gentle Dwarf!

He rushed towards the enemy with the strength and vigor of a lifelong warrior, plowing into the enemy while swinging his battle hammer wildly. It crashed into the sides of the demons with incredible speed and efficiency, sending them flying like rag dolls.

"This is easier than I thought!" he said, laughing hysterically as he proceeded to pummel a nearby demon that had tried to flee from the raging dwarf.

The Dwarves were mighty folk, and they were not to be easily dismissed!

Meanwhile, King Tybrin was surrounded by a group of large demons with great, spiked clubs. They were slowly closing in on him, placing him in a dire situation. He tried to swing at one, but their clubs were too long, and he was easily pushed back.

Seeing their King's desperate situation, Darryn and a few others quickly rallied and rushed to his aid in a ferocious charge while screaming at the top of their lungs.

The brutes, surprised by the sudden attack at their flanks, turned their attention to the incoming dwarves. King Tybrin used their distraction to his advantage and rushed towards the nearest brute, his back now to the King. He swung his mighty battle hammer with all his strength, crashing it into the back of the demon's knee and knocking its feet right out from under him. When the beast fell backwards and to the ground, King Tybrin smashed his hammer into its head, squashing it like a bug.

He quickly joined in the fray with his defenders, helping them take on the remaining demons. They had recovered from their sudden confusion and had now cornered the rest of the dwarves with their backs against the far wall of the mountain pass.

The King rushed towards the nearest demon, diverting its attention long enough to give the others a chance to make their desperate break through its legs. The brutes were large and strong, but they were slow to react to the smaller and faster moving dwarves.

Once they regrouped, they charged the demons together in a ferocious attack, catching them off guard and swiftly taking them out one at a time.

The ebb and flow of the battle continued on for hours as more and more demons flowed in from the Great Plains below and into the narrow mountain pass. The losses were staggering on both sides, but at last, as the sun started to sink lower in the Western sky, the giant battle hammer of King Tybrin Hammerclaw struck down the final demon in the pass. Its devilish howls echoed through the cool mountain air, ending in a dramatic gurgling before it fell motionless to the ground.

He lifted his great hammer into the air and let out a hearty cry, "FOR THE CREATOR!" he said, shouting their customary victory cheer.

An enormous cheer erupted from the Dwarves as they watched the final enemy fall, echoing their leader and King's triumphant call, each raising their weapons to the air as they chanted.

***

Reingard and Holzer, watching as the enemy marched towards them down the Eastern slope of Draco's Pass, suddenly saw a flash of metal rushing down the slopes just above the demon army. They could barely hear the roar and clashing of battle in the distance at the top of the mountain pass.

He pointed to the commotion and Gilric Ellisar only smiled. His elf eyes and ears better than theirs, he could see and hear what it truly was – the Dwarves had come out of their holes.

"Charge!" he screamed, and they all drew their swords and broke out into a full sprint towards the advancing enemy lines.

The Wolves, seeing them coming and hearing the commotion in the flanks behind them, broke out into a run on all fours, bounding down the road and across the foothills at incredible speed, with the bulk of the demon army following closely behind.

The two armies clashed with great force, sending demons, wolves, and elves flying backwards with the impact. The two sides quickly melted into each other, breaking the once distinguishable forces into a huge mass of brutal combat. Swords and shields were crashing against flesh and teeth and the long scythe-like weapons of the Wolf Guard.

Reingard and Holzer fought side by side with great tenacity, swinging their newly forged battle axes with a strength they had never known before, sending demons and wolves flying backward and in pieces with every mighty swing of their axes.

They fought with all of their might, determined to send each and every one of the enemy hordes back to the dark halls of the Dark Abyss from whence they came.

Gilric Ellisar, his long, curved blade flashing left and right with incredible speed and precision, was dispatching enemies as quickly as they came, tearing through their ranks at the front of the battle, leaving a wake of death and destruction trailing behind him that was quickly filled with forces from both sides, locked in combat.

Eventually he caught up with the leader of the Wolf Guard who snarled fiercely as he approached, bearing his big yellow fangs threateningly before jumping toward him at breakneck speeds.

Their blades clashed as they met, sending sparks flying in every direction. Their attacks were a flurry of steel and fur, hammering again and again in an endless rhythmic dance.

More than once the wolf's blade struck home, but Gilric's armor proved to be the stronger of the two metals and deflected the attacks.

Emboldened by his seeming superiority, the Wolf lunged ferociously at Gilric, but he had been anticipating this moment and side-stepped quickly out of the way before bringing the full might of his sword down on the back of the wolf's head – severing it completely. It fell to the ground with a sickening thud, rolling several times before coming to a stop, his tongue hanging halfway from his mouth. The leader of the Northern Wolf Guard was dead.

After hours of tireless fighting and heavy casualties, the demon army began to wear thin just as the sky began to dip behind the mountain range to the West. The final remaining enemies were quickly dispatched by the elvish forces, and the ones who had tried to flee were quickly hunted down and slain. When they saw that they had finally triumphed, they all cheered together in victory.

They had suffered great losses, but they had ultimately won the battle.

Gilric, Reingard, and Holzer looked up together towards Draco's Pass where the last of the sun's rays was starting to disappear, sending a brilliant array of golden light scattering throughout the painted sky. In the distance they could see the silhouetted outline of the Dwarven army, all holding up their weapons in victory.

"It appears our friends have also been victorious!" said Gilric, a clear expression of relief etched onto his face as he approached Reingard and Holzer who were both covered nearly head to toe in sticky demon blood. He looked to Reingard and Holzer and tilted his head towards the mountains, "Shall we go congratulate them?" he asked with a rare smile, which they both returned in full.

"Aye, we shall!" replied Reingard, clasping hands with the Elven Prince.

And they began their ascent with the remaining Elven forces up the mountain pass to greet their new allies and prepare for their march to Ravenfell's aid.

Chapter XXIII

Look out!" shouted Rex, as a ten-foot-tall demon came charging over the top of the wall, tearing off the arm of one of his soldiers before lunging at General Owen.

General Owen turned just in time to dodge the attack and quickly decapitated the demon with his two-handed sword, sending it tumbling off the back of the wall and into the spikes below.

"That was too close!" he replied, laughing more out of relief than anything.

They had been fighting constantly for over twelve hours straight. The first of the three defensive walls had been overrun, forcing them to retreat to the second tier, but it too, was quickly becoming overrun.

The men had been fighting tirelessly and valiantly, many refusing to rotate from their shifts or leave to seek medical attention despite their wounds, but the demon army was relentless and greatly outnumbered their own.

It was only a matter of time before they would have to fall back to the third defensive wall, leaving them to defend the final barrier between the increasingly violent enemy and their main forces. It seemed the more they fought on, the more ferocious the enemy became, as if they were in a bloodlust battle rage intent on killing anything and everything that got in their way.

The defenders on the other hand, were growing weaker with every passing hour – they simply couldn't continue at this pace for much longer, even with the constant rotation every few hours with fresh troops. They just simply didn't have the numbers, and with each passing hour, they had more and more men killed or forced out of the fight from their wounds.

"Fall back!" yelled Rex, indicating it was time to move out to the third and final barrier.

The men quickly complied, filing out one by one down the stairways to the ground level and moving their way through the maze-like barricades as they had done several hours before when they had been forced to abandon the front line. While the majority of the forces retreated safely to the third barricade, several others stayed back to hold the line and keep the demons from getting through.

Finally, Rex, General Owen, General Ryan, and Orin were all that were left on the middle wall. Seeing that everyone else had safely escaped to the final barricade, they each slowly made their way to the final defensive position, fighting back demons and undead every step of the way with archers from the wall behind supporting their escape and helping hold back the enemy hordes.

When they reached the wall and got into position, Orin held up his hand with a ball of fire, the signal for the archers to light the barricades.

Immediately, hundreds of archers each dipped their arrows into the oil filled gutter and Orin sent his flame into the pitch, igniting each of their arrows before they sent a volley into the pitch-soaked barricades below.

The entire area ignited into a roaring blaze, catching hundreds of demons and undead afire who had been pursuing Rex and the others through the barriers, sending them flailing around and screaming, trying to escape the inferno. In their frenzy, some of the demons managed to impale themselves on the spikes, causing them to scream even further in anguish, while others simply trampled one another into oblivion. The trap had worked, but in the end, they knew it would only slow them down. The hundreds who died would quickly be replaced by equal numbers as soon as the blaze subsided.

With the pit below afire and preventing any enemies from crossing the gap for the time being, Rex looked over to General Ryan and Orin who both agreed the time had finally come to utilize the elixirs that Orin had prepared.

He began running up and down the lines, telling his men to drink the contents of the little vials, and prepare for their final stand. One by one, the men took out their vials and began downing the clear liquid. The effects would last anywhere between twelve hours and forty-eight hours, depending on the size of the user and how much energy they were using. Given the ferociousness of the fighting thus far, Orin suspected they would be lucky if they got half of that before crashing, but the alternative was for their men to begin falling down exhausted before the fight was over – something that would certainly bring their doom.

Immediately, a surge of energy and strength flowed back into the bodies of the defenders. Their wounds no longer bothered them, their tired limbs no longer ached, and their minds were clear as if they had just woken for the day – they were prepared for the next wave of attacks.

Within minutes, the men had regrouped and prepared to face the onslaught – and it came in full force.

The flames finally subsided, the enemy forces let out a devilish high-pitched howl and charged at the wall full force. They were running so quickly and carelessly that they were climbing over the scorched bodies on the barricades, refusing to wait their turn to fit through the maze, but instead using them as steppingstones to keep from becoming impaled themselves. They were charging with such reckless abandon that they were pushing each other over and impaling the slower ones on the barricades, creating more and more paths across the field.

Orin and the others could see this becoming a problem as it allowed the enemy forces to attack them in greater numbers, thereby thinning out their forces on the walls.

General Ryan, thinking quickly, instructed the catapults to fire their remaining cannisters as close as they could to the front of the wall.

"But sir, that would put the men in danger." objected one of the engineers firing the devices.

"Just do it, soldier!" shouted General Ryan.

The men sprang into action and after making the necessary adjustments, began sending volley after volley of flaming cannisters into the opening between the two walls and a short distance in front of the defenders.

The entire area before the wall erupted in a series of explosions, sending demons flying in every direction, sometimes in unrecognizable pieces.

The defenders behind the wall braced for impact, covering their heads, and hiding behind the crenelations to protect themselves from the flying debris and powerful blasts.

In the span of just a few minutes, over a thousand demons and undead soldiers were obliterated. Not a single soldier had been killed, while only a few had suffered severe burns on their hands or arms from the blaze.

When the smoke cleared, they could see the now pothole ridden field filled with the charred remains of countless enemies. When they had seen the effectiveness of the barrage, the rest of the forces had stopped pouring into the pit, waiting for the rain of death to cease. Now that it was finally over and they could see no indication of any further attacks, they grew emboldened once again and one by one started rushing through the still smoking field, navigating around the flaming pits and scorched bodies.

When the ladders started hitting the wall, the defenders were ready.

Over the course of the next several hours, the defenders held back the enemy waves with surprising efficiency, kicking off the ladders, lopping off their heads and arms and any limbs that they could reach. The stench of demon blood filled the air. The smoke from the still blazing fires blocked the midday sun of the second day, giving the air an almost dusk appearance.

Men and demon screamed alike, fighting viciously for their lives for what felt an eternity. The sun began to set in the distance, and the fighting still raged on, as ferocious as ever.

That's when they first caught sight of him.

General Krauss came in like a bulldozer, faster than a charging bull, and ten times as strong.

He was glowing an eerie green and seemed to be larger than they remembered, but his evil smirk and his dark features let them know that it indeed was the General.

The archers sent a flurry of arrows flying towards him in an attempt to knock down his charge, but he just waved them off with a flick of his hand, sending them flying back at the men and taking out several of them.

Orin sent a fireball blazing toward him. He simply batted it aside as if it were a firefly, giving it even less thought than he would an annoying insect as it deflected off into the side of the mountain pass, exploding like a bomb and taking out several demons in the process.

Rex and the two generals looked at each other and immediately knew what must be done.

They signaled for the men to fall back into the main forces that were waiting just behind the walls, then followed quickly in pursuit, prepared to make their final stand in their last-ditch effort to keep the enemy forces from breaking through into the valley and spreading out like wildfire. They knew if they got that far, their chances of survival would drop significantly. It would be the end of Ravenfell.

Just as they got off the wall, it exploded with such force that it knocked them all several feet through the air. They landed hard just before their main line of forces, several soldiers running forward to help up their fallen generals and king.

When they got to their feet and turned around to see what had happened, suspecting they already knew the answer, General Krauss was standing in the midst of the rubble, a great cloud of dust still clearing from the air as it settled back into place.

"He's far more powerful than he was before," said Orin, seeing the incredible force he had displayed, "He must have been enhanced by his connection with the Defiant One. Now that he's no longer in the Dark Abyss, their connection appears to be stronger than ever!"

"Great..." replied General Ryan, "so how do we stop him?" he asked.

They each looked to Orin, his face covered in dirt and sweat and his eyes wide.

"We fight together, with everything we've got!" he said defiantly.

With that, they each nodded, knowing they were in this together until the end. If they were going to die, at least they would die fighting with their friends and for their people, and they did not plan on going down easy.

General Krauss stepped through the opening, letting the horde of demons and undead flood through the clearing towards the eagerly awaiting army of defenders.

"This is it men! Prepare yourselves!" shouted Rex above the roar of the incoming demons. "This is where we make our final stand. For freedom!" he screamed.

The remaining combined might of Ravenfell and Eldergate cheered with their King and Generals and rushed into the incoming horde, clashing into them with such fury and ferocity that a shockwave seemed to erupt between the two forces.

General Krauss locked eyes with Rex, General Ryan, and Orin, while General Owen fought on with his men around them.

Orin was the first to strike.

He rushed into a flurry of casting, sending a series of powerful attacks at General Krauss with terrifying results. The ground and area around the General exploded with a variety of elemental spells, fire, ice, wind, lightning – it was a relentless attack in a display of power the likes of which the mage had never shown before – a clear indication of their desperate situation.

He jumped into the air and spun his staff around, slamming it to the ground, causing the earth to shake beneath their feet as a large crack began to snake its way towards the General who at this point was obscured behind the smoke left over from his flurry of attacks. Finally, out from the earth shot a geyser of fire that would have melted the flesh off a normal opponent. And it did. Several demons unlucky enough to be caught in the blast fell screaming as the liquid flame contacted their flesh, sending stinking smoke into the air as it melted their skin and bone.

But General Krauss was not a normal opponent.

When the smoke began to dissipate, the figure of the General stood unharmed within the shadows and they could hear a harsh laugh emanating from within. A scorched perimeter surrounded him where the earth had been obliterated, but within it he remained seemingly unaffected by the powerful attacks.

Immediately, Orin was lifted into the air by an invisible force and thrown backwards several feet through the air, landing hard on the ground. His staff slid from his grip and rolled to a stop several feet from where he lay. He didn't get up.

Enraged, Rex and General Ryan rushed into the fight, charging at General Krauss with renewed ferocity and in synchronized attacks.

The General met their attacks with large twin swords, one in each hand, deflecting wave after wave of their attacks with ease. His movements were impossibly fast and coordinated, despite taking on two opponents of substantial skill and strength simultaneously.

They increased their efforts, and still he gave no way or any indication of faltering. All the while the endless battle continued around them, the screams of demon and men alike falling by the thousands.

In the distance Orin began to finally stir, trying to shake off the ringing and dizziness in his head as blood trickled slowly down his face.

He looked around for his staff, locating it just a few yards away in the midst of a group of soldiers fighting back a couple of demons.

He stumbled slowly towards the group, catching himself from falling a couple of times, completely oblivious to the shouting and screaming of mortal combat surrounding him on all sides.

The staff was suddenly kicked in the scuffle between the soldiers and the demons, but fortunately it spun closer to him and he reached down and grabbed his staff, gripping it firmly in his hands.

He cleared away the pain with a quick spell and turned just in time to see General Krauss rushing toward him in a full-on sprint, swords held behind him. General Ryan and Rex were sprawled out on the ground behind him, each sporting what looked like pretty serious wounds and neither one seemed to be moving.

Overcome with rage, Orin screamed and released all of his power at once in a desperate attack to avenge his friends, focusing it on General Krauss. He tried to block the attack with his blades, but the impact hit him square in the chest, sending him flying backwards a couple hundred feet through the air, landing hard on the pile of rubble from the crumbled wall.

Relieved his attack had worked, Orin rushed as quickly as he could to check on Rex and General Ryan.

They were both alive and breathing, but they were severely injured. General Ryan had suffered a few cracked ribs and a deep gash in his side, while Rex had a few cuts on his arms and back and was bleeding profusely. They would both need medical attention soon or risk passing out from loss of blood.

He quickly wrapped the wounds as best he could and helped them up, trying to get them out of harm's way. Several of the men, after seeing what had happened to their King and their General, had formed a protective circle around them, staving off the enemy forces the best they could and providing Orin time to get them to safety.

As they started their retreat, slowly moving down the valley towards the castle, Orin heard the men screaming behind him in horror. He turned just in time to push away Rex and General Ryan before throwing up his staff and casting a defensive barrier around himself.

General Krauss had come back in full force, enraged at having been struck by Orin's attack. It seemed to have injured him slightly, as he had blood trickling down his forehead and a large scorch mark on his chest that had broken his armor plate at the point of impact.

His double blades crashed down on Orin's magical shield, knocking him to the ground. He continued his attack, time and time again swinging forcefully with all of his might at the old mage. Orin was doing all he could to block the attacks and keep from being cut in two. He focused his energy on strengthening his barrier so it wouldn't break under the force of the blows, but it was all he could do. He knew it was only a matter of time before he would lose.

When all hope seemed lost and a defeat was everything but sure, a horn blew somewhere in the distance near the mountain pass.

The demon army began to turn around and face an unknown threat to their rear, giving up on their relentless pursuit of the men in the valley who were scattered and fleeing for safety.

Confused, the fleeing men turned to see what had caused their attackers to abandon their pursuit. They could see the demons fighting something, but they couldn't tell what it was, until finally a vanguard of elves in brilliant armor came rushing through the enemy forces, led by a pair of raging barbarians wielding heavy battle axes.

They were screaming fiercely and sending demons and undead flying with every swing of their axe as if they possessed super-human strength.

As they neared, the men began to shout and cheer. They could finally see who it was leading the charge – it was Reingard and Holzer, and they had come back with an army of Elves and Dwarves at their side!

With the sudden sound of the horn behind him and the abandonment of his force's pursuit of the defenders, General Krauss let up on his relentless attack to turn and see what was happening.

Just as he did, Orin gathered what strength he had left in him and sent a powerful attack towards the General, knocking him back several feet. Exhausted beyond all hope as the effects of his elixir finally wore off, Orin gave in to his weariness and dropped his staff to the ground. He could fight no longer as he embraced the end that would soon come his way.

Enraged and seeing the old mage apparently defeated, General Krauss walked back to Orin to finish him off with a final blow. With a smirk on his face, he looked down at his opponent before lifting his swords high into the air and driving them down with all of his might. Orin looked up at the coming attack defiantly, determined to face his end with honor.

Suddenly, a streak of silver flashed behind General Krauss and the attack immediately halted. Slowly a thin line of blood began trickling from his neckline as his head casually tilted and toppled over before falling to the ground. His body fell to its knees and likewise toppled to the side, falling into a lifeless heap.

Confused and overwhelmingly relieved, Orin propped his head up to see what had happened. Rex was standing over the body of General Krauss, holding his blood-soaked battle axe horizontally as he followed through with his deadly swing.

The old mage just lay his head back and let out a hearty laugh. He couldn't believe what incredible luck he had.

Rex and General Ryan carefully helped Orin onto his feet as he took a look around the valley.

The last of the demon army was quickly being chased down and hacked away by the elves and dwarves along with what remained of the defenders of Ravenfell – they had actually done it – they had won the battle!

Ravenfell would live to see another day.

Chapter XXIV

With the demon army defeated and General Krauss no longer a threat, the remaining forces of Ravenfell, with the aid of the Elves and Dwarves, began the long and difficult task of sorting through the carnage of the battlefield.

They roamed through the wreckage and massive field of bodies for hours, finding the wounded and carrying them to the infirmary while the dead were taken to a field and prepared for a great funeral to be held that evening.

The battle had taken a massive toll as expected, but the number of demons and undead easily outnumbered the fallen men ten-to-one. Still, they had lost a sizeable portion of their forces and knew that it was only a matter of time before the demon army would rebuild – being constantly supplied by the underworld with fresh recruits of demons and undead.

This thought, although distant at the moment for most of the men – whose primary focus was sorting through the mixed emotions of having survived the battle only to have to bury many of their friends and family members – it remained constantly in the minds of their leaders.

Nearly as soon as the battle had ended, the men were given orders to take care of the wounded and dead. Rex, Orin, General Ryan, General Owen, and King Eldergate then met with the Elven prince, Gilric Ellisar, and King Tybrin Hammerclaw of the Dwarves, to thank them for their courage and assistance and to create a plan for the path ahead.

As they were walking to the castle for their discussion of their remaining forces and future battle strategy, the sun was setting behind the mountains once again as it had done twice already since the battle had first begun. Suddenly, the sound of distant yelling came from the road leading up the valley towards the mountain pass.

They turned and could see a lone soldier running quickly down the path towards them, arms flailing as he screamed.

All they could hear were his words, "He's coming!"

For a moment they were startled and confused, but the uncertainty lasted only a moment, for shortly after they saw a bright green streak fly high above the mountain pass before barreling down at incredible speeds and plummeting into the castle upon the hill. The impact was so powerful it imploded the entire structure and sent a shockwave reeling outward at incredible speeds that knocked everything in its path backwards and through the air.

In a matter of seconds, the entire stronghold of Ravenfell was obliterated to nothing but a pile of rubble surrounding a crater where the castle once stood.

In the middle of the crater, floating just high enough for all in the valley to see, was the Defiant One.

His voice, ethereal and fierce, echoed throughout the entire valley, bouncing off the mountains around them.

Man, Elf, and Dwarf alike covered their ears against the sudden onslaught, but his voice still resounded in their minds – there was no escaping it.

"All who oppose me will fall like a wave against the shore. To resist is futile. You may have had the strength to fend off the first wave of my army, but you will not survive the next. Find me the boy, bring him to me, and I will be a merciful ruler. If you fail, you and your people will suffer the likes of which you have never seen before."

With this, he rose high into the sky and jetted across the mountain pass once again, creating a shockwave through the skies that shook the air and ground around them as he headed back to his fortress atop the mighty rock where Eldergate once stood.

***

When they recovered from their shock and awe at the immense power of the Defiant One, the leaders all stood together discussing their options.

"We don't stand a chance against that kind of power, not without David." said Rex calmly, looking

233

around at the others as they stood in a makeshift command tent. They had been going over various plans to confront their enemy, and so far, nothing was looking promising.

Reingard and Holzer had informed Rex and the others of their journey with David, Tyrius, and Erin and of David's eventual capture by Jakob Zander of the Southern Kingdom's Guild. They said Tyrius and Erin had gone after him, but that they suspected he was somehow taken by magic to Brineport where he would be under the mercy of the bandits and their leader, whoever that was.

"They rode South on the morning of the battle of Draco's Pass just three days past," said Gilric. "They were on the backs of two of our fastest horses. With luck and the Creator's grace, they should be in Brineport by now. What they will find there, only time will tell." he said.

"What do you suggest we do? We can't wait here until the next wave of enemies come. They will surely destroy us where we stand!" said Tybrin Hammerclaw, clearly still shaken by the show of force he had just witnessed.

"He's right. Our defenses are all but destroyed, our fortress is obliterated, and we have less than half the numbers we had. We can't withstand another direct assault." said King Eldergate, shaking his head.

The situation was dire indeed, and they all knew it.

"Well, he's giving us a chance to get David to him, right?" asked Orin, wincing from the pain in his side as he tried to stand up. Rex quickly helped him to his feet, giving him the support needed to address the others.

"That must mean he doesn't yet know that David is captured in the South! If he did, he wouldn't have asked us to bring David to him, because his minions in the South would be doing it for him." he said, looking around the room. Everyone nodded in agreement, suddenly a glimpse of hope on their faces.

"It also tells us, for some reason, the Defiant One is not traveling too far from Eldergate to search for David himself. Why do you think that is?" he asked, searching the eyes of everyone at the table.

When no one seemed to have an answer, Orin spoke up again, "I believe, and I may be wrong...but I believe it's because he can't!"

With that, everyone looked up, shock and confusion on their faces.

"What do you mean, old man?" asked Gilric, his expression for the first time showing a rare hint of emotion.

"What I mean is, maybe he can't travel too far from Eldergate because the spell that once banished him to the Dark Abyss still has a hold on him, however slightly. What if he is bound to the area until David is defeated, thereby destroying the last remnants of the power that sealed him away and freeing him at last – the power of the Mystics of Creation. The power that, although dormant it seems, David now possesses and keeps a part of this world."

Everyone looked around the room, each judging the merits of the information Orin was proposing. Could the Defiant One truly still be in chains?

Orin, seeing that his message was making an impact, decided to reveal his final bit of information.

"Did anyone else notice that when the Defiant One first arrived, after his initial display of power, that his aura had dimmed significantly? When he was on his way, his light was as bright as a star, but when he was leaving, it was barely noticeable at all. He merely glowed the way the orb now glows in David's hand – as if it is sleeping, dormant. I believe this is because he had expended his stored energy in that powerful blast. Had he continued so far from his source of power, the Dark Abyss where he is still bound, he would have run out of strength. That is why he has been staying in Eldergate instead of leading his armies like he once did so many years ago." said Orin.

With this, the light seemed to turn on with Gilric and Tybrin, both of whom had fought in the Mystic Wars and had seen first-hand the might and power of the Defiant One.

"He's right!" said Tybrin, eyes wide with recollection. "Before, the Defiant One always glowed bright and he took pride in personally leading his armies. It didn't matter where he went, he was always fighting alongside them!"

"Indeed, it is true." said Gilric pitching in. "The Defiant One was never one to shy away from a battle. After all, he was bred for destruction as a means of balancing the creations of the other Mystics. It seems now he has a reason to remain hidden away, at least until he has David in his grasp. What you suggest, Orin, may have some merit." said Gilric, nodding his head in agreement.

"So, what does that mean for us?" asked Rex, looking to Orin for guidance. "Do you suggest we go into hiding until David can regain his powers and defeat the Defiant One once and for all?"

With this, everyone turned to Orin, waiting for his advice on what to do next.

"No. I think that we should gather what supplies we can and go to the Southern Kingdom to help Tyrius and Erin find and rescue David. Without David, our future is bleak indeed. We must find him and get him to the Crystal Caverns no matter the cost. He is our only hope of survival. So long as the Defiant One remains on this earth we will never be safe, and there's no telling how long he will remain chained like this. David is the only one who can face him, and he must do it sooner rather than later" said Orin gravely.

"If we can get our people to the Southern Kingdom, we can rebuild our forces without the threat of the Defiant One showing another force of power like he did today. That is, if Orin's hypothesis is true. Once David recovers his powers and returns from the Caverns, we will then be ready to take the fight to the Defiant One with David by our side!" said Rex, looking to King Eldergate who nodded in agreement.

"Yes, I believe that is the best course for the time being. We have nothing left here for our people." said King Eldergate. "This valley will be our doom if we stay here and have to fight again" he said gloomily. "No, we will go to Brineport and reunite with our people who have gone before us"

"King Kane, Prince Gilric, King Tybrin, what of your people? Will you accompany us through the Southern Tunnel?" asked King Eldergate.

Rex, the Elf Prince, and Dwarven King shared a look of mutual agreement before answering. They would all bring their forces through the Southern Pass. It would be safer to travel South through the mountains, than risk a confrontation again in the open fields of the Great Plains.

"It is settled then. We will gather what supplies we have left and, after we bury the dead and send them off properly, we will begin our journey south through the mountain. May the Creator's blessing be with us all!" shouted Rex, to which everyone joined in the blessing before dispersing to spread the message to their respective people.

They spent the next several hours preparing for their coming journey and gathering the last of the dead for the funeral pyre while a group of Dwarves worked to clear the rubble from the Southern Tunnel that had been blocked before the battle.

When the dead had all been gathered, they lit the massive pyre, each leader giving their blessings and saying a few kind words to commemorate the thousands of brave warriors that had given their lives in the battles of Ravenfell and Draco's Pass.

The mound was great, and the light of the fire lit up the valley in a radiant hue of yellow and orange, casting long shadows across the landscape of the men, elves, and dwarves who circled around to honor their fallen comrades. Millions of little sparks danced and flittered through the cool mountain air as the fire burned away its fuel, sending them high into the air to join the countless stars littered across the cloudless night sky.

In the early morning before the fog had even lifted, they gathered the last of their supplies and began their descent into the Southern Tunnel, many wondering if they would ever see their homeland again.

Chapter XXV

David watched helplessly as he was being pulled away from his friends as their captors were taken out one by one by rogue arrows flying from the shadows among the trees. He was bound tightly and no matter how much he struggled he couldn't break free.

He watched in horror as arrow after arrow flew in his direction, several narrowly missing David's body as he was being dragged mercilessly across the forest floor. The ground was rubbing his arms raw and more than once a protruding root jabbed into his ribs, knocking the breath from his lungs.

Eventually he was dragged beyond the tree line and his captor took out a small glass ball the size of an apple from his pocket before throwing it harshly to the ground, shattering it into a thousand little fragments that glittered in the moonlight.

A plume of smoke rose from the debris, engulfing the two of them and blocking the view of the forest and their pursuers out of sight.

Suddenly, David felt a strange rushing sensation as he felt his body become weightless. The sound of the forest and whizzing arrows vanished and was replaced with absolute silence. Then, just as suddenly as if no time had passed at all, he landed hard on a stony floor, knocking his head hard on its surface before his vision went completely black.

When he awoke, David found himself in a small, square room with sandstone walls and ceiling that were rough and gritty. He was lying on a straw covered cot with his head bandaged and propped up on a straw pillow, its rough bristles pricking his head and body in various places.

He sat up to take a look around and saw that he was in a prison cell of some kind. The air was humid and hot, unlike anything he had felt before – indicating he was far away from where he had been the night before.

The light shining into his room from a small, barred window on the wall gave him the indication that it was sometime during the day.

He stood up and walked to the door which was more of a wall of bars with a section that opened and closed. He gripped the cool metal bars and took a peek outside his cell. They were rough on his hands and slightly rusted but were spaced far enough that he could reach his arm through the gaps. Not that it would do him any good – he was locked in there with no apparent way of escaping.

From what he could see as he peered through the bars, his cell was apparently one of many and was located in a long, hall-like room with a small plain looking door at the middle leading to what David assumed was the exit.

His cell was located somewhere between the end and the middle of the hallway, from his best estimate.

"Hello?" he called into the hallway, hoping to figure out why he was captured and where he was being held.

"Eh, there's no use boy" came a raspy voice from the cell to his right, "They won't hear you. They only come here twice a day, if we're lucky, and that's to drop off the slop so we don't die before our execution" he said, followed by a rough, wet sounding cough.

"What do you mean, execution? Where am I being held?" asked David, moving closer to the side of his cell that the voice came from.

The man just laughed until he was stopped by his ragged cough, then finally he responded.

"What, you don't know where you're at?" he mocked, "Surely, you're innocent, then?" he asked, before breaking into another hysterical laugh.

David shook his head, realizing he wasn't going to get any real answers out of the man to his right, and headed back to sit on his bed.

As he sat down, he heard another voice from the cell on his left. It was deeper and younger sounding.

"I saw them bring you in last night. You looked banged up pretty good" the voice said.

David rushed to the wall near the voice.

"Who brought me in, did you see who it was?" asked David.

"Oh yeah, it was Jakob Zander. You must have really rattled his feathers for him to bring you down here himself." said the man, chuckling softly.

"I didn't do anything to that lunatic!" replied David, "He was the one chasing me and my friends around the whole countryside!"

"Hmm...are you the one they've been talking about, then? The "Outsiders" they've been calling you." said the voice, suddenly seeming more interested.

"Wait...are we in Brineport?" asked David, suddenly recalling where Jakob had said they were taking them before they had been attacked in the woods.

"That's right, where did you think you were?" asked the man to his left.

"It doesn't matter now, does it?" said David, discouraged.

He had spent over a week heading North to the Crystal Caverns, only to have been captured and taken back all the way to the Southern Kingdom. How would he ever get his powers back in time to stop the Defiant One now? He let the people of Ravenfell down, and more importantly, he let his friends down. He worried deeply for their safety, not knowing what was to become of them now that he was still so far from his goal of reaching the caverns and getting back his powers.

Feeling something was wrong with his new cellmate, the man decided to press the issue.

"So...what was Jakob so interested in you for, anyway?" he asked.

"He says we got his brother killed...but the truth is, it was his men who attacked us first. Apparently, since he failed to capture us, he was executed."

243

replied David, recalling the story Jakob had told them when they were ambushed.

"I see...and why were they after you in the first place?" asked the man.

"He said it was because we were outsiders. We're from the Northern Kingdom, but we weren't here to cause trouble – we were just passing through." replied David quickly, remembering the hostility they faced in Ashmire when the locals figured out where they were from.

The man just chuckled gently to himself.

"You don't have to worry about that here, boy. I'm no stranger to the wider world. I've been around in my days and come across all types of people. Seems to me that people are people, doesn't matter where they're from. Sometimes they are nice, other times they are scumbags like Jakob and his gang. What brought you and your friends to the Southern Kingdom anyhow?" he asked.

David sat silently for a moment, considering how he would answer. He couldn't tell this man the truth about their mission, it would reveal that he was the bearer of the Orb and that would put his life in even more danger than he was already in. Instead, he made up a lie that he figured would be good enough for a prison-mate.

"We were traveling merchants, trying to reestablish the Southern Tunnel trading route that once thrived between our kingdoms." said David.

It seemed to work.

"Oh yeah...I remember hearing about that route when I was a kid. It used to benefit both of our kingdoms. I remember most of our salt was sent that way and was traded for precious metals and gems from the Mystic Mountain region. Very valuable stuff if you got your hands in the market." he said.

"So, what are you in here for?" asked David, curious to know why the man in the cell to his left was in a similarly precarious situation as he was.

"Me? Oh, well... I suppose I deserve to be here more than you do. I was a part of a rebellion trying to take out the current leadership – if you want to call it that. What we really are is patriots trying to take back our lands and our rights to live free." he said. "My name's Riyan, what's yours?" he asked, holding out his hand through the bars. His skin was dark and rough like leather.

"David...David Bishop" replied David, reaching out and shaking the man's hand.

"Good to meet you, David Bishop" said Riyan.

The door to the hallway opened and much to David's surprise in walked a couple of wolves that closely resembled that of the Wolf Guard.

The cloth around their waist sported the emblem of the Southern Kingdom – a black raven in a blood red circle. The fabric was a tannish color and had frayed ends where the cloth was unwinding. David wondered if that indicated their class was a much lower class than the wolves David had encountered in Eldergate, who sported higher quality garments and weapons, or if there was another reason for their appearance.

They walked up to David's cell, baring their teeth in warning as they unlocked his door and opened it, indicating for him to follow but not try anything stupid or suffer the consequences.

He took their warning seriously and cautiously followed their directions as they led him out of the hallway and into a large open chamber with high vaulted ceilings. The walls, floors and roof were all made of the same sandstone blocks as his cell. They were tannish with a rough, grainy texture and were much larger towards the base of the walls, some as large as small buildings, growing smaller as they rose up to the ceiling.

The room he was in reminded him of the great pyramids of Egypt, their ceilings sloping upward in a diagonal fashion before leveling off and flattening in a high point at the center of the structure.

This left the majority of the building as a single, wide open room where he was being led to.

As he followed the beasts through the center of the structure, he could see they were taking him to a set of great stairs leading to a second and third level within the great chamber. The stairs had several landings and were lined with thick, blocky rails that supported a large bronze brazier on each side of the landings, each blazing hot with a bonfire that provided lighting for the surrounding area.

As they reached the third and final floor, the ground leveled off to a long, smooth walkway leading up to a great stone doorway that was open, as if inviting them inside. Through the doorway was a smaller chamber filled with wolves standing at attention, each holding their large, curved scythe-like blades in front of them and decked out in elaborate bronze-colored chest plates and headgear that David hadn't seen on the wolves' before.

As he was led between the row of guards, the surrounding wolves watched him with their great yellow eyes as if he were a piece of meat ready to be devoured. He could feel their gaze upon him, leaving a trail of sweat trickling down his back that was from more than just the sweltering heat.

As he entered through the final doorway, he found himself standing before a great stone throne and the largest wolf he had ever seen sitting casually upon it.

When the wolf saw his expression, his lips curled up in a grotesque smile, baring his great fangs and his blood red tongue.

"Hello, boy" said the wolf in a deep, snarling voice. "My name is Bloodvayne, and I've been expecting you."

"And why is that?" asked David defiantly, although he felt about as small as a bug before the great wolf.

"Oh, feisty, this one?" said Bloodvayne to the other wolves, laughing in what sounded more like a dog panting. "No bother, we will break that spirit soon enough." he said coldly. "You are here because our master demands it, and that is reason enough." he said, finally.

"So, even the great Bloodvayne answers to someone else? You sit on that great thrown, but you're just as much of a pawn as the others, doing your master's bidding without question. How pathetic." said David, taunting the great wolf.

"I do what my master says because I know what's best for me, boy. Just like you will find out soon enough!" spat Bloodvayne angrily before he calmed himself and continued. "But I admit...I brought you here today to see what was so special about you, and sadly, I see nothing. Nothing special at all."

With that, David slowly hid his orb hand behind his back to keep it out of view, but Bloodvayne's eyes were too keen and David saw them flick to his hand immediately as he silently cursed himself for being so stupid.

"Ahh...what is that you're hiding behind your back, boy?" asked the wolf, growling as he spoke. He got up from his throne and began stepping towards David in great big strides, licking his lips instinctively as he neared.

"Nothing..." lied David, gritting his teeth.

Bloodvayne quickly reached out surprisingly fast and grabbed David's hand before he could pull it away, twisting it painfully towards him so he could get a good look. His sharp claws dug painfully into David's flesh, little droplets of blood oozing out slowly from the tiny wounds as David grimaced with the pain.

When he saw the orb pulsing dimly in David's hand, his eyes lit up with recognition.

"Ahhh...It all makes sense now why my master would have been so interested in some boy from the Northern Kingdom. He will be most pleased when he finds out that I, Bloodvayne, have captured the warrior of legend!" said the wolf.

He let go of David's hand, and David pulled it away quickly, rubbing his hand where Bloodvayne's rough, calloused paws had rubbed his skin raw and doing his best to wipe away the blood with his sleeve. The wounds were shallow, but they stung like fire.

"Take him away and send our fastest messenger at once to Eldergate. Tell the master that I have captured the warrior of legend and will be bringing him to Eldergate within the coming week. We will leave in the morning."

"Yes, your highness." said one of the wolves who had been escorting David.

Then the two wolves quickly turned around and grabbed David by the arms before leading him back to his cell once again.

When they reached the door to his cell, they threw him roughly to the floor and slammed the door shut behind him, locking it securely before exiting the room.

"Ouch, you okay David?" asked Riyan, having woke from a light nap when the guards had brought him in.

"Yeah...just a few scrapes and bruises, nothing major" replied David, rubbing his skinned knees and bruised elbows.

"What did they want with you?" he asked.

"They are going to take me away to Eldergate..." said David, giving up on any attempts at secrecy. His secret was out, and it was no good trying to hide it any longer.

"Eldergate? What for?" asked Riyan, curious.

"They are taking me to the Defiant One, probably to be executed." said David somberly.

"Woah, woah, hold on there, kid. The Defiant One? As in the Mystic of Destruction? The powerful being who was imprisoned long ago at the end of the

249

Mystic Wars?" asked Riyan, suddenly far more alert than he had been.

"Yup, that's the one..." said David.

"What would he want with – unless...you were the warrior from the legends who bears the Orb of Power?" said Riyan.

David heard the clinking of the bars from the cell to his left and he got up and walked to the bars to see Riyan's hand stretched out from between his bars as far as he could reach towards David's cell.

David pushed his orb-hand through the bars for Riyan to see the orb pulsing faintly in his skin.

"Well I'll be...you *are* the warrior of legend! What are you doing all locked up in here then? Can't you just...I don't know...blast your way out of here or something?" asked Riyan in awe and confused why David was locked up in the first place. He had heard of the legends all his life, like most people in Hurea had, and he was confused at how such a powerful warrior could be taken prisoner like David had been.

"Once, yes...I could have. But since the Defiant One has been released from his prison, my powers feel so distant. I can't access them. Believe me, I've tried many times." said David, slumping his shoulders and sliding down the wall into a sitting position. He didn't know what he would do now. Without his powers, he would never get away.

Sensing his new friend's dilemma, Riyan sat down on the wall opposite from David, with his back up against the same wall.

"I tell you what. You coming here – this changes everything..." said Riyan.

"What do you mean?" asked David through the wall.

"Nothing. You just focus on getting some rest. Come morning, you'll see." he said, then he grew silent.

"What do you mean, Riyan?" asked David again more forcefully, trying to get an answer, but all he would say was to get some rest.

Finally, David gave up on his interrogation and decided it was best to get some rest. After all, there was nothing else he could do but sit around and wait for the Wolf Guard to come and get him in the morning. They would then take him north a few days before turning west through Draco's Pass on the final stretch to Eldergate, where the Defiant One would be eagerly awaiting his arrival. It seemed that his fate was sealed now unless some miracle happened to break him free.

David lay down on his straw covered cot, trying to ignore the itchy hay as his mind wandered off. The sun was sinking lower in the sky and was no longer shining directly into his cell. Instead, a gentle orange glow took its place and covered his cell walls in its light, indicating the day was almost spent and would soon be replaced by the cool darkness of the night.

As he lay in his bed, all he could think about was Erin and the others, hoping they were safe wherever they were now. Eventually, too tired to continue brooding, sleep overcame his worry and he drifted off into a deep sleep.

***

Sometime in the early morning David woke to the sound of his cell door being opened. In walked two wolves of the Guard before slapping shackles on his wrist. They quickly grabbed David's arms and hauled him out of his cell and into the hallway before leading him through the large chamber from the day before.

They took him out into the open air where he caught his first site of the city of Brineport. He found himself standing before a great pyramid structure to his rear from which he had just exited, its great stone steps leading down into the courtyard below. Before him sat a great open square that was surrounded by a high limestone wall.

Within the wall was a group of similarly built structures, each large and ornate, but not nearly as big as the pyramid and not so oddly shaped. Instead, they were all rectangular and had great balconies with highly decorative pillars supporting their load that created a highly sought out space beneath their cover that was cool and in the shade. A valuable addition to any building within the desert environment such as Brineport.

This was definitely the wealthy district of the city, David figured, as just outside the walls he could see the buildings were not so grand or elaborate, and with their positions being outside of the walls it was clear their owners were not of the same elite class as the wolves and surrounding people.

The people themselves were all clothed in loose garments that were colorful and festive looking. They all had dark, brown skin and equally dark hair, many of which was curly and shiny with the women mostly having their hair put up in some elaborate fashion while the men all covered their short cropped heads in cloth to protect them from the intense heat of the sun.

Inside the busy courtyard a group of Wolf Guard stood waiting in a long line of roughly a dozen or so warriors. In the middle, waiting for David, was Bloodvayne seated on a great cart being pulled by a few members of the Guild. The citizens of the city all crowded around watching and gossiping about what was going on and who this strange prisoner was that warranted such an escort.

Bloodvayne's lips curled up in a smile as David approached. He was eager to get David to his master so he could reap his reward. David found himself wondering what reward would merit bringing the warrior of legend to the Defiant One. Whatever it was, it was clear that it was valuable enough for Bloodvayne to have gone through such great lengths to capture him and bring him back to Brineport.

"Don't look so morbid, boy" snarled Bloodvayne as David approached the caravan, "It's going to be a few days before we get you to Eldergate. No harm will come to you until then, you have my word." he said.

As soon as David was chained to the back of Bloodvayne's cart, they started off through the city walking at a much faster pace than David would have liked. He was having a difficult time keeping up with the cart pulling him along at the other end of his chains.

As they made their way through the heart of the city, David could see the large pyramid shaped building fall away in the distance behind them, along with the sturdier built buildings that surrounded it.

The road before them was surrounded by poorly constructed homes that more resembled huts and shacks than proper houses. Despite their materials still mostly being the same kind of stone, they were built in a much more careless fashion, and their roofs were covered by sticks and dried reeds covered in mud or clay rather than the more sturdy and durable stone roofs in the city's central district.

It was apparent to him that the wealth in the city flocked around the central building that housed the Wolf Guard and those loyal to them, whereas the rest of the city was living mostly in poverty. There were a few areas that seemed to be a little better off than others, but these were clearly the specialists who were selling a skilled labor of some kind such as ceramic pottery, specialty tailored clothes, and the likes. They were few and far between, however, which meant that the wealth was too.

Soon they came to a point in the road that was being blocked by what looked like a merchant and his mule pulling a cart of goods. The mule was stubbornly sitting in the middle of the road, blocking the way with his cart, while the merchant was screaming at the animal apparently trying to get it to move out of the way.

When the Wolf Guard approached, the man's eyes grew wide with fear and he tried to shove the un-budging mule off the road, but much to his discomfort, the mule refused to move.

"What's the hold up? Get that animal off the street!" yelled Bloodvayne, annoyed that his trip was already being delayed so soon after their departure.

Suddenly, dozens of men and women came rushing from the buildings from all directions, some from the tops of the structures, some from within, and some from the surrounding allies. As they rushed inward, the back of the covered wagon was flung away, revealing even more armed men as they quickly jumped from the back of the cart and into the fray.

They all carried weapons of some kind, swords, axes, pitchforks, hammers, and they were screaming loudly as they charged towards the procession of Wolves, immediately attacking them and the Guild members with extreme ferocity.

The Wolf Guard, surprised by the sudden attack, lost a few soldiers from the initial onslaught, but quickly regrouped and began fighting back against the attackers in a coordinated fashion.

Distracted by the sudden ambush, David's two guards forgot their guard duty and took up their weapons, jumping into the action.

David tried to run, but his chains were securely fastened to the back of a cart that was filled with supplies for the trip north.

He pulled with all of his might, but the chains wouldn't budge.

Suddenly, two of the warriors came rushing towards David with their weapons raised.

David threw up his hands to prepare for the attack, only to hear a loud metallic ring and the sound of the chains dropping to the ground. He could feel the weight of the chains drop from the bands around his arms.

He opened his eyes and saw the two warriors standing before him, urging him to follow them before rushing into the alleyway and away from the skirmish. David, startled but recognizing a chance when he has one, saw that his chains had been cut and bolted after the two men.

He ran with all of his might, eager more than ever to get away from the scene of the fighting and, more importantly, Bloodvayne.

He cut corners after the two men who were still rushing through the narrow corridors between the rundown shacks. They clearly knew where they were going and weren't wasting any time getting there.

Exhausted, he pushed on, afraid of losing sight of the two men until finally they disappeared down an alley to his right just before what seemed to be a dead end.

When he turned into the alley, the men were there waiting for him. One of them grabbed David while the other pulled a cloth bag over his head. He tried to resist, but in the struggle, he fell and hit his head against something hard before everything went black.

Chapter XXVI

Erin and Tyrius had been riding through the wilderness nearly nonstop since they had left the outskirts of the Forest of Immortals, stopping only when necessary to rest the horses to prevent them from becoming too exhausted and keeling over, and to take short rests for themselves so they could continue on their search for David.

It had been a long journey, but they finally reached the crest of one of the hills just outside the great desert city of Brineport. They could see the sprawling port in the distance with dozens of white sails moving up and down the river, and the winding dusty road leading up to the main entrance of the city.

The city was built mostly of sandstone and clay bricks, being located in the hot, dry climate of the Southern Lowlands. The only reprieve from the constant heat was the long winding river that snaked down the Draconian Mountains from the north and into the South Sea a few hundred miles to the south. It gave the city a cooler feel than the surrounding areas and allowed a wide swath of vegetation along its banks that wouldn't grow anywhere else in the region.

The river, apart from the obvious relief from the sun, was also the city's lifeline to the abundant natural resources of the sea – fish, crab, shrimp, and of course, sea salt. It was once the most trafficked trade route of the Southern Kingdom, having a direct route from Brineport to Ashmire and the Southern Tunnel that led through the mountains to the Northern Kingdom.

Erin and Tyrius shared a quick look of determination before urging their steeds onward. They galloped for a little over an hour, heading down the hills and through the flatlands before reaching the outer slums of the city.

The sun was high in the sky by the time they reached the first of the buildings, and the heatwaves could be seen rising from the scorched ground like ripples through the air. They quickly found an inn where they could tie off their horses and get them some water at a trough, while cooling off and getting some refreshments of their own at the bar inside.

As they entered the dusty tavern and their eyes adjusted, they quickly found a couple small stools near the bar and took a seat, ordering a set of light-colored ales from the bartender as they did so.

He gave them a quick look down before shaking his head and passing them a pint each and walking to the other end of the bar to converse with some of the locals. The ales were refreshing, with a hint of zesty fruit that neither Tyrius nor Erin had tasted before.

"I don't like the looks of this place," said Erin, eyeballing the crowd around them who seemed to be glancing their way frequently and whispering under their breath.

"Me neither, but that heat is just unbearable, and the horses needed a rest as much as we did." replied Tyrius, wiping the sweat off his forehead with his sleeve.

"Where do you think they're holding David?" asked Erin, "It's been several days since he was taken from us. I fear we don't have much time to waste." she said, worry in her voice as she glanced nervously around the room for any signs of trouble.

"I know, child, I know. I fear for him too, but trust in the Creator God. His blessing is on our side, we *will* find David." replied Tyrius determinedly.

"Yeah..." replied Erin, looking down at her mug not as convinced, "Do you really think so?" she asked, glancing up at her mentor and friend.

"I do, child. Now, finish your drink and let's get back to our search. Something tells me we are headed in the right direction." said Tyrius.

When they finished their drinks and left payment for the bartender, they exited the building and returned to their horses. A woman was standing by Erin's horse, whispering softy to the animal, and tenderly brushing its long white mane with her fingers.

When she saw the two of them approach, she smiled kindly and asked where they had found such beautiful animals.

"They were gifts to us, and only borrowed" replied Erin, smiling in turn.

"I see..." said the woman, "Where are you heading? Do you have shelter for the night?" she asked.

Erin and Tyrius exchanged looks before Tyrius answered her, "We are just passing through, looking for a friend of ours who may have come this way. Have you seen a boy, roughly her age?" asked Tyrius, gesturing towards Erin. "He would have had a brown tunic on, with dark brown shaggy hair and fair skin that had the cares of a traveler worn from a long journey."

"Hmm...you know, I think I may have seen him. He came through here just this morning. Would you like me to bring you to him?" asked the lady eagerly.

Erin and Tyrius eagerly agreed, feeling fortune had finally come their way but remaining skeptical in case it was some kind of trap. One could never be too careful in the city, Tyrius knew that much.

They followed the woman through the dusty streets of the city for several minutes before they reached the part of town that was clearly where the poor took up residence. The buildings were poorly built, made up of a variety of materials that were probably just found lying around. They looked as if a strong gust of wind would knock them down, some even leaning dangerously far, but somehow still stood tall.

Two men suddenly came out from behind one of the side alleys and stopped the woman in her tracks.

"Missy, Missy...up to no good today, are you?" asked one of the men.

"I don't know what you mean." she replied, smiling, and glancing nervously back at Tyrius and Erin who were both now on edge.

"You know exactly what we mean. Now get out of our territory before we send you back home with a reminder of what happens to traitors such as yourself" threatened the man.

Missy grunted in disgust and spit at his feet before she turned and quickly ran past Tyrius and Erin headed back the way they came.

The man shook his head as if he were disappointed before addressing Tyrius and Erin.

"Sorry about that. Missy's one of the folks who's loyal to the Guild. She lures unsuspecting travelers such as yourself into a secluded area where members of the Guild are waiting to ambush them and throw in prison. But not until they get what they can from them. You're lucky we saw her when we did." he said.

Tyrius and Erin looked at the man skeptically, they didn't know what to believe at this point. For all they knew, he could be one of the Guild himself, and this could all be a part of their tricks.

"The name's Kal, and this here is Ty. We're part of the resistance." he said, holding out his hand for Tyrius and Erin to shake.

They each shared a look of caution before taking his hand in turns and asking him if either of them had seen a boy matching David's description come through these parts recently.

As soon as they described David, both men shared an equal look of understanding before getting really excited.

"You two must be the friends he's been talking about!" said Ty, nodding his head enthusiastically.

"Come on, we'll lead you to him! He's not far from here, actually." agreed Kal.

The two men led them through a series of interconnected alleys before they came to a section that crisscrossed through the center of the makeshift slums, before stopping as they reached a plain looking building made of sandstone with a red clay roof and a wooden door. The door was composed of several wooden planks that had been nailed together to make a panel, and it was placed unevenly on its hinges.

Ty knocked on the door three times, then opened the door and walked in, urging them to follow.

When they entered the small building and their eyes adjusted to the dimmer light, Erin's heart almost leapt with joy.

There in the corner of the room, seated at a small table, was David.

He hadn't seen her yet, as his head was resting on the top of the table with a wet cloth over his neck.

She couldn't hold in her excitement and rushed over to the table, only for the men around the table to quickly jump up with their weapons drawn, pointing towards Erin in a threatening gesture.

"Easy does it!" said one of the men towards the front.

With the commotion of the men jumping up and the swords being drawn, David lifted his head to see what had suddenly caused all the excitement.

When his eyes found Erin he nearly jumped from the bench and knocked over the table, startling the men around him.

He quickly urged them to put down their swords and ran over to Erin, embracing her in an enormous hug, lifting her off the ground and spinning her in a circle.

When he finally put her down and let her go, he held her at arm's length to make sure it was really her, then pulled her in for a passionate kiss.

Finally, Tyrius had to gently remind David of his manners, loudly clearing his throat in the process, to which David pulled back from Erin, smiling sheepishly.

"Sorry, Tyrius." he said, ears beet red. "I'm just so happy to see you both!"

"No need to apologize, David. I'm just as happy as you are!" said Tyrius, smiling. "How did you get away from Jakob?" he asked as they picked up the fallen table and sat down, two of the men giving up their seats for Erin and Tyrius to sit.

"These men rescued me." said David, looking around the room at the men seated beside him. "When I was thrown in prison, after I had been taken here by Jakob Zander, I met a man named Riyan who was also being held prisoner there. He found out who I was and that I possessed the Orb of Power, and that night while I slept he told his crew through the bars of his prison window of the Wolf Guard's plan to lead me out of the city the next morning. They set up an ambush and the next morning when I was being led through the slums, they rushed us from all sides. It was enough to provide a distraction long enough to free me from my chains and lead me away from the fight.

"When I caught up to the men who led me away, they tried to cover my face so they could take me to their headquarters and question me without revealing the location of their headquarters, to make sure I was indeed who Riyan said I was, but I fought back not knowing what was going on. In the struggle, I knocked my head against the wall and when I woke up, I was here!" he said, holding up his arms.

"Thank you all, truly. You've done an incredible service to us all!" said Tyrius, looking around the room at the men and women who were now standing throughout the small building.

They were a rough looking bunch of people, but they seemed to be good natured and honest.

"They need our help, Erin." said David as the room finally quieted down. "They've been oppressed by the Southern Wolf Guard and the local Guild for a long time. That's why they helped me escape – they think I can make a difference in their fight for freedom. That I can be a beacon of hope that will inspire the locals to rebel." said David, the men and women in the room all nodding in agreement.

Seeing the look on Erin and Tyrius' face as David revealed the news, Kal spoke up.

"We heard about his powers, how they are being blocked. We don't need him to fight, we just need him to be seen, so the people can see that he is on our side and he is here to help them claim their victory. The legend of the bearer of the Orb is one that our people have been told for generations. If the people knew we had David on our side, we think that is all they will need to become inspired enough to fight back against the Guild and Wolf Guard and bring us victory. If even just half of the population fought back, the Wolf Guard and Guild would be outnumbered by far." he said.

Tyrius looked at David and the others before responding, "David, I understand you want to help these people, but we have a greater mission than this that is at stake. We have to get you to the Crystal Caverns to awaken your powers so you can stop the Defiant One. We can't afford to put that on hold, no matter what the circumstance. We've already been delayed long enough as it is. You know this..." he said, sadly.

"Look, I understand that...I do. But these people need me, and right now, I am in a position to help them. I can't turn my back on them now, not after all they've risked to free me." said David, his jaw set and a look of determination in his eyes.

"Please..." he added, grabbing Erin's hands in his own.

Erin looked over at Tyrius and shrugged, smiling.

Tyrius let out a long sigh and after a moment of silence and much internal debating, finally caved in and agreed to help in whatever way they could.

If they were going to inspire a rebellion without sacrificing too much time from David's main quest, they would need to get started immediately and had no time to spare.

They spent the rest of the day plotting out their course of action.

They determined that in order to get the message around they would need to send out small groups of rebels to infiltrate the population and spread the word quietly that the warrior from legend had come to free them from their oppression. In addition, David would reveal himself to small, isolated groups of the strongest believers. His appearance would reinforce the rumors going around town that the bearer of the Orb had in fact arrived to lead them out of bondage, and the news would spread throughout the city like wildfire.

It was important that they remain careful with who they reveal the information to, as it would be unwise to try to solicit those who were loyal to the Guild or the Wolf Guard – as some, hard to believe as it was, were happy with the way things were being run.

For some, the reduced crime due to the fear of retribution was enough to keep them content. For others, it was the increased business they earned from being located close to the headquarters in the central part of the city where most of the wealthy people took up residence to have their voices heard by the Guild and the Wolf Guard as well as to remain under their protection.

If any of these people were to find out about their plot, and the knowledge that they had David still hidden within the city, they would certainly go running to the Wolf Guard and Guild in order to betray their cause in hopes for a sizeable reward.

Once they decided what they needed to do to spread the word to as many people as they could without risking being exposed, they started to plan their uprising.

"How long do you think you will need to gather enough people to make a large enough force?" asked Tyrius, ever conscious of their main task and how it was being delayed.

"It should only take a day or two max. Word spreads quickly in the slums, we are all living so closely and have a very interconnected network used for spreading information – mostly for keeping everyone informed of important events happening in the city that may affect us, or when there is a group of Guild members or Wolf Guard headed our way causing trouble – that way we can always stay ahead of their moves." replied one of the leaders named Natan.

Like most of the men and women in Brineport, he was dark skinned, with bright eyes and short, jet black hair. He was roughly middle aged and thin, but healthy, his muscles cut like chiseled rock from a lifetime of manual labor on the docks moving supplies to and from the fishermen to the storehouses for salting.

People in Natan's status were never allowed on the boats – they were only for the wealthy. They were the ones who owned and manned the ships, taking them out to sea for long expeditions and bringing back their catch of thousands of fish and, sometimes, whale.

It was a lucrative business, as it supplied the majority of the meat to the city, and those who controlled the food supply, controlled the wealth. The first of the selections would always go to the

Wolf Guard, then to the Guild members, before reaching the owners and their friends and families. Finally, the last of the scraps, and always the worst quality, went to the slums.

Like most of the population, Natan had been born and raised in the slums and lost his parents in a similar uprising when he was young, forcing him to live off the streets and depend on the care and help of the community around him to survive.

They all worked together like one large family, always helping one another as needed, never having much but always willing to share with those in need. It was a simple life, but hard, not just on the body, but also on the spirit. It was common for men and women to be taken away on a whim, without any cause or reason, by the Wolf Guard – most never being seen or heard from again.

This is what led Natan to begin recruiting the other rebels and begin their resistance. For their people, their children, and for their future to be free of such uncertainty.

"Once we have word that the people are with us, we will spread the word for everyone to prepare to gather in the three main marketplaces, the North Sector, the Eastern Sector, and the Western Sector by the fish market. That will have the central headquarters surrounded when we begin our strike." said Natan, pointing to a small makeshift map he had drawn in the sandy floor.

"Do your people have enough weapons to support this kind of rebellion?" asked Tyrius, concerned of the prospect of arming thousands of people living in poverty with weapons effective enough to take on a militarized Wolf Guard and Guild consisting of trained warriors and seasoned fighters.

"We will have them covered, yes." said Natan, "We have many tools we use throughout the city – fishhooks, harpoons, shovels, axes, hammers, and some swords we have managed to pick off over the years." he said, smiling.

Tyrius, Erin, and David shared equal looks of concern. Fishhooks and harpoons were effective tools for their trade, but to use them against the Wolf Guard who had those long, curved blades that would easily cut through the wooden handles of such tools, that was a different story, not to mention the short swords used by the Guild.

"Pardon my concern, but fishhooks and harpoons and shovels are not weapons, they are tools. The Wolf Guard and Guild members have real blades that are designed for war. These are poor substitutes..." said Tyrius, concern in his voice.

"I saw the people fight in the streets when they ambushed the Wolf Guard. These people are brave and determined. Even with such inferior weapons, they will pose a formidable threat to the establishment." replied David, nodding towards the others in the room, who all stood up straighter as they heard his praises.

They clearly all admired David and took his words to heart, something David knew he would have to use to his advantage if needing to rally the people behind him.

"Their sheer numbers and determination will be their greatest weapon. The most important thing will be making sure they don't lose their resolve once they get into the action and start to see their friends and family fall beside them in battle. Morale will be the key deciding factor if we are going to come out of this on top" said Erin, chiming in.

"Have any of your people been in combat, Natan?" she asked.

"Yes, many. Many have had to live in constant threat of the Wolf Guard and the Guild, many times having to fight their way out of dangerous situations before running away. These are the ones who come to us for protection. Once you run away from the Wolves or the Guild, you can never show your face again or they will take you. Those who survive are lucky, many do not survive, and many more still are taken away." he said, clenching his teeth in anger.

"Our numbers have grown recently. People are angry, and people are fighting back more and more, knowing that to give up is to die. The people know that when the Wolf Guard or the Guild take you away, you are a dead man. This has caused many to stand up and fight, instead of giving up easily. Now our numbers have more than doubled in the past month alone. And with David here, our ranks will grow even faster." he said, looking to David with admiration.

David was not used to this kind of attention, but he sympathized for Natan and the others and wanted more than anything to help them achieve their goals.

After hearing David's account of the ambush, and seeing Natan's determination, Tyrius seemed to relax a bit on his stance and instead focused on the task at hand.

"So, once we get the numbers and everyone is in position, how will you start the attack? We have to make sure we have the element of surprise, and we can't risk word spreading too quickly of the rebellion or the enemy will have time to mobilize and respond in a coordinated attack." said Tyrius.

"Yes, this we have thought of too." said Natan. "We wait until the market hour, where the Guild and Wolf Guard send many of their soldiers to the markets to see that they get their first picks. When they are looking over the shipments, we catch fires around the market, closing them off and keeping their soldiers blocked off from the rest of the city.

"This is when we rush all three groups toward the central headquarters and take them by force. If we take the central building and take out their leaders before the main forces return from the markets, we can free Riyan and the others."

David suddenly chimed in with an idea, "The central barracks, the pyramid shaped structure. That's where I was being held and it had a heavy presence within its walls. I bet you that's where they are storing their weapons stash too! If we can take that, we can get their weapons from within, giving us a greater chance to take the rest of the city." he said, to which everyone nodded eagerly.

"If we do this, the rest of the people will see we have won and will fight back, but if we don't show them our strength by taking the main building, they will not join us. I know this – it was where my parents failed before. They had gotten to the steps of the main fortress, only to fail in taking out the leader of the Wolf Guard. The rebellion died soon after, and the members were all beheaded in a public execution for all to see what punishment awaits those who resist." said Natan.

"Their leader's name is Bloodvayne," said David, "he's much bigger than the Wolves we came across in Eldergate and the Great Plains. That's who was going to take me to Eldergate, and he would have, had I not been rescued. I think we will also need to make sure Jakob Zander is taken out too – he is the leader of the Guild. So long as he lives, your people will not be victorious."

"This is true, we must eliminate both leaders to cause the most confusion to the enemy. But their building is not in the central pyramid with the Wolves. They are further east. They take shelter in a compound made of large timbers. It surrounds their main building like a great wall." replied Natan.

He looked over to a woman who was standing off to the side and waved his hand for her to come over.

She was tall and skinny with long black hair that flowed down the length of her back. She wore shabby clothes like most of the others consisting of plain trousers and a light, flowing robe that covered her head and was customary for the women in the area to wear, as it allowed the air to flow through the fabric and cool the skin while protecting them from the intense sun.

"This is Anita, she will show you the compound so you can see what we are facing with Jakob. Maybe you can find a way for us to get through their gates?" said Natan. "So far, no one has ever tried."

"Yes, that would be great" said Erin, smiling and nodding to Anita.

David chimed in "I'll come along too!" He was eager to spend some more time with Erin and catch up after being away for the past several days.

"You two go ahead, I will stay here and continue going over the plans with Natan and the others. We must make sure we are truly prepared for everything, there's too much at stake if we fail." replied Tyrius.

"Alright, see you in a bit then" said Erin, hugging Tyrius and waving goodbye to Natan.

Anita led Erin and David through the maze of narrow corridors between the buildings until they reached the main road.

The sun was on its last stretch of sky heading towards the horizon in the West, casting longer shadows and signaling that the end of day was growing nearer.

With the air beginning to cool off from the scorching heat of the day, more and more people were beginning to gather in the streets to enjoy the reprieve and get their work done while socializing with their neighbors.

The endless chatter of people busy at work echoed around them as they made their way through the crowded, dusty streets.

They passed several noisy vendors that were yelling at them as they passed, trying to get them to come take a look at their goods. Some were selling various spiky fruit and vegetables, and some were selling different types of outfits and face coverings for the dusty storms that plagued the region. It was a very chaotic market.

Children ran throughout the streets laughing and playing, while others sat on the sides holding out their hands, hoping for a gesture of kindness from the passerby's in the form of food or coin.

David even caught a few of the children trying to reach their hand into his pockets. He quickly shooed them away, telling them he had nothing to give them, at which they quickly scattered off, fearful of a rebuke.

Eventually they reached an area where the buildings stopped looking so ragged and frail and instead were much better built. There were hundreds of sandstone brick or adobe structures that Anita said had been standing for many years and would be still for many years to come. Buildings that lasted more than a couple of years were apparently a luxury that most of the population couldn't afford – including Anita and her family.

Anita explained that they were now in the wealthier middle district that formed a ring that separated the poor outer slums from the rich inner circle.

She said the city was much like a circle, with the outer edges being the poorest, and the inner most section being the wealthiest where the pyramid of the Wolf Guard stood along with the Guild's compound which they would soon be reaching.

The three major markets that they would be setting blaze to in the coming days each existed in these middle-income sectors, as they were within reach of the wealthiest members of society but didn't impede on the wealthy class' privacy and grandeur. This strategic position still gave access to the poor and middle classes, whose money really fueled the economy as the majority of the population fell within these classes.

Finally, Anita brought them to a place where there were large, sandstone walls with great arched openings being guarded by members of the Guild.

"This is one of the gates separating the wealthy inner district of the city from the rest of us. It is guarded at all times by two Guild members at each entrance. They rotate shifts twice a day and twice throughout the night, so they are always fresh and alert. When the uprising begins, we will need to take out these guards quickly so they don't ring the bells at the top of the gates and alert the rest of the city." she said, pointing to the large bronze bell positioned at the top of the arched opening in the gate.

It was connected to two long ropes that were rung through rings along the wall and hung just behind each of the guards. They were well within reach so it would be easy for them to sound the alarm in the event of any trouble.

"If you look through the archway, you will see the Guild's compound. It is that large wooden building there, just beyond the street." she said.

Erin and David looked to where she was pointing and could see the structure she was referring to. It was a great, walled structure surrounded by wooden fencing that rose nearly eight feet tall. They could see a wooden gate that was currently open but had the ability to quickly shut in the event of an attack.

They silently noted the number of guards before the entrance and began formulating plans on how they could get through the front gate and to the structure before any alarms went off, causing the gate to be securely shut.

"Anita, are there any basements in the city?" Erin asked, "Particularly near the Guild's compound?"

Anita thought for a moment to herself before answering, "We know of a merchant who sympathizes with our cause. She owns a small shop a couple of streets down that specializes in perfumes. She keeps her stores in a cellar to keep the flowers and other ingredients cool, so they don't spoil."

"Do you think she would be willing to help us?" asked Erin.

"How would she help us?" asked Anita, "She isn't a fighter."

"I don't mean to fight with us, but if she could give us access to her cellar, we could easily burrow through this soft rock in a matter of a day or so. If we planned it right, we could tunnel under the wall and beneath the compound. Then, when the uprising begins, we can break through the floor and take them out from within." she said, looking at David for confirmation.

He thought for a moment, considering Erin's idea. "That could actually work." he said, finally. "What do you think Anita?" he asked.

"I think that we should go see her and find out." she said bluntly.

She led them back down the street and a couple minutes later they were entering a small building roughly the size of a two-bedroom house. As they looked around while Anita spoke to the owner, David realized the back of the shop was actually shared by the wall separating the two districts, meaning as soon as they tunneled just a few feet into the wall, they would already be into the inner district and would only need to tunnel roughly fifty feet or so before they reached the compound. It was a perfect location for Erin's plan.

The walls on the main floor were lined with shelves filled with hundreds of little vials of glass, each containing a variety of different colored liquids that when opened released a pleasant aroma.

Erin was walking down the aisles, smelling each of the bottles before finally deciding on one she liked. She put a dash of the liquid on her neck and wrists.

When David walked past her, her scent was intoxicating and made him wish they were in a more private location, but he knew that was a far-off fantasy and they probably wouldn't have a chance for such intimacies until the Defiant One was defeated – if ever.

Instead, he just sighed and shrugged off the thoughts, replacing them with the more pressing concern of the rebellion and, ultimately, heading back north to the Crystal Caverns and stopping the Defiant One.

Eventually, Anita returned with an elderly woman with gray, frizzy hair wrapped up in a tight bun and a nice looking, flowing dress that stopped mid-calf. Despite her old age and countless lines etched in the corner of her eyes and around her mouth from years of smiling, her skin was still otherwise smooth and flawless, and her eyes twinkled brightly.

"David, Erin, this is Francesca, but we all call her Frannie. She's agreed to help us. We can start digging tonight" said Anita, smiling.

Chapter XXVII

When David and Erin finally got back to the rebel headquarters, the sun was almost completely set, and the warm air was beginning to rapidly cool. The streets were all lined with torches protruded out from the walls of the buildings, giving a nice warmth to the encroaching night.

Tyrius and Natan were sitting at the table with Ty and Kal, eating a small meal of bread and chunky soup filled with local vegetables while going over the final plans for the operations when David and Erin walked through the door.

"How did it go? Did you find a way into the Guild compound?" asked Tyrius, getting up from the table to greet his friends.

"Yes, we think so." said Erin.

She explained to Tyrius, Natan, and the others around the room of their idea to tunnel from Fannie's cellar into the ground beneath the compound, giving them a way to quickly enter the Guild after the fighting begins without the risk of being shut out at the gates.

"If we can get in there quickly and surprise them, that would give us an even bigger advantage. They would never expect us to come from beneath the ground like that!" said Natan, excitement beaming on his face.

"Exactly what we were thinking." said David, "The chances of us being able to get through the main gate into the inner district *and* through the Guild's gate are pretty slim. We would have to really move fast, and even then, the odds aren't in our favor."

"Agreed, I think this is our best shot at taking the compound. We will have to dedicate a separate force from the main attack to make this happen. How far is the distance from the shop to the compound?" asked Tyrius.

"Roughly a stone's throw" said Anita, after mentally gauging the distance. "The material of the bedrock is the same grainy stone used throughout the city" she replied. "It gives way easily under a minor amount of force. Pickaxes and chisels will easily cut through it. With a small group of men cutting away and another handful actively clearing the debris, it shouldn't take too long to prepare the tunnel."

"That's great news" said Natan, "Anita, go and gather some of the men and get them started on this at once. We can't afford to delay any further. We must get this tunnel ready for when we are ready to strike."

Anita nodded and quickly exited the room to recruit the force needed for the operation, while David and Erin stayed behind to get a bite to eat and finish catching up with Tyrius and Natan.

After eating, Erin pulled out her pack and grabbed a long object that was wrapped in a blanket and twine.

"David, I forgot to tell you about this earlier, but this is for you." she said, holding out the long, wrapped object for David to take and open.

Seeing the look of confusion on his face, she said "It's a gift, from Gilric Ellisar."

David took the object from her hands and from the size and the feel of it in his hands, he immediately knew what it must be. He quickly unwrapped it, excited to see what lay beneath the thick cloth.

When the hilt of the sword was revealed, he placed his fingers around it and slid the rest of the blade out of the scabbard beneath the blanket.

The sound of steel being drawn rang throughout the room, turning heads of everyone in attendance.

David held up the blade and inspected the intricate carvings in its side, running his fingers along the edge of the ancient ruins.

"It says '*Here lies the sword of legend, forged for the bearer of the orb*'" said David in awe, to which Erin and Tyrius both looked at each other in wonder.

"When did you learn how to read ancient Elvish script?" asked Tyrius, bewildered and double checking the inscription on the side to confirm it was, in fact, in the ancient language.

"I don't know, I just know what it says, somehow." said David, equally in wonder. He was still running his hands over the hilt of the sword, getting familiar with its every curve and detail.

He finally put the sword back in its scabbard and thanked Erin for keeping it safe, making a mental note to remember to thank Gilric if he ever saw him again.

"I've decided that I'm going to fight" said David, looking at Erin and Tyrius.

"I knew that you were going to say that." said Erin, "and that's why I had already decided to fight too." she said, smiling.

"You two are about as troublesome as they come!" said Tyrius, shaking his head and smiling despite himself.

"But I suspected as much. After all, you are the chosen one for a reason, and that reason is to liberate the world from tyranny. That tyranny doesn't have to only be from the Defiant One." he said, his heart brimming with pride at the display of courage from David and Erin.

"So be it, we will fight together. May the Creator God be forever on our side!" he said, to which they all agreed.

They spent the rest of the evening pouring over their plans and the following day traveled throughout the city with Natan and his men, spreading word of the coming operation the following evening, and giving the people small glimpses here and there of David and his orb-hand.

By mid-afternoon of the next day, the day before the planned revolt, they had gathered enough men and women to form three equal groups of two hundred each, and a small infiltrating party of fifty men who agreed to take the tunnel into the Guild compound and strike from within.

All together they had amassed a total of six-hundred and fifty men and women, all prepared to lay down their lives for the chance of freedom.

The rest of the afternoon they spent preparing for the next morning when they would begin their march to the markets and ignite the flame of rebellion.

***

The morning had come faster than David had expected, and the sun was just starting to grow higher in the sky, it's first rays of light peaking over the horizon and spreading its fiery tendrils across the pinkish sky.

The groups were all positioned just outside of each of the three major markets and were waiting for the time to come to begin their strike.

The procession of Wolf Guard and Guild members entered on time, as was expected, to gather for the first shipment of supplies from the docks and make their selections to bring back to the central district for disbursements.

David and the others looked over to Natan, who nodded that the time had come.

In the distance across the market, several of his men grabbed their torches and started setting the market ablaze in the predetermined locations.

Instantaneously flames erupted around the perimeter of the market, sending the inhabitants into a panicked frenzy, and setting the Wolf Guard and Guild members on high alert, who were now scanning the area for the perpetrators and any coming threats.

Seeing that the enemy was now blocked in the market behind the wall of flames, David, Erin, Tyrius, and Natan, along with their band of roughly two-hundred rebels started running through the streets towards the central district.

When they reached the inner-city gate, they plowed through the two guards standing duty before they were able to ring the bells, but somewhere in the distance at one of the other gates, they heard the distinct sound of bells ringing.

David turned to Erin in alarm, "They must have seen the smoke rising from the markets throughout the city and began ringing the bells in alarm!" he screamed as they rushed through the gates.

"It doesn't matter now! We have to press on to the central pyramid!" she yelled back in reply.

They pressed on through the city until they caught sight of the main steps leading up to the entrance of the central Pyramid. Out from the main entrance poured a procession of armed wolves, ready to face the incoming threat.

They turned to David's band of rebels, ready to face them head on, when suddenly behind them one of the other groups came running up, screaming wildly and crashing into their flanks.

With the wolves distracted and caught off guard, David and the others charged into their ranks and the mayhem of battle, quickly cutting away anyone who dared step in their path on their way up the stone staircase and into the main building.

When David, Erin, and Tyrius reached the top, Natan and his rebels following quickly behind, they were confronted by a group of wolves being led by Bloodvayne himself.

They were armed and ready for battle.

David and the others didn't waste any time rushing into the fight while a few of the men broke off from formation and down the corridor that David had told them led to the prison cells.

As the rush of the battle filled David's mind, he suddenly noticed for the first time since Eldergate that his body was reacting faster than he could think. His movements were smooth and collected, his response to every assault was calculated automatically without any thought or worry, as if his body were responding to the threats all on its own.

Emboldened by the sudden awakening of his powers, David pressed on his attack, twirling around a swinging blade and slashing the back of a wolf, sending him howling in pain before he pressed onward through the ranks to get to Bloodvayne.

He had had enough of the Wolf Guard; it was time to end this once and for all.

As Erin watched David gliding effortlessly through the lines of Wolves, she realized his powers must be returning and screamed out in renewed strength as she rushed into a flurry of attacks, sending her opponent reeling on his hind legs despite him being twice her size.

He tried to recover, but she was too quick and nimble, easily maneuvering around his heavy blows, and finally, after rolling under his legs, she plunged her sword into his back before he fell to the ground defeated.

Quickly moving on to her next opponent, she fell into a trance-like battle rhythm, weaving in and out between swings from her opponents, ducking and dodging and spinning around like a dancer, hacking, and slashing in a mindless frenzy.

Wolves fell behind her, one after another, in a bloodbath of ferocious attacks.

Meanwhile, Tyrius was just as busy swinging his staff with strength and precision to knock his opponents backward or to the ground for others to take down with their swords, harpoons, and fishhooks.

In a matter of just a few minutes, the majority of the wolves were either dead or severely wounded, while only a handful of the rebel forces had been taken out.

David, having dispatched the final opponent between him and Bloodvayne with ease, began walking towards the giant beast, prepared to take him on.

Just then, another sizeable force of Wolf Guard came rushing from one of the interior hallways, breaking the fight into renewed frenzy. The rebel forces charged into the incoming Wolves, keeping them occupied while David and Bloodvayne locked their swords in a powerful show of force.

Another group of rebels came rushing from the hallways to their left with Riyan and a few other men at their side, armed to the teeth and ready for battle. The fighting that ensured was vicious and bloody.

Meanwhile, David and Bloodvayne had locked in combat. The wolf tried using his superior size and strength to his advantage, sending powerful, man-crushing blows at his opponent one after another, but David, being smaller and nimbler, simply dodged and deflected the attacks, causing Bloodvayne to roar in frustration and renewed rage. He rushed at David in a flurry of brutal attacks, causing David to second-guess his sudden confidence of his newly kindled connection to the orb, putting him on the defensive.

He raised his sword time and time again, trying to block the powerful blows aimed at his face, his midsection, his legs, just to barely get his blade up in time to keep from being gutted by the wolf's curved blade.

David didn't know how much longer he could keep up this level of assault, as his arms were growing weak from the constant barrage of attacks. He glanced to his side to see Erin still fighting with the other forces, holding the wolves at bay, but completely unaware of his dire situation.

It seemed he was on his own.

Desperately trying to figure out a way to keep from being killed, David felt deep within for the presence of the orb. He could almost sense its presence, far away, pulsing faintly within a deep recess of his being, ready to be released.

If he could just get to it, he would be able to access his powers and take out Bloodvayne once and for all.

He could see the look in Bloodvayne's eyes as he continued his relentless attack. His confidence was building, and a smirk was growing on the corner of his black, glossy lips, revealing his yellowed fangs and plump, red tongue.

He knew he was winning.

In a last-ditch effort for survival, David gave up on his attempt to reach his powers and lunged out of the way of a deadly thrust, causing Bloodvayne to stumble beneath the weight of his own blow. He had overcompensated, anticipating a resistance that never came.

Seeing his opening, David rolled out of the dive and onto his feet, spinning quickly as he landed on his feet before hurling his blade with both hands and putting all of his weight into the lunge towards the back of the big wolf.

He watched as the blade twirled over and over, blade over hilt, as it soared gracefully through the air.

Bloodvayne, seeing the flash of metal from the corner of his eye as it flew through the air, had little time to react as he tried to turn to avoid the attack. But he was too late.

The tip of the blade pierced into his side, gouging his lungs, and rendering them useless as the edge cut into his flesh and between his ribs.

The beast reared up in pain, howling and clutching at his side, until the cry was abruptly silenced with a loud gurgling as the blood filled his lungs and throat, cutting off the sound.

The great beast fell to the floor, panting heavily as his lifeblood spilled across the floor.

The rest of the rebel forces, having finally dispatched the last of the enemy wolves, quickly ran to David's aid, checking to make sure he was okay before cheering loudly for their victory.

Natan, seeing Bloodvayne lying lifeless on the floor, walked over to him, and cut off his head before carrying it out to the front entrance and holding it high into the air for all to see.

"Your leader is dead! Surrender now or face a similar fate!" he screamed, to which everyone stopped their fighting and turned to see the poor orphan turned rebel holding up the decapitated head of the great leader of the Southern Wolf Guard.

One by one the wolves dropped their weapons and bowed their heads in defeat. The surviving rebel forces bound their hands and round up their weapons before they all lifted their hands into the air and cheered, elated in victory.

Suddenly, the roar of tens of thousands of men, women, and children could be heard echoing through the streets. A large procession of citizens came marching through the streets from all directions, headed towards the central courtyard before the pyramid shaped headquarters. They were holding weapons of all kinds, mostly tools, and were chasing the last remaining forces of men and wolves towards the central district.

When the enemy forces reached the main gates and saw their brethren and leaders were defeated here as well, they stopped running and simply dropped their weapons, allowing the crowd to push them into the center and round up their weapons and bind their hands like the others.

The remaining citizens, seeing the severed head of Bloodvayne held high in the air by one of their own and the remaining forces bound at the steps of the great pyramid, began cheering loudly, raising their weapons in the air, and chanting at the top of their lungs "Victory! Victory!"

David and the others watched as the crowd marched the remaining forces of wolves and Guild members, of which they happily saw Jakob Zander among them, to the edges of the city, forcing them to flee into the wilderness never to return again.

The city was finally free – the people of Brineport would live in fear no more. They were now all makers of their own destiny.

***

That night they held a great feast in celebration of their victory over the enemy.

David, Erin, and Tyrius were held as honored and esteemed guests of the highest regard as stories of their heroic deeds were told in dramatic fashion by a group of men and woman, acting out the events of the past few days accompanied by lively songs and dances for all to partake in.

They laughed and danced through the night, happy to have been able to help the people of Brineport rid themselves of their oppressive overlords.

Later, when David finally had a moment to speak with Tyrius and Erin alone, he told them of his moment in the battle where he felt the orb's power once again.

"That is great news, David!" said Tyrius, patting him on the back heavily. "Do you still feel it now?" he asked eagerly.

"A little...it's nothing like I felt during the battle. It still feels so far away, but when I was fighting, I could tell it was directing me like it used to before. I think something about the fighting was rekindling the connection somehow." replied David.

Tyrius stood for a moment in silence, thinking over the past few weeks before he finally responded, "David, I think I know what may be going on." he said, to which David and Erin both leaned in closer to hear what he had to say.

"When the Defiant One was released, you put a lot of the blame on yourself. You have carried that weight with you, blaming yourself for the destruction and dangers we've been facing since that fateful day." said Tyrius.

David nodded in acknowledgement, he had in fact blamed himself for what happened. Without David's powers, the Defiant One wouldn't be a threat today, as it was his powers that gave General Krauss the surge needed to perform the ritual and break open the seal between their world and the Dark Abyss, setting him and his army of demons free.

"With that guilt, came a lack of confidence in yourself and your own worth. I think that has led to a blockage of sorts in your connection to the source of your powers." he continued.

"That makes sense..." said David, thinking it over, "But then why am I now starting to feel it again?" he asked Tyrius.

"I think it is because you are starting to believe in yourself again," said Tyrius. "These people's faith in you has inspired you enough to make you question the doubt you've been carrying and is giving you a new sense of confidence and purpose that is dissolving that barrier." he said. "I believe, with time, your powers would come back as you push away those feelings of doubt and release the blame you hold on yourself. However..." he said, "We don't have the luxury of allowing you the time needed to do that by yourself." said Tyrius.

"This is why we must get you to the Crystal Caverns as soon as possible. Their restorative and amplifying properties will help speed along this process of healing, giving you the surge needed to reestablish your connection to the orb, and possibly make it even greater than ever before." he finished.

"I know what must be done," said David, "Now that we have accomplished what we set out to do, we can return to our journey north. We will leave at first light."

Both Erin and Tyrius agreed, and seeing the conversation was over, decided to leave their worries for the coming days and instead focus on the festivities of the night.

They spent the rest of the evening learning the local dances and songs, partaking in their excellent zesty ales, and letting the mood of the celebration take them away from the worries of the world, if only just for a few more hours.

Chapter XXVIII

The following morning David, Erin, and Tyrius woke and were beginning to gather their things for the long journey north once again, when Natan and Anita asked them where they were headed so soon.

"We have to continue on with our journey, Natan." replied Tyrius, "It is a long way to the north where we are headed, and we do not have the luxury of time on our side I'm afraid."

"My friends, we would be honored to help you on your journey. Please, let us take you there on one of our great ships. We will take you wherever you please!" he said, grinning and holding out his arms in invitation.

Tyrius and the others exchanged hopeful looks and each nodded in turn, agreeing to accept Natan's gracious offer.

"We would be grateful for such assistance." said Tyrius, accepting his offer, "But, I thought only the wealthy had ships?" asked Tyrius, remembering Natan's explanation the other day of how the shipping industry operated.

"This is true, but that is the old way. We are making a new way now, a way that benefits us all. We will break up the shipping industry and give the ships back to the people. Come, let us gather you some supplies and find you a ship!" he said, leading them to the doorway.

He led them through the city, which now was livelier than ever. Everywhere they looked and went, people were moving about busily throughout the streets with confidence. A smile stretched across everyone's faces, and they were no longer wearing looks of fear or uncertainty regardless of where they were at in the city.

It was a good feeling knowing they played a part in the cause that led to such happiness and joy among the people.

When they reached the docks, there were a series of great fishing ships with massive masts that stretched to the sky. Each ship was being loaded for the coming trips out to the South Sea that would bring back masses of fish and other sea creatures for distribution among the newly freed population. They were all eager to begin their day as free men and women that would all benefit from the day's hard work.

Natan walked up to one of the men who was holding what looked like a supply list, checking off each item as it was being loaded.

It was one of the men who had been fighting with them during the uprising, and he apparently was now in charge of the ship docked before him.

"Hello Robert! Good day to sail, yeah?" asked Natan cheerfully.

When Robert saw who it was addressing him, and that David and the others where there as well, a large grin quickly spread across his face and he walked up to each of them, eagerly shaking each of their hands and thanking them for everything they had done.

He was a middle-aged man with a round face and a big belly from his love of heavy ales. His hair was short and curly, and twice as dark as his skin, peppered with patches of grey here and there. He had a great big smile, and an even bigger personality, as he had owned and operated a vendor in the slums nearly all of his adult life selling anything from fruits and vegetables to pick-pocketed jewelry.

"It is an honor to have you here to see me off on my first fishing expedition!" said Robert in his deep booming voice customary of a market salesman.

"Actually, that is not why we are here," said Natan, "I have a favor to ask of you, Robert." he said to the man.

"Anything, anything for you!" replied Robert eagerly.

"Good to hear it, old friend! I need you to take David, Erin, and Tyrius, along with their horses and whatever supplies they need, along the Eastern Shore beyond the Forest of Immortals. They are headed to the Birthplace of the World." said Natan.

"The Birthplace of the World? Where is this?" asked Robert, a confused look on his face. "I do not know this place on the maps."

"No worry friend," said Tyrius, "I can show you the way. It is north of the Land of the Immortals, just beyond the northern forest beyond a cluster of mountain ranges covered in snow." he said.

With this, Robert smiled again and agreed to take them wherever they like, thanking them again for their help in the rebellion and telling them how much of an honor it is to have them sail with him.

They fetched the two horses that they had borrowed from the elves, a mule to carry their supplies once they set foot back on land, and the rest of the supplies they would need for their journey north along the coast and to the Birthplace of the World.

Within just a few short hours, they had gathered all that they needed and were standing at the bow of the ship as they sailed south. The mists of the great winding river crashed on the bow, sending salty spray high into the air as they cut through the waters at a fast and steady pace.

Less than an hour later they reached the mouth of the river and entered the vast blue expanse of the South Sea, before turning up the coast to head north as Tyrius had instructed. Water stretched as far as the eye could see, with white caps slowly gliding across the surface of the waves as the wind rustled over the top of the water.

David and Erin both looked in wonder at the sight before them – neither of them had seen the ocean before and it left them both in awe.

The front of the ship rocked up and down as they crashed over the waves, sending a rush of exhilaration through the two of them, making them feel like kids once again. David wrapped Erin up into his arms, holding her tight as they closed their eyes, letting the gentle sea breeze rush through their hair while holding on to the side of the deck to make sure they didn't fall from the constant rocking.

The sound of the rushing wind and the crying gulls reverberated through the salty air as they charted their course along the rocky coastline.

With the sun to their right, rising ever higher into the sky as it made its journey across the vast expanse of cloud-dotted blue, David and Erin basked in the moment, happy to be together once again.

***

After what felt an eternity of traveling through darkness and wet, damp tunnels, Rex and the others finally saw the light at the end of the Southern Tunnel, indicating that their journey through the dark mountain was finally coming to an end.

When they crossed the threshold into the open air, the sun was high in the sky. By the time they gathered up the rest of their caravan and supplies and made it down the mountain path to Ashmire the sun had nearly set in the west.

When they reached the outskirts of the mountain village, some of the men were greeted by loved ones who had seen them coming from the entrance of the tunnel and had been eagerly awaiting their arrival.

Others, who had been waiting beside them and were expecting to see their husbands, fathers, brothers, and sons come down the path, were left in sobbing wrecks, having discovered that they would not be coming, as they had fallen in the battle.

When they had all set up camp around the city, as the Inn and other homes were already too full from the refugees much to the dismay of the old innkeeper and some of the villagers who still held grudges against the Northerners, they sat around late into the night telling tales of the heroic men who had given their lives defending the valley of Ravenfell and catching up with the rest of the citizens who had fled south over a week prior.

Songs were sung of their fallen brethren's courage and valor while minstrels played upbeat tunes to match the battle scenes, and somber songs to set the mood of the story when the heroes would fall.

It was a night of mixed emotions – joy for those who made it out alive and were reunited with their loved ones, and sorrow for those who were left with emptiness in their hearts and lives, having lost friends and family in the great battle against the demon horde.

When the festivities were over, they each got some rest, knowing the next day would bring more tiresome travel as they made their way down the mountain road to Brineport in search of David and the others.

The next morning, they woke early and packed up their belongings before heading south down the foothills of the mountain on their long march toward the city of Brineport.

When they finally reached the city, it was already late into the afternoon the following day. They were greeted by the newly freed citizens of Brineport, all happy to see the new arrivals and eager to sell them their wares. When the citizens discovered they were from the Northern Kingdom and were friends of David, Tyrius, and Erin, they were heralded as heroes and given a great welcoming and provided a whole section of the city where they could take up residence for as long as they pleased.

Rex and the others, including King Eldergate, General Ryan, and General Owen, as well as King Tybrin Hammerclaw and Gilric Ellisar, were all caught up on the recent events that night during the feast by none other than Natan himself. He told them how David and the others helped inspire a rebellion, freeing the city from decades of harsh rule by Bloodvayne, the Southern Wolf Guard, Jakob Zander, and his Guild of misfits.

When Rex and the others learned of David, Erin, and Tyrius' departure the morning prior to their arrival, they were faced with the hard choice of going after them to assist in whatever way they could or staying behind to regroup their forces and plan for whatever the Defiant One might send their way.

After much debate, Rex and King Eldergate determined it was best for them to let David and the others go off on their own, and instead, focus on rebuilding their homes in Brineport in order to prepare for the coming battle that would inevitably come their way.

Prince Gilric Ellisar of the Woodland Elves and King Tybrin of the Dwarves both decided to part ways with the humans for the time being in order to head back home and prepare their own kingdoms for war. They each promised to gather once again in the coming days for their final march against the demon army and their Mystical ruler once David and the others had returned from the caverns.

The Elves and Dwarves, saying their goodbyes, headed north the following morning to their respective kingdoms. Rex and the others watched them slowly disappear beyond the rolling foothills of the mountains before returning to the care of their people.

The time would come where they would fight together again, they knew, and much sooner than any of them would have liked. They only hoped that when that day came, David would be by their side with his renewed power, prepared to take on the Defiant One and send him back to the depths from whence he came.

Chapter XXIX

It only took them three days to reach the northern shores beyond the Land of the Immortals. Taking the route by sea rather than land proved to be a real timesaver, cutting their journey of what would have been over a week into less than half of that time.

They pulled up as close as they could to the land without running the ship ashore, and Robert lowered them down in a small boat for David and the others to depart in. He lowered a second, larger boat for their horses and a couple of mules to carry their supplies along the rest of their journey into the mountains and beyond.

The sun was nearly halfway along its journey across the sky when they reached the shore. They waved goodbye as the sailors rowed their boats back to the main vessel, and then David, Tyrius, and Erin started off toward the mountains on foot, leading the horses and mules by rope. As they passed the outskirts of the forest to the south, the horses, catching scent of their homeland, broke free from their ropes and darted off towards the woods before disappearing from view into the thick trees beyond.

Erin and Tyrius were sad to see them go but knew that they had fulfilled their purpose and were thankful to have had their support during the long journey to Brineport a week earlier.

They spent the rest of the day hiking across the cold, rocky land leading up to the foothills of the distant, snowcapped mountains.

The winter months were fast approaching, and the wind was whipping past them across the mostly barren plains as they walked, making for a very miserable journey. The frost on the ground this far north was nearly permanent this time of year, causing what little grass there was beneath their feet to crunch with each grueling step.

Pointing to the mountain range in the distance, Tyrius indicated that was their destination, beyond which lay the Birthplace of the World. Tyrius knew that there was a cavern there that was filled with crystals, but he wasn't certain it was the same Cavern from the book. Although he was convinced that it must be, guessing there weren't too many caverns filled with crystal that the Mystics of old would have chosen to lay their brother to rest in, a part of him inside was still uncertain and hoped more than anything they were in fact the same caverns that David had read about in the library back in Ravenfell.

To David, that time spent in Ravenfell, in the safety and warmth of its halls among all of his friends, felt like a lifetime ago. He was eager now more than ever to finish his journey in the north where he hoped to restore his powers. Powers he needed in order to face off against the Defiant One and have a chance at stopping him. He was terrified of the prospect of fighting him, especially knowing he was a divine being made by the Creator God for the sole purpose of death and destruction, but he also knew what needed to be done to keep his friends and this new world safe – a world he had become quite fond of and was ready to experience without the constant threat of danger looming on the horizon.

He hoped, once his mission was complete, for a life with Erin by his side. Nothing made him happier than the thought of a future with her, one free from constant dangers and war, where they could spend their time together as they saw fit. Maybe even get married and have a family of their own. But right now, in that moment, even that prospect seemed far off – almost too far to imagine clearly. For now, David knew his focus must remain on his mission if he were to ever see it through to the other side.

After walking as far as they could bear, they chose to set up camp for the night before the sun had reached the point beyond the mountains when it would cast the land in a blanket of darkness. Once they finished setting up their tents provided to them by Natan, they ate a filling meal before calling it a night. In the south, the tents were used for protection against the sandstorms when traveling. Up here, it would serve to protect the travelers from the constant and bitter wind while they rested.

Despite the cold and the constant howl of the wind, the companions rested easily, knowing that they were in a land safe from any real dangers, as it was protected by the Elves to their south.

When the morning came, they broke camp and started again on their way.

This routine of hiking through the day and camping for the night continued for several days as they made their way across the desolate landscape, through the rolling foothills, and up the rising mountain range of the north.

Finally, they reached a valley between two great mountains with peaks higher than the mountains surrounding Ravenfell. They could see a long, almost imperceptible path that snaked through the valley and up the side and around one of the great mountains. Tyrius indicated that this was the old path that would lead them across the mountain to the other side where it would eventually wind down into the opposite valley and to the stone structure at its center.

They hiked the remainder of the day until they reached a stopping point just at the base of the mountain before the steep climb up and over its ragged side. They set up camp near a small stream fed by melting snow from the peaks of the mountain. It wouldn't be much longer before these mountains were completely covered in snow, as the light, dancing snowflakes that now fell from the skies only to melt shortly after reaching the ground, would eventually be replaced by a torrent of heavy blizzards that would be settling in for the winter.

Tyrius said they were fortunate to be traveling this way when they were, or the pass would almost certainly be impossible to traverse in the coming months.

After getting the fire going and having a warm meal, they each got some sleep, too exhausted to stay up for any meaningful conversation. The following day would contain a rough journey up the side of the mountain and back down to the opposite valley, and each of them were ready to get it over with, knowing it would likely be the hardest part of their journey.

That night David had some strange dreams.

He was walking through a fog so thick he could barely see his hand in front of his face. The ground was smooth and free from obstruction, but he could feel the hard rock beneath his feet, so he knew he was somewhere rocky, or maybe underground in a tunnel.

As he walked, searching for something just out of sight, he heard a voice. It called to him, beckoning him onward into the fog, so he complied, curious to see who it was that was speaking to him.

After some time, David could see a light in the distance penetrating through the thick misty air. It was pulsing slowly like the orb had done long ago when he found it in the temple in the Outer Woods.

When he neared, he could see the shadows of a great circular structure surrounded by pillars of stone that rose high above his head. The light was coming from within the structure, somewhere in the middle.

David walked onward, ever toward the increasing bright light, entranced as it pulsed faster and faster with each step he took.

The voice rang out in his head, *Welcome back, David.*

"Who are you?" said David startled, "Where am I?" he asked the mysterious voice.

You are home, where you belong. Can't you feel it? came the voice.

David did notice a strong sense of belonging deep within, but he couldn't explain it. It was as if he were on the horizon of a profound discovery, one that he had been waiting to find his entire life.

He noticed his heartbeat was increasing and his breath was becoming more labored.

"What do you mean *home?*" asked David, suddenly wondering if he already knew the answer.

Search within your heart David, and you will find the answer you seek. said the voice.

Then suddenly, the fog cleared, and David could see the temple, clear as day. The orb was resting on a pedestal like the one it had rested on in the temple before. Its light exploded in a brilliant display of power, blinding his eyes in pure white light so bright it hurt.

A series of visions began flashing before his eyes, too quickly to discern what they were trying to show him. All he knew was that his chest began to hurt, like his heart was being ripped out and he could hear the sound of Erin's voice screaming to him, calling his name, begging him to come back.

As he focused on Erin's voice, her face suddenly appeared in his mind's eye. She was crying and holding her arms out to him, running towards him as he drifted away. For some reason, he knew he had to leave. He didn't want to, but he *had* to, and it was breaking his heart. Erin fell to her knees, defeated, sobbing heavily into her hands as she faded away in the distance.

Then something grabbed his shoulder and began shaking him fiercely.

"David! David, wake up!" came a distant voice.

David opened his eyes and Erin and Tyrius were kneeling above him. She had her hands on his shoulders, shaking him gently.

"David! Wake up!" she said, a hint of alarm in her voice.

When she saw he had opened his eyes she sighed in relief and plunged herself into his arms.

"Don't do that to me again!" she said, sitting up and looking down at him.

"Do what?" asked David, confused.

"You were screaming, like you were being attacked or something. It looked like you were in pain." said Tyrius, a look of concern etched on his face as well.

David decided to keep his dream to himself, feeling it was better left unsaid. He didn't want to worry Erin any more than he already had, and for some reason, he felt like now was not the time to reveal to her what he had seen. There would be a time for that later.

Instead, he decided to quickly get up and start breaking camp. The other two eventually abandoned their attempts to get more information out of David and followed suit, keeping a cautious eye on him as they worked.

The rest of the day was spent hiking up the mountain and David kept mostly to himself. He couldn't shake the feeling that something was wrong, that he was heading towards something he wasn't going to like. He knew he had to do it, that much was certain, but he also had this deep feeling in the pit of his stomach that what he was going to find at the end of the road was something that he wasn't really prepared for.

They crested the side of the mountain where the path crossed over from one side of the valley to the next sometime around midday. The chilling wind was whipping past them violently at this height, sending shivers down David's spine and Erin's hair flapping wildly like a dark banner. The sky was mostly overcast, as it had been for days now, and the sun was giving off little to no warmth, leaving them in a bitter cold that seemed to sink to the bones.

In the distance they could see the bottom of the path as it wound its way down the mountain and through the flat bowl-shaped valley. In the center of the white expanse of snowy ground, just barely visible in the distance, stood a solid black structure.

They reached the structure just as the sun was beginning to set. Its tall columns sporting sconces with ever-burning flames indicating it was in fact the one Tyrius had been brought to with the Master Elder and the King what seemed like a lifetime ago.

They hastily entered the protection of the structure, eager to escape from the increasingly violent winds that had been picking up as the day drew to an end. It had been causing wisps of snow to swirl around in twirling little whirlwinds as they made their way across the bleak valley floor and made it difficult to keep their cloaks wrapped around their faces, let alone see more than a few feet in front of them.

When they entered the doorway, they saw a stairway descending into the heart of the structure. As they descended, the air began to change from the cool, crisp mountain air to the still warmth of the underground.

David and Erin were fascinated by the ever-burning flames that lined the stairwell, wondering how such things could be burning for so long without any apparent source of fuel. Tyrius told them that those flames had been burning just as brightly when he had walked down these stairs with the Elders and King Eldergate, and that he, too, had been just as entranced as they were.

As they neared the end, David's sense of dread that he had felt throughout the day was growing increasingly more persistent. His stomach began to cramp with anticipation of what was to come – he somehow knew that his time in this world was slowly coming to an end. He didn't know how, but something told him that the powers he came here to find would also bring with them a price that was far beyond anything he had been prepared to pay.

When they descended the final step and entered through the doorway into the space beyond, they stood before a great chasm filled with enormous clusters of crystals across the walls and ceiling the likes of which David and Erin had never seen before. They were illuminated from within, glowing softly and creating a greenish blue aura throughout the vast cavern that allowed them to see far within its depths.

David could feel the power within his mind roaring to life. It was exhilarating and filled him with a sense of strength and vitality that he hadn't felt in a long time. Not since he first awakened the power of the orb on the mountainside while heading back to Eldergate with Rex and Orin at his side. A feeling he had only been able to experience for a day or two, as it had disappeared once the Defiant One had been released.

Suddenly and without warning, David dropped to the ground unconscious like a rag doll. Erin and Tyrius quickly ran to his side, trying to wake him and see what had happened. No matter what they did, he wouldn't wake, it was useless.

Realizing that he must be in a trance induced from the presence of the crystals, Tyrius gently urged Erin to stop trying to wake David.

"It would appear that our assumptions were correct. These must in fact be the same Crystal Caverns used to create the Orb and the Mystic Crystals. They seem to be responding to David's presence, forcing him to face his inner demons by putting him into a deep sleep. Wherever he is, he is lost to us now. Come, help me get him to the temple" said Tyrius to Erin, who looked as if she could cry with worry.

Ever since they had been nearing the structure, and since the other morning when he had awoken from that nightmare, David had been acting more and more unlike himself. He had been distant, keeping to himself mostly, and seemed to be cold to Erin and Tyrius. This worried her greatly – she was worried she was losing him.

They lifted his limp body and carried him slowly down the black stone path spanning across the lake and into the magnificent temple at the heart of the chamber.

They set him on top of the tomb of the fallen Mystic, where he lay motionless and still, the only indication of life was his erratic breathing and racing heartbeat. As he settled into place on the tomb of the Mystic, the orb in his hand began to glow brighter than ever before. It was like a shining beacon in the middle of the dimly lit temple, filling its space with its light as it pulsed slowly between varying levels of intensity.

"His powers are being amplified," said Tyrius, "It must be related to the crystal's effects on the Orb – he's searching for its power, deep within his consciousness. We must let him be. He will work it out and return to us when he is ready."

Tyrius and Erin stayed by David's side for several days as he tossed and turned. They took turns on watch, making sure David was still breathing, giving him water every so often and making sure it went down without issue.

On the third day David's eyes suddenly shot open and he quickly shot upright in a heavy sweat, gasping heavily.

"I know what I have to do" is all he said, then he looked at Erin and wept.

Chapter XXX

Erin held David in her arms as he wept uncontrollably for several minutes. When he finally settled down and was able to speak without being interrupted by gasping sobs, she asked him what had happened.

"I saw the Creator God," said David, eyes distant and glossy as he recalled the visions.

"He showed me the history of the world... the creation of the Mystics, their decision to bring life into the world in the form of the Elves, the Dwarves, every living thing. I saw when the first man and woman were created by the Creator God, how from them spawned the vast history of mankind that we see today, and the jealousy that it brought upon the Defiant One." he said.

Tyrius and Erin exchanged looks before urging David to go on.

"He was once good, you know. He worked with the other Mystics of Creation, he was the balance for life, so it didn't go unchecked and overcrowd the world. His actions were never malevolent and cruel, but simply necessary. But, when the Creator God made mankind, he grew distant and jealous, eventually that turned to anger, then hatred... that's why the war began, he wanted to eradicate all of mankind, erasing them from the earth. He hated them..." said David.

"When the war broke out the Mystics of Creation gathered together, along with the forces of their creations, to help the race of man defeat the Defiant One and his armies. The fighting was unlike anything I could have imagined...his power, it was incredible. They only just managed to subdue him before they were able to banish him into the Dark Abyss. History nearly went the other way." he said, horror across his face as he recalled the visions of the battle between the forces of creation and destruction.

"Yes...the accounts of the Mystic Wars are very descriptive, I've read nearly all of them" said Tyrius, "and their images alone used to haunt me in my dreams."

"After the Defiant One was imprisoned, I saw the Mystics of Creation gather their fallen brother and seal away his life force in the Orb. At first, they were unsure of how to go on without their brother, knowing without him they were not strong enough to contain the Defiant One forever, that eventually he would wear down the barrier and once again break free from his chains.

"That is when they decided to seal away their powers, along with their lifeforce, into the Orb alongside their fallen brother, so that when the one worthy to reclaim their powers finally came, as they foresaw that he would...that I would...that he would then possess the full might of all of the Mystics of

313

Creation and would therefore have the power necessary to face the Defiant One and defeat him, banishing him for good into the Dark Abyss. So long as his powers remained in this world after their brother was banished, the seal would never again be broken."

"That certainly makes sense and corresponds with the history as I've been taught it," said Tyrius, looking at David and Erin in turn, "Did you find it? The source of your power?" asked Tyrius, seeing again how the orb in David's hand continued to glow strong and eager to hear the answer they had both been waiting for. If he didn't, then all of what they had been through over the past couple of weeks was for naught.

"I did..." said David, looking down and away from Erin as he said the words.

"So, what is the problem? Why are you so downtrodden all of a sudden?" asked Tyrius, confused at David's mood since he woke.

"The power...it comes with a price that I'm not sure I'm willing to pay." said David bluntly.

Erin's stomach dropped as she heard the words depart from David's mouth.

"Do you...do you have to sacrifice yourself?" she asked, afraid of the answer.

"No...not exactly." said David, dancing around the truth. "I don't really want to talk about it right now. I need time to process everything. I promise, when the time comes, I will tell you everything." he said, grabbing Erin's hand and squeezing gently, gazing into her eyes. They locked eyes for a few moments before she finally responded, recognizing that he was being sincere and not wanting to press the issue.

"Okay..." said Erin, still concerned for her friend. She loved David fiercely, and at the moment she was terrified for him and for herself. What did he mean when he said *not exactly?* Was he having to sacrifice something else? Her mind was racing with the implications of his final words. They were making her sick to her stomach with worry.

"Fair enough," said Tyrius, thinking over David's words, "So what is our next move, then? The orb, it has certainly sprung back to life it seems. Do you have any of your powers back?" he asked David.

"Yes... I can feel the power, it's definitely there." said David, "I feel it like I did before...before Eldergate" said David.

"That's good!" said Erin, hope slightly restored at the positive news.

"I think it's time we go. We need to get back to the others and prepare for the final march to Eldergate. The Defiant One is amassing an army even greater than the one he had before. He's going to be sending his army towards Draco's pass within the next few days, but it is large and therefore won't be moving very quickly.

"He had received a report from a scout when I was captured saying that I was being taken to him as Bloodvayne's prisoner. Since we never showed up, he now knows something went wrong and is planning on taking the fight to Brineport. We have to make sure we are ready to face him before his army gets that far or we risk losing countless lives of innocent women and children in the fighting. The

Defiant One is ruthless and will use our love for friends and family against us and it won't end pretty." said David, shaking his head as he recalled the countless versions of the future he had been shown.

"When the time comes, I need to face him at Eldergate. It's where the barrier between the world of the living and the Dark Abyss is at its weakest. If I'm ever going to seal him away, it has to be done there. We can't let his army through Draco's Pass – the battle must take place in the plains" said David, standing up with a look of determination on his face.

"How do you know this?" asked Tyrius, alarmed at the news.

"I've seen it." said David.

"Seen what?" asked Tyrius.

"The future." he said. He picked up his pack and started heading out of the temple towards the winding path across the lake.

Tyrius and Erin exchanged mutual looks of confusion before they quickly grabbed their things and followed suit, wondering what in the world had just happened.

David was back, but he was different somehow, and Erin wasn't sure she was ready to face the consequences of what that meant.

***

When David, Erin, and Tyrius finally reached the stretch of land between the Eastern range of the

Draconian Mountains it had already been several days since they had left the Crystal Caverns.

They had been traveling at a constant pace, and thanks to their mules hauling the majority of the supplies and therefore the heaviest burden, they were making incredibly good time all things considering.

There had been little to no conversation from David, so Tyrius and Erin mostly kept their distance and talked quietly amongst themselves, their worry for their friend growing more and more with each passing day.

As they moved further South, they passed the road leading up to Draco's Pass on their right and the Forest of Immortals on their left.

This is where they caught their first glimpse of Gilric Ellisar's forces as they were marching home from Brineport.

When they neared, the army of Elves stopped short and a lone rider began galloping toward them at a fast but steady pace.

"Prince Gilric! Is that you, old friend?" called Tyrius across the way, squinting to try and see the rider more clearly.

The rider approached and atop the great white stallion he could see that it was indeed Prince Gilric of the Woodland Elves.

"Good day, Tyrius!" said the Prince, smiling slightly at the sight of the Elder. He never was keen on showing much emotion.

"David, Erin, good to see you both in good health!" he said, acknowledging the other two with a formal nod of his head.

"Prince Gilric, I have to warn you that the Defiant One has been amassing another army of demons, far greater than the one you have recently faced." said David, jumping straight to the point.

Gilric frowned slightly at the news, "Yes, we suspected as much. That is why we have come to prepare our people for the coming war. We have just come from Brineport where the survivors of Ravenfell have taken refuge and are rebuilding what's left of their lives the best they can. The Dwarves parted from our group just last night and are headed back to Emerald Keep preparing their people as well." said the Prince.

He caught them up on the battle of Draco's Pass and Ravenfell, skipping the heavy details and getting straight to the point. He told them of the show of force from the Defiant One shortly after their victory over General Krauss and his forces, and how it had destroyed what remained of Ravenfell and sent the rest of the survivors with no choice but to fall back through the Southern Tunnel to Brineport where they had hoped to find David, Erin, and Tyrius.

"We had agreed to meet in the coming days, if all went well on your quest to the caverns, as I presume it did since you are standing here before me." said Gilric.

"Yes, it went well enough." said David, dodging the subject from any further scrutiny. "What of Rex, Orin, and the others?" he asked, eager to hear the news of his friend.

"They have started gathering as many men as they can who are fit and willing to fight, while the elderly and the women and children stay behind to rebuild."

said Gilric. "They are a valiant bunch and have suffered greatly, but still they wish to fight on. I admire their courage." he said.

"Will you join us for a feast tonight in the White City?" asked Gilric, "Your friends have agreed already to meet us in the valley with the Dwarves no more than two days from now. I'm sure you could use the rest and we would be honored to host the bearer of the orb and his friends." said Gilric, nodding respectfully.

David knew they would be cutting it close. The enemy would be on the move soon, if not already, and it was of paramount importance they stopped them before they reached the pass through the mountains. Everything he had seen depended on the final battle occurring in the Great Plains around Eldergate if they were to have a chance of surviving the coming battle.

He looked to Tyrius and Erin, who were watching him for confirmation, before agreeing and they joined ranks with Gilric as they made their way through the Forest of Immortals toward the White City.

When David saw the city for the first time, he didn't seem to be impacted as much as Erin had expected. Before the caverns, he would have been amazed at the great ancient tree and its marvelous white bark and golden leaves. Instead, he seemed unaffected by its grandeur as if it were just another place, just as ordinary as the rest.

She tried her best to hide her worry, but no matter what she did, that feeling in her gut continued to grow the more distant David seemed to become.

That night they enjoyed a great feast as wonderful as the last time they had been in the city. The great dining hall was even more packed with elves than the last time. This time, however, they were all trying hard to get a look at David and introduce themselves to the great warrior of legend.

He was polite and humored them all with grace and kindness, but Erin could tell that his mind was off somewhere else, distant from the party around him. He smiled and bowed when he was expected to and partook in various conversation and idle talk with all of the elf lords and ladies, but she knew him well enough to see that the real David, her David, was not at all present.

When the party quieted down enough for her to get a chance to speak with him in private, Erin led David to an outer balcony that was quiet and secluded from the rest of the party.

It was nestled near the outer edge of the canopy of the great white tree and they could see the clear night sky dotted with a million stars shining brightly above.

Hundreds of little fireflies flittered around the branches around them, lighting up the area in a soft glow that was truly spectacular, but David barely seemed to notice.

"What's bothering you, David?" asked Erin softly, concern etched in her face. She gently placed her hand on his hand that had been resting on the railing – he didn't move it, which was promising she thought.

"It's nothing..." said David unconvincingly.

"Is it your visions?" Erin asked, gently prodding him for more information. She took his hands into hers as she faced him, forcing him to look at her. She was looking in his eyes, and he kept diverting them from her gaze, trying to hide his inner feelings.

"David...you can talk to me. After all we've been through, I'm here for you, no matter what." she said, lifting his chin with her finger and forcing him to look in her eyes.

He did, and finally the faintest hint of a smile began to form on the corner of his lips, but then faded almost as quickly.

"I know, it's just..." he started, struggling to find the words to say to her. He knew she was frustrated with his unwillingness to tell her what he was thinking, but he was only trying to protect her.

In truth, David wanted to tell her how much he loved her, how much she had come to mean to him, but he knew that if he were to do so, it would only make things that much worse...that much harder, when the time came. But Erin didn't know any of this, how could she?

She leaned in and quickly pressed her lips against his. At first it seemed as if he was going to resist, but he eventually gave in, returning her kiss passionately in kind.

They stayed locked together for what felt an eternity, until finally their lips parted, and their heads rested together, reveling in the moment.

"David, I love you." said Erin softly.

For a fleeting moment, David hesitated, unsure if he should tell her how he felt, but he quickly gave in deciding it was better for her to know, than for it to remain a mystery forever and risk breaking her heart even more.

"I know...I love you too, Erin. I've known for some time now. You are an amazing woman..." said David, looking into her big blue eyes. He could see the light of the fireflies, reflecting dimly in her pupils. She looked so beautiful, like always. So strong, yet so delicate. His love for her was so fierce it felt like it was burning his insides and would explode if he let it.

He leaned in and kissed her again, slowly, gently, then turned and leaned up against the rails, watching the fireflies as if seeing them for the first time.

"They're beautiful, aren't they?" he asked, watching the little lights blip in and out throughout the canopy.

Erin nestled up next to him as he wrapped his arm around her, pulling her in close. She had her David back again, and she planned on relishing it as long as she could.

They stood there for some time, enjoying each other's company while watching the fireflies and basking in the light of the stars.

Chapter XXXI

O ver the course of the next day, the remaining forces of men, being led by King Reximus Kane of Ravenfell and King Eldergate of the Northern Kingdom, along with a great host of men from the city of Brineport who had agreed to come along and fight by their side, began pouring into the valley between Draco's Pass and the Forest of Immortals.

As the day waned on, the Dwarves began filing out of their tunnels from deep below the surface, marching in long lines down the mountainside before joining in making camp with the rest of the human forces.

By the end of the day their forces filled the entire space between the forest and the mountains, and with what remained of the Elven forces, hosted a combined might of a few hundred-thousand strong.

When David, Erin, and Tyrius saw the masses gathering they decided to go and meet the others to catch up on all that had transpired since they last saw each other.

They walked to the large central tent that had been put up as a command post in which the Kings and Generals gathered to discuss the final plans for the coming battle.

When they entered the flap, they all turned to watch David as if he were some reverent king who had returned from a faraway journey.

He ignored the looks and instead walked right up to the table where Rex and Orin were standing near General Ryan and General Owen who were looking over the battle plans.

They turned and looked up to see David approaching and big smiles stretched across each of their faces, especially Orin's.

"David, my boy! How good to see you again!" he said, wrapping his old, frail arms around David's neck. Despite his frail appearance, the old mage was much stronger than he seemed, and his embrace nearly took the breath from David's lungs.

"And Erin dear, you've been gone for so long!" he said, giving her an equally strong embrace to which she finally escaped, gasping for air.

"Orin, good to see you!" said Erin and David, smiling and rubbing their necks where he had been squeezing.

Shortly after, a set of powerful, muscular arms wrapped the two of them up in a great big bear hug, squeezing the breath out of their lungs once again.

"REX!" they shouted through gasps, "We can't breathe!" they said together.

When he finally put them down, they all started laughing. It was good to be together again, and for the first time since he had left the Crystal Caverns, David felt like his old self again surrounded by his old friends.

324

They broke away from the planning, leaving it to Gilric and the others to continue while they sat down and enjoyed a few drinks and shared tales of their adventures.

Rex gave a very lively reenactment of their battle of Ravenfell, with Orin helping out here and there and paying particularly more attention to his battle with General Krauss. When he finished, he puffed up his chest and said loudly that he was the true hero of the day while Rex just laughed and agreed, remembering how he had indeed saved them from the powerful General's attacks.

David, Erin, and Tyrius caught Rex and Orin up on their adventures through the Southern Kingdom and the Dwarven mines, going over David's capture by Jakob Zander and their roles in the uprising in Brineport before finishing off their story with their journey by boat up the coastline to the Crystal Caverns.

"Ahh, so you've finally reconnected with the orb, just as we had hoped would happen!" said Orin as they finished their story.

"Yeah, you could say that." said David, suddenly remembering why he had been so down lately.

Sensing she was about to lose him again to the dark mood that had been hanging over him, Erin changed the subject to the coming battle, "So, now that we're all together again, what's the plan for stopping the army headed our way?" she asked.

"Yes...David said he saw a vision of the army amassing at Eldergate. It is troubling indeed, but if history is any indication of our strength when we unite as we are now, I have no doubt we can take on this army and come out victorious!" said Orin confidently.

He had also had several drinks by this time and was smiling much more than normal, which was a lot for Orin. Erin suspected he may indeed be slightly drunk.

"I agree," said Rex, equally as optimistic, but unlike Orin, very much in control despite having had several pints already. "The combined might of our forces will be a formidable match for any army, no matter how large. The demons fight ferociously but recklessly, and that is their weakness. They aren't very skilled, and without caution or fear of death, they make mistakes that expose their weaknesses far too often. We used this to our advantage in the battle of Ravenfell, and we will do it again in the coming fight." he said, slamming his mug onto the table, sloshing the foamy liquid over the sides.

"Agh! Another drink wasted!" he said angrily, as he got up to get another.

Erin and David shared a mutual look of amusement before continuing their conversation with Orin.

They talked and laughed long into the evening until they finally decided to turn in for the night, knowing that in the morning they would begin their long march over Draco's Pass and into the Great Plains below towards Eldergate, where they would face off for the final battle. The battle that would ultimately decide the fate of Hurea.

Erin and David walked back to the White City hand in hand and made their way to the hallway before Erin's quarters that the elves had prepared for her the night before.

They stood outside the doorway in silence for a long moment before Erin finally spoke.

"David, I want you to stay with me tonight." she said, looking up at him and searching his eyes.

"I don't know..." he said, worried it would only make things worse and still uncertain of how to tell Erin the full truth of his vision.

"I don't want you to hold anything back from me," she said strongly, "Whatever it is, I can take it. I'm strong enough." she said, tears building up in her eyes.

David tenderly caressed her cheek with his fingers and kissed her gently before wiping away her tears.

"I know you are...and you're right. You deserve to know the truth." he said finally.

He took her hand and led her into her room, sitting beside her on a bench near the window at the back of the room.

After a long moment of trying to sort out his thoughts and carefully choosing his next words, he began revealing the rest of his visions.

"Erin, I'm not of this world" he began.

"I know, you're from your world" she began, but he put his finger up to silence her, indicating he wasn't finished.

"I'm not from that world, either." he said, "In fact, I never was. That world was an illusion, created by my Father to give me a sense of being. An illusion that would give me the necessary humility and, in the end, lack of attachment, to do what was necessary when the time came." He let those last words sink in a bit before continuing with his explanation.

"When I was in my trance, and speaking with the Creator God, He revealed the truth of my origins to me. Erin, I am His son. He created me for the purpose of filling the void left by the other Mystics of Creation. The void that was created when they willingly gave up their lives and their powers to ensure the survival of this world. They too, were His children, and when their brother died at the hands of the Defiant One, it created an imbalance in the world.

"I am the answer to restore that balance. They knew that I would come, because they understood that balance was necessary for life to continue to exist." he said.

Erin searched his eyes, trying to understand how his words were going to ultimately lead to the sacrifice that he had mentioned was necessary to regain his full potential.

"When I discovered the truth, it all started to make sense. That is why I never knew my parents, because if He gave me parents to remember, I would have never wanted to leave them. That is why he made me from another world that had nothing for me, because if it did, I would have never wanted to leave it so eagerly behind for this one. My Parent has always been there watching me, guiding me, directing me towards the final goal of finding the Orb and uniting with its power to take my rightful place as the Final Mystic of Creation. There is one thing, however, that He didn't intend. He didn't intend for me to fall for you." said David, his eyes starting to well up with tears.

"I can feel His presence more each day, but the more I drift towards Him, the further I feel myself drifting from the life I've come to cherish, the life I've come to want more than anything to be real...and the more I feel myself drifting from you." he said, the tears starting to fall from his eyes.

"David, I won't let this affect what we have, I promise!" said Erin quickly.

"You don't understand, Erin." said David, regaining his composure. "In order for me to gain my full powers needed to confront the Defiant One and seal him back within the Dark Abyss, I need to give up everything that holds me back from becoming the final Mystic of Creation. I can't be a Mystic *and* a boy that's madly in love with a girl – that reluctance to leave you would prevent me from accessing my true powers, because it would be accompanied with a fear of losing you, a fear that would always keep a part of me focused on protecting you instead of giving myself completely to the sole duty of protecting the world of the living."

"No...no that can't be. By protecting the world of the living, you *are* protecting me, David. The two are one and the same. You can have both!" said Erin, fighting back the tears.

"I tried to fight it too. I questioned Him over and over again, but He always had the same answer. '*No David, you can't have your life as a human, and a Mystic. You must choose, and the fate of the world will be determined based on your choice.*' I spent what felt like an eternity going over everything He said, but at last I finally realized that it was useless. He was right, how could He not be? He is God, after all." said David, slumping his shoulders in defeat.

With this, Erin had heard too much, and she collapsed into David's arms sobbing uncontrollably. She couldn't stand to hear it, to bear the thought of losing him after all they had been through together. He had become her best friend, her confidant, and she loved him too much to let him go.

"I can't lose you, David, I just can't!" she said through chest-racking sobs.

David held her in his arms, tenderly stroking her hair as tears fell freely down his face.

They sat together for a long while and cried together, holding each other until the sobs finally subsided and were replaced with a deafening silence.

Erin finally sat up and looked into David's eyes, her beautiful face red and puffy from crying.

"I stand by what I said. Stay with me tonight? If I can't have you forever, let me at least have you tonight." she asked, looking up at him eagerly.

How could he deny her such a thing? David smiled and nodded.

That night they spent together, that last night, Erin would cherish for all eternity.

Chapter XXXII

The next morning Erin and David set off through the forest and into the campground to find the others. The morning had come for their march to battle and they were as prepared as they ever would be.

They found Rex and the others in the command tent, each dressed in their most splendid armor and prepared for the coming battle as if it were their last – and it would be. Whether they won and the Defiant One was sealed away once again, or they lost, and the world was destroyed – one way or the other their time at war was about to be coming to an end.

When they saw the look of resolution on David and Erin's face, they knew the time had come.

Together, they marched their army of men, Elves, and Dwarves up the Great Road towards Draco's Pass and over the snow dusted mountain. When they reached the crest of the pass, marking the divide between the eastern and western sides, they got their first look of the amassing army of demons far below in the Great Plains. They were marching from the Outer Woods near what remained of Eldergate, flowing across the great grassy fields like a black flood of death.

Their masses covered the landscape for miles between the edge of the tree line to the north and the foothills of the mountains to the south, while the air above was littered with winged beasts of war, circling above like vultures, ready for the coming battle.

David and Erin shared a look of determination before pressing on to the other side of the pass, heading down the mountain path and into the Great Plains below.

The once green, grassy field had now turned to dry grass from the changing seasons, mixed with trampled muddy ground from the hundreds of thousands of marching feet that had been crossing back and forth on its surface over the past couple of weeks.

The air was cool and dry with the sky mostly overcast to match the gloomy atmosphere of the pending battle below.

The allied forces reached the bottom by mid-day and gathered into three great divisions at the foothills of the eastern slopes. Each group had two battalions of Dwarves in the front lines with their great halberds and lances standing at the ready for the coming charge, standing behind two long rows of mounted warriors with long spears and short swords on their hips.

Behind them stood several battalions of men and elves, laden with the decorative armor of their respective kingdoms and each carrying their preferred weapon of war. The rear of each battalion consisted of several companies of archers from all of the races, prepared to release volley after volley of magically crafted arrows designed specifically for the demon horde that would fly farther and faster than ordinary arrows – allowing them to soar through the air to their target from the safety of the rear. They were ordered to focus first on the flying enemies to protect the others from being picked off by the winged beasts before targeting the masses on the ground.

Each division was being led by one of the Generals or Kings of each race. The left division would be led by Kings Eldergate and Reximus Kane, with their Generals Nathaniel Ryan and Cornelius Owen at their sides. The middle division would be led by Prince Gilric Ellisar of the Woodland Elves. And the right division would be led by King Tybrin Hammerclaw of the Dwarves of Emerald Keep. Together, they made a formidable force, but before the great sea of darkness their numbers were but a fraction of the size and paled in comparison. It would be a desperate battle indeed.

The plan was for the main forces to keep the demons occupied and at bay long enough for David to find the Defiant One and take him out. Once he did so, he would be able to unleash the spell of banishment, sending the Defiant One back into the Dark Abyss, along with the remaining forces of Demons and undead soldiers. In order for the spell to work, the Defiant One would have to be in a weakened state, and they knew this would be no easy task – even for David with his newly regained powers.

Their whole plan rested on David's success. If he failed, or if he took too long, their defeat was all but certain – it was a risk they were all willing to take.

Seeing that the fight was about to begin, David and Erin took one last moment to say goodbye and wish each other luck in the coming battle.

David leaned in with a passionate kiss before parting for the last time.

"I love you, Erin Alderan. I always will." he said, trying his hardest to smile and be strong while fighting back the tears.

"And I love you, David Bishop. You have come into my life and changed it for the better. I will never forget you, and I will carry you in my heart forever." she said, smiling as tears welled up once again.

"Now go and save the world!" she said with a weak laugh, wiping away her tears and trying her best to look strong.

David smiled in kind before he took off towards the middle of the central group. Erin watched him him disappear into the ranks of men before she finally gathered enough strength to turn away and join with Rex and the others on the left flank.

It was one of the hardest things she had ever done, for she knew in her heart that things would never be the same again.

Suddenly, the ground began to tremble, and the massive force of demons began charging full throttle towards their front lines.

It had begun.

"Here they come, boys!" shouted Tybrin Hammerclaw, "Let's give 'em what they came for!"

he said, raising his battle hammer high into the air for all to see.

"CHARGE!" he screamed, and he took off along with the rest of their forces at high speed, headed straight towards the front lines of the demon forces.

The riders quickly sped away from those on foot and, closing the gap at incredible speeds, crashed into the frontlines of the demon forces, sending them sprawling into the air or flattening them into the ground. They pushed deep into the enemy lines, breaking into their formations, and scattering them behind with their deadly charge.

The rest of the forces caught up and started hacking away at the still recovering demon horde, dispatching thousands in a matter of a few minutes. When the demon horde finally recovered from the initial impact, what ensued was a battle the likes of which the world hadn't seen since the Mystic Wars nearly two millennia ago.

Sword clashed with sword and shield, blades and teeth met flesh, tearing it asunder, and the screaming of both man and beast could be heard for miles as the two forces clashed with unwavering tenacity.

As the fighting waged on and intensified with every passing moment, David scanned the distance, trying to find any indication of the Defiant One.

He crashed through the enemy lines, slashing and blasting away demons left and right with his sword and incredible power, but no matter how many he destroyed, more always took their place, filling the void of the blast area just as quickly as it had cleared.

Behind him, Rex was swinging his double-sided battle axe ferociously back and forth, taking off limbs and heads with every powerful swing, unleashing his pent-up rage for the deaths of thousands of his people at the hands of these monsters. The area around him began building mounds of fallen demons, and the earth beneath his feet was blackened as their sticky blood flew through the air in swirling arcs, following the path of his axe.

"Is that all you got!" he shouted in rage, crushing the skull of one who he had just dispatched and was still crawling towards him.

In the distance to Rex's left, General Ryan stuck close to King Eldergate and Erin, protecting them from the onslaught of enemy forces, while each fought valiantly and without tire.

"I forgot how exciting this could be!" screamed the King over the roar of the battle, cutting down a nearby demon that had jumped from the fray into his reach.

"I'm not sure that's the word I would use, Highness" shouted General Ryan in response while taking on another demon to his right.

In the middle rank, Gilric Ellisar was dancing and twirling with his long, curved blade, creating a wake of destruction in his path as he spun in and out and between the enemies around him. With each swing of his blade, two more demons fell. The enemy couldn't get closer than a few feet from him before falling from several gashes as he slashed at lightning speeds and with the frightening efficiency of a lifelong warrior.

He could hear the laughter of King Tybrin not far to his right, as he was spinning wildly with his battle hammer, crushing any enemy that dared approach him.

He looked over and saw the Dwarf King taunting a demon closest to him, causing it to lunge at him before he dodged just in time and swung his hammer onto its head, pushing it into the ground with a sickening crack.

"Tybrin, you're one crazy Dwarf!" he said to the Dwarf king, before having to quickly deflect an incoming attack from an undead soldier. King Tybrin just laughed heartily as he rushed towards his next opponent who was scrambling to get away and was unsuccessful.

David, encouraged by his friend's apparent success, but knowing time was not on their side continued to frantically search the battlefield for their true enemy. After spending as long as he dared searching and seeing no indication of the Defiant One anywhere on the battlefield, David finally decided to instead take the fight to him.

He held out his hand and rushed through the battlefield towards Eldergate, blasting away and slashing anything that got in his way.

When he reached the final stretch before the giant fissure surrounding the rocky outcrop that was Eldergate, he finally caught a glimpse of him for the first time.

A flash of green light streaked from the highest tower of the palace, soaring faster than lightning through the air before landing heavily on the ground not fifty feet away. The force of the impact created a crater around him and sent debris of rock and earth flying high into the air.

When the dust cleared, David found himself standing before the Defiant One – the Mystic of Destruction.

He was taller than David had expected, standing nearly eight foot tall or higher. He was completely naked and muscular, not a single hair on his body, and his eyes were a haunting milky white – absent of all emotion. Despite his appearance, he had handsome features and would have been an attractive man had he not had that sickening greenish hue to his flesh.

"You were foolish to come, but I expected nothing less from a boy such as yourself" said the Defiant One.

His voice was deep and commanding and seemed to echo everywhere all at once.

"You know why I'm here, and I intend to finish this once and for all." said David, getting straight to the point.

"A man of little worlds, I like that." said the Mystic, a smirk on his face. "So be it!"

With his last word, he rose slightly off the ground and rushed towards David with incredible speed, landing a powerful blow that sent David flying backward hundreds of feet before crashing into the trunk of a nearby tree, cracking it nearly in two. His sword flew from his grasp and disappeared somewhere deep into the tree line.

"This is starting well," gasped David, trying to catch his breath.

Stunned, David tried to recover, but the Defiant One was too quick.

He quickly rushed towards David again, landing a flurry of attacks that were too fast for David to comprehend, let alone deflect. They just looked like blurs to David's untrained eyes. All he could feel were the incessant impacts landing securely at his midsection and the numbing pain growing from the attacks.

He couldn't keep this level of beating up for much longer.

David, sensing his desperate situation, recovered his wits and reached to his power within, sending a powerful blast outward toward his attacker, causing the Defiant One to be pushed back long enough for David to regroup and prepare for the next assault. He checked his body and was surprised to see that he was relatively unharmed.

Relieved, he looked up at the Defiant One who was recovering from the unexpected show of force. David smiled.

He could actually do this; he could fight the Defiant One.

Simultaneously, the two leapt into action, crashing into each other in a brilliant show of force that sent a shockwave around them so large it blasted away all of the trees within a hundred-yard radius and created a crater equally large beneath their feet.

As they clashed time and time again, David suddenly realized they were fighting in the air, high above the Outer Woods. He could see the armies below, still locked in a deadly struggle, but his mind was quickly forced back to the fight when the Defiant One sent a powerful blast of energy his way and he had to quickly dodge away. The energy flew through the air behind him and blasted away the entire peak of one of the surrounding mountains.

Huge boulders flew through the air and plummeted towards the forces below. Seeing one of them falling towards Rex and the others, he rushed through the air and blasted away the rock just before it crashed into their forces, sending hundreds of small fragments flying through the air and saving the lives of countless men - but it came with a price.

His distraction made him lose sight of the Defiant One, and suddenly a powerful attack came from behind, sending him hurtling through the air like a rag doll and falling heavily to the ground.

David...you have to let go of your friends. You must choose now, or risk losing this fight. Came the voice he had come to know as the Creator God...his Father.

David shrugged it off, he knew what he had to do. If he kept losing focus like this, he would surely lose. And if he lost, the world would fall to ruin, along with Erin and everyone he had come to love. He had to stay focused.

As he turned his attention back to the Defiant One he was instantly thrown into the surrounding mountains, pummeled by a series of energy blasts the Defiant One had unleashed on him while he was distracted. Over and over again his body was impacted by a series of blows, pushing him deeper and deeper into the rockface.

When the attacks finally subsided, David's head was dizzy, and his body felt weak. He could feel the blood dripping down his hairline and from his chin.

Fearing the Defiant One was on his way to finish him off, David tried to quickly shake off the attack. He had to keep fighting, he couldn't give up, there was just too much at stake and too many people depending on him.

He slowly crawled his way out of the tunnel of crushed rock back towards the battlefield.

When he reached the opening, he could see the Defiant One across the plains, pummeling his way through the Dwarven forces with his powerful attacks. They didn't stand a chance against him. He was too powerful. With every swipe of his hand, dozens of men and Dwarves went flying through the air, their bodies crushed and crumpling as they landed on the ground. It was a terrifying sight to see, and one only David could stop from continuing.

David gritted his teeth and pushed himself up off the ground, brushing off the dust and blood as it smeared across his hairline.

He looked around and could see that the battle was starting to turn, and their forces were being overrun little by little. Slowly but surely, they were all going to die.

He couldn't let that happen. He knew what he had to do, no matter how much it hurt him. He knew that he had to let go. He had hoped ever since he had his visions that he would be able to compete with the powers of the Defiant One without giving up his humanity, but now, after seeing his incredible power firsthand and being beaten so badly despite his best efforts, he knew he was outmatched and there was only one way to even the odds.

"I'm sorry Erin...I tried. I love you...I will always love you." said David, tears flowing down his face.

Finally prepared to do what must be done to save his friends, David set his jaw and closed his eyes, pushing away all of his feelings one by one.

Memories of his time with Erin came rushing to his vision. He could see the first time he saw her in the Forgotten Temple, their first kiss in the Great Plains before the battle of Eldergate and all of the wonderful times they spent together since, and finally, the last night they shared together as lovers. He mustered all the courage he had and each time he painfully pushed them away, out of his mind, out of his heart.

He did the same for the images of Rex and Orin, of their time together in Ravenfell, the battles they had fought together, and the laughs they had shared, slowly letting them fade from his heart and mind, until all that was left was his mission and purpose – defeat the Defiant One, save the world of the living, become the final Mystic of Creation.

Finally, as he pushed away the last of the thoughts of his friends, no...his family...he felt a sense of freedom that filled his body and mind. It was as if he were weightless. His thoughts cleared, and his heart raced. His body surged with a power unlike anything he had ever felt before.

He opened his eyes, and he could see and feel everything around him as if he were intimately connected to every living thing. The grass, the fields, the birds flying high in the sky, the people fighting for their lives. He could feel their fear, their sense of uncertainty as they struggled with a foe far greater than they. It was time to ease their fears, it was time to finish this.

David could see his skin glowing intensely with the same light as the orb. His skin no longer it's normal hue, but bright and luminous, like the orb had always been. Something about him had changed, he could tell, but for now, he didn't have the time to inspect it.

Feeling renewed by this sudden surge of energy, David rushed into the sky, flying faster than a streaking bolt of lightning, before crashing into the unsuspecting Mystic who had just obliterated a group of warriors in the field far below with his powerful blasts of energy.

***

Erin looked up from the fighting to see a streak fly overhead and crash into the Defiant One, sending a shockwave through the air and knocking down those demons and men unfortunate enough to have been beneath him.

A smile stretched across her face as she realized what it must mean. David finally did it. He had accessed the full might of his powers. She was filled with pride for her David. At the same time, a gut-wrenching pain went reeling in her chest, breaking her heart with the realization of what it meant. He had let her go; he had let them all go.

She knew David had done what he had to do and knew that it took great courage and sacrifice for him to do it, but that realization did nothing for the pain that was now ripping out her heart. For the moment, she would have to push it away, just as David did. They had a battle to win.

She rushed back into her attack with renewed energy, knowing David now had the power to finish this once and for all.

***

David clashed time and time again with the Defiant One, keeping him on his heels as they fought for control of the world below.

His powers were incredible, but he still seemed evenly matched with the Defiant One, despite having now possessed the combined might of all six Mystics of Creation. He assumed it only made sense, after all, they were a balance to each other. David was now the light, the Defiant One was the darkness. David possessed the power to create, whereas his counterpart had the power to destroy.

Their struggle to overcome one another continued for what felt an eternity, each side landing powerful blows and taking incredible hits, until finally David had had enough. His righteous rage had been building to extreme limits that he could no longer contain.

His people below were dying, and they were depending on him to get the job done. He had to finish this now, or risk losing even more lives to the endless horde of demons below.

He gathered all of his strength and rage and released a flurry of attacks on his opponent, who was unprepared for the sudden onslaught. The Defiant One held up his hands in defense, trying to block the blows, but David was moving too quick and landed a series of strikes that sent the Mystic of Destruction flying through the air and landing hard into the ground below.

David pursued his opponent relentlessly, never giving him a moment to breathe, a moment to think, a moment to react.

Finally, in a desperate moment of righteous rage, David threw out his hands and released a blast of energy so bright it blinded the forces below, causing them all to break from their fighting and look up in wonder at the show of force above.

A great beam of white light shot out from his hands, soaring through the air towards his target in a brilliant twisting beam of Mystic energy.

Inside the light, David could see the spirits of the last Mystics, circling around each other like dancers, rushing through the air towards their doomed brother.

In suspended time, David could see the Defiant One's eyes open in shock as the incoming projectile neared ever closer, helpless to stop the attack.

It struck him with such force it blasted a hole through his chest, leaving a great gaping cavity where his green, glowing flesh used to be, sizzling with smoke rising slowly from the wound.

He looked down at his fatal wound then back up at David, an expression of horror on his face as he fell backward to the ground with a thud.

David, knowing he had not a moment to spare, quickly summoned the energy needed to reopen the rift fully between the world of the living and the dead and cast the spell of banishment.

As he forced the rift apart, holding it open, a great spiraling vortex of dark energy began to escape from the fissures around Eldergate, pulling in the demons that were still pouring out from the cracks. The vortex slowly began increasing in size and strength, eager to feast on the forsaken beasts who had managed to escape its depths.

Eventually, the vortex grew to such strength that the entire army of demons began sliding across the ground, their claws desperately trying to grip the earth before being pulled mercilessly through the air and into the vortex, their horrendous screams finally disappearing beyond its veil.

The Defiant One, seeing the events unfolding around him as they had so many ages ago, screamed as his body began sliding across the ground towards the rift, his hands flailing around trying to grip anything to keep him from falling backwards into the Abyss once again.

His efforts were useless, and he fell away, back into the eternal chambers of the Dark Abyss as the vortex swallowed him whole. At last, the Defiant One disappeared from the world of the living once again.

When the final enemy had been cleared from the land of the living, David focused his energy, causing the rift to slowly close and the scars in the ground to heal. In a matter of moments, the great fissures of darkness vanished without a trace.

As David drifted above the battlefield, exhausted from his momentous struggle, he could see the thousands of bodies of men, Elves, and Dwarves lying lifeless on the ground. They had lost so many...if he had only been able to defeat the Defiant One sooner...

His heart ached for the countless lives lost.

As he succumbed to his exhaustion, he felt his body slowly being lifted higher into the air as the clouds parted in the skies above and enveloped his body in a shaft of gentle light.

His work was done, he was going home. His mortal fears would finally be no more.

***

Erin and the others watched in awe as the demons were being pulled across the ground towards the dark vortex that had sprung up suddenly from the fissures around Eldergate.

They had seen the powerful blast that had sent the Defiant One flying into the ground. Shortly after, the ground began to tremble, and the great vortex appeared before growing large enough to start pulling in the vast army of demons.

The fighting ceased as they all stood in awe and watched as the intense winds of the vortex whipped around them, pulling enemy forces away and into the Dark Abyss beyond the rift. Their cries were followed by the haunting screams of the Defiant One as he was dramatically dragged across the ground before vanishing without a trace.

David had done it! He had defeated the Defiant One along with his great army of demons.

Shortly after the vortex disappeared, she could see a shining white figure high in the sky above. The figure was that of a man and appeared to be naked, hovering high in the air with great wings of light. He hovered there above the battlefield for a brief moment before collapsing midair. It was David – no, the Mystic of Creation. Her David was gone as she had known him, and he had grown into something more.

Suddenly, the clouds parted, and a great shaft of light enveloped the Mystic of Creation, catching him in its track.

He slowly rose with the beam of light until finally he disappeared beyond their vision and out of sight.

When everyone shook off their awe and wonder and realized what had happened, that the battle was finally over and they had won, the entire army erupted into cheers, raising their hands into the air in defiance of the Mystic of Destruction that had threatened their world and lost.

All but Erin, who fell to her knees and wept.

She wept for David and his selfless sacrifice.

She wept for their love that would never know what fruits it could have blossomed.

And she wept for the thousands of brave men, Dwarves, and Elves who had given their lives for the righteous pursuit of freedom.

But most of all, she wept because he was gone. He was gone, and she knew in her heart that she would never see him again.

Epilogue

In the several months after the battle in the Great Plains where David had defeated the Defiant One and his vast army of demons, a conflict that was now termed the "Battle for Hurea", the people of Hurea were finally starting to recover from the war.

The Elves and Dwarves had parted from their human allies shortly after the battle and returned back to their respective homes, and the men and women of Ravenfell, Eldergate, and Brineport were starting the incredible task of rebuilding their great civilizations.

King Eldergate, having been gravely wounded in the battle after he had taken a demon's claw to his chest, lay on his deathbed after the medical staff had determined there was nothing else they could do except to help ease his suffering until he passed. He had been in and out for weeks but was finally awake and, knowing his time was near, had beckoned for his men to get Erin and bring her to his side as quickly as possible.

His room was in one of the great chambers of the pyramid located at the center of Brineport where they had set up a makeshift medical center to care for the wounded.

When she entered his room, he waved for her to come closer.

General Ryan and Tyrius were standing by his side and smiled slightly when they saw her.

"You called, your highness?" asked Erin, confused at why the King would ask for her at such a time.

"Your highness..." said the King slowly repeating her words between labored breaths, "That's quite a name to call your father." he said bluntly, no longer having the luxury of time on his side.

Erin, completely caught off guard and eyes as wide as a doe, looked up at General Ryan and Tyrius for confirmation of what she thought she had just heard.

"Yes, Erin. It's true." said Tyrius, smiling.

She turned and looked again to the King, the man on his deathbed that was now claiming to be her father.

"*You're*...my father?" she asked, still in shock and having a hard time believing what she was hearing.

The King laughed and then started coughing harshly, taking a few moments to regain control before he responded.

"Yes, child...I'm so deeply sorry for keeping it from you all this time." he said, sorrow etched across his face.

"But a King must do as he sees fit to protect his people, especially his daughter." he said, taking a brief pause to steady his breathing after another coughing fit.

"When I found out your mother was pregnant with you, I had already been warned of the prophecy and the dire threat that would be growing within our kingdom. The only way I knew to keep you safe, was to keep you a secret." he said.

"That is when I asked General Ryan here to keep an eye on you," he said, gesturing to his side where General Ryan stood.

"I instructed him to help train you in combat so I knew you would remain safe and could protect yourself in the event the need arose. I also had Tyrius agree to make you his apprentice, so he could teach you the wisdom of a true leader, so that one day, when the time came and you were ready, and our kingdom no longer lived under the shadow of the threat from the Defiant One, you would be prepared to take my place, your rightful place, as ruler of the Northern Kingdom." he finished, closing his eyes for a moment as a wave of pain rushed through his body. It was clear the effort of speaking was taking a toll on the already weakened man.

"I...I don't know what to say..." she said, overwhelmed with the sudden revelation of life-changing news. "I always knew my mother had been secretive about my father, but I never suspected..." she trailed off.

"I realize this is a lot to take in," said the King. "Please, take your time to let it digest. I don't have much time left here, I'm afraid, but I have already drawn up the necessary documents revealing your true lineage to the world. When you are ready for it, the kingdom is yours." he said, grabbing her hand

and gently patting it with his other hand. His hands were cool and weak.

It was the first time she could recall that he ever touched her, it would also prove to be the last.

He looked at her longingly, like a man with many regrets and so much more to say but not enough time to say it properly, before he eventually closed his eyes and fell fast asleep.

In the following days, King Eldergate peacefully passed from his wounds. That night they had a great funeral in his honor where it was revealed that Erin Alderan was in fact, Erin Eldergate, the living heir of King Eldergate and rightful successor to the throne of the Northern Kingdom.

She was crowned the next day in a great pompous ceremony, where she vowed to unite the kingdoms of the north and south in an era of peace and prosperity and, with Rex's blessing, reopen the Southern Tunnel so their kingdoms could openly travel and equally share in their great wealth and resources.

King Reximus Kane of Ravenfell, Prince Gilric Ellisar of the Woodland Elves, and King Tybrin Hammerclaw of the Dwarven Kingdom were all present for the ceremony, along with her friends Orin, Darryn Faircloth of Emerald Keep, and Natan from Brineport. Each of the leaders of the free people of Hurea gave her their blessings and promise of continued trade among their respective kingdoms. The free trade would allow all the races to grow and prosper to heights they hadn't seen since before the first Mystic War when trade had been more frequent between their lands.

It was during this ceremony that Erin began to feel something wasn't quite right. Her cycle hadn't started yet, and she was beginning to wonder why when it had suddenly dawned on her. She was with child – David's child.

The rest of the evening she couldn't help but smile, eventually spilling the news to Orin and the others, who were all immensely thrilled.

Over the next several months, the plans began to be developed for the future city of Eldergate. It would be built back on the same plot of land as the former city, only in a grander fashion that would better reflect the combined might of the united kingdoms of Man, Elves, and Dwarves.

Once Erin approved the plans, the building began immediately, and with their combined skill and resources the city was rebuilt within a few short years.

A great gold-plated fountain was commissioned in the center of the new marketplace dedicated to David Bishop, the boy who had come to their world and become the final Mystic of Creation. A boy who had saved not only the people of Brineport from their tyrannical overlords, but the entire world from the brink of destruction.

For ages to come that fountain would serve as a symbol of hope for all who traveled from the far corners of Hurea to see it, knowing that because of David's sacrifice, and the sacrifice of all those who lost their lives in the war, they were able to live their lives free from conflict and destruction.

During Eldergate's construction, while she was still living in Brineport, Erin gave birth to a healthy set of twins: one boy and one girl.

The boy she named David, after his father. The girl, Elena, after her mother.

They each grew to be strong, intelligent, and compassionate rulers and over time began to slowly take the reigns from their mother, preparing for their eventual rule of the kingdom when she no longer could carry the burden of rule alone.

Over the years, the various races of the world all gathered in the metropolis that became Eldergate, which once again was the crown-jewel of the Northern Kingdom. They shared in its wealth of natural resources and knowledge, bringing in a new era of prosperity that was enjoyed by all for ages to come.

As for Erin, she never did find love again – that is, apart from the love she shared with her children. Instead, she dedicated her long life to her kingdom – ensuring its prosperity and security for decades to come. It was her pride and joy to watch her children grow into adulthood, ever safe from the threat of war, but she never forgot the price that was paid for that security – or the anguish that it left in her heart. Some wounds, she told young David and Elena, just never heal.

One night, many years down the road when the cares of a lifetime were permanently etched on her once delicate face, and her dark hair had been completely overridden with grey, Erin lay in bed in her palatial tower.

She dreamed she was young again and was standing at her balcony in the quiet of the early morning, overlooking the newly built city of Eldergate. The first of the sun's gentle rays stretched across the sky, blanketing the landscape in its golden light. The sky was clear and there wasn't a cloud to be seen from horizon to horizon as the church bells far below sounded their first call of the morning.

As a warm breeze gently brushed a fallen strand of hair from her face, she felt a familiar presence standing behind her. She wasn't afraid, as there was something serene about this presence that made her heart flutter with excitement. She turned around slowly, holding her breath with anticipation.

Behind her, just as she had hoped, stood David. He looked as he once was, young and vibrant with his shaggy brown hair brushed slightly over his brow and his boyish grin stretching wide across his face.

His eyes were twinkling with such love and warmth that her heart was instantly filled to the brim, threatening to burst at the seams.

Overwhelmed with the sudden emotion rising within, she erupted into chest heaving sobs as she ran to his arms. He quickly stepped toward her, enveloping her in a heartfelt embrace.

They were together once again, as they had been in her dreams nearly every night since they had parted, only this time she wouldn't be waking.

At last, after all these years, Erin had found her peace – she was finally home.

Special Thanks

Dear Reader,

Thank you for taking the time to read *David Bishop and the Mystic of Creation,* the second book and epic finale to the David Bishop series.

I hope that you enjoyed reading David's story and that it sparked a sense of adventure within your heart that will stay with you throughout your life, maybe even inspiring you to take an adventure of your own.

If you enjoyed going on this journey with David and his friends, I hope that you would take the time to submit a review about your experience reading *David Bishop and the Mystic of Creation.* It not only will help other readers such as yourself to find David's story, but will help my efforts in continuing my career as an author and my pursuit in writing the next great adventure.

May the Creator God watch over you and all of your future travels.

Sincerely,
T.C. Crawford

Printed in Great Britain
by Amazon